THE ALIEN WHO PREFERRED FISH

THE ALIEN WHO PREFERRED FISH

Blaine C. Readler

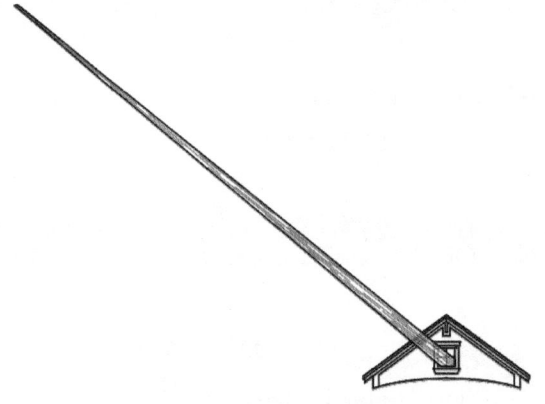

Full Arc
Press

THE ALIEN WHO PREFERRED FISH

Published by Full Arc Press

Visit us at: http://www.readler.com

E-mail: blaine@readler.com

An acknowledgement and thanks to Lulu Enterprises, Inc. for making the publishing of this book possible.

This book was previously published as "Monsters in the Attic: Aliens, Terrorists, and One Voluble Raccoon" (ISBN: 978-0-615-41141-5).

ISBN: 978-0-9834973-1-8

Printed in the United States of America

First Edition: 2011

For my brother Ken who, via miniscule scrawl spanning many pages of many letters, showed me that every day our lives reveal humor worth getting down on paper.

ACKNOWLEDGEMENTS

Bucketfuls of thanks to MTB for wrestling the initial draft of the story into something resembling a novel.

Also, bushel baskets of thanks to Christina Wilson for advice and help in creating the cover.

And it turns out that all of the information that man has carefully accumulated in all the books in the world can be written in this form in a cube of material one two-hundredth of an inch wide—which is the barest piece of dust that can be made out by the human eye.

—Richard Feynman, There's Plenty of Room at the Bottom, 1959

After I give lectures—on almost any subject—I often am asked, "Do you believe in UFOs?" I'm always struck by how the question is phrased, the suggestion that this is a matter of belief and not of evidence.

—Carl Sagan, The Demon-haunted World

Chapter 1

Tuesday morning

Gabe snapped awake. Echoes of an unidentifiable sound faded among the nooks and crannies of his brain. He was looking at his guitar case leaning in the corner, draped with his clothes where he'd tossed them the night before. His eyes moved to the floor where they met another pair staring back. These were black and shiny, and lay along the backside of a snout. Black fur framed the eyes, and was itself edged top and bottom by a white band that melded to an animal-gray. The effect of a masked little bandit was so effective that Gabe marveled at evolution's apparent sense of whimsical mimicry.

The black eyes blinked once. Gabe blinked in return.

"Hello, Gabe," the mouth said in a gravely little voice.

This jolted him from his befuddled stupor and he sat upright with a cry of despair, covering his eyes with his hands. He looked down, but of course there was no raccoon. It had been over a year since his last flashback, and he'd thought that he was finally free and clear of the lingering effects of the bad LSD trip. The fact that he'd been a little drunk when he'd fallen into bed the night before was beside the point, which was that whatever he thought he saw was now history.

Punky came trotting in to see what the ruckus was all about. Barely ten inches high, the Toy Poodle held the unshakable opinion that by sheer conviction alone he could convince the world that he was a Doberman. The tiny titan's original name had been Pinksty, bestowed by his previous owner, Mrs. Crabnuckle, and this was one of the reasons why Gabe now owned him, and why Mrs. Crabnuckle was an ex-client.

"Sorry about that," Gabe said, rubbing his eyes with his palms. "I thought I saw a poody-cat."

Punky tilted his head back and forth, lifting each ear in turn.

Gabe patted the bed next to him. "Come on up and say good morning."

Punky leaped forward. He failed his first attempt and fell back out of sight, but an instant later Gabe saw the determined little head appear above the side of the bed as the poodle struggled to hang on.

"Come on, big boy," Gabe encouraged and reached out to pull him up by his front paws.

The dog set about feverishly reapplying a fresh coat of saliva on Gabe's face as he fended him off, laughing at the earnestness of the struggle.

Punky suddenly froze except for a probing twitch at the end of his nose. He jumped to the far edge of the bed and looked at the floor next to Gabe's guitar case. With one excited bark, he leapt down and sniffed back and forth, searching, searching.

"Huh," Gabe uttered, intrigued. He wondered if this was some sort of man/dog telepathy. Maybe Punky had picked up some subtle clues from him. "If so," he said to Punky, "I apologize for dragging you into my bad trip."

Gabe slid out of bed, stepped into slippers, and went to the kitchen to make coffee. He slapped at an ant racing across the counter. The dry climate of San Diego prevented the spawning hoards of flying bugs that infested the east coast. The void was nearly filled, though, by those that crawled. Gabe had spent his whole life in the old house surrounded by armies of tiny marauding ants and platoons of spiders waiting patiently to feast on them. The ants had always been black, but the ones he'd been squashing for some weeks now were of a light hue, almost silvery. The black natives attacked in mass, an endless line of thousands of tiny critters marching resolutely towards some dropped bit of jam. These new silver fellows, however, preferred to strike out alone. Also, whereas fallen comrades of the black old-guard were eventually carried away by their replacements, the squashed silver carcasses lay there until

Gabe finally wiped them away with a paper towel. Their breed apparently didn't believe in "No soldier left behind."

He flipped on the radio sitting next to the coffee maker and was greeted with static. Silver ants and static: the latest irritants of his life. He turned the tuning dial back and forth until he could make out the announcer above the hiss and crackle. The static had started about the same time that the silver ants had suddenly appeared, and it was getting progressively worse. Maybe the old radio was finally dying. Maybe the silver ants were responsible.

The announcer's words were sinking in. She was talking about an explosion, a nuclear explosion.

What? He must have heard wrong. No, both the USGS and the Pentagon were reporting a large explosion—presumably nuclear—in the Pacific Ocean, two hundred miles west of Panama. It had happened just a half-hour before.

Gabe fiddled with the dial. Anonymous sources within the government were speculating that it was one of our submarines on maneuvers in the area. They guessed that one of the missiles on board had blown. This, of course, was supposed to be impossible.

Well, apparently not.

The phone on the kitchen wall rang. Gabe picked up the receiver, expecting it to be the fire department telling him where to find the nearest bomb shelter, but it was the power utility company. They were finally returning his call from two days before when he'd complained about a high bill. Gabe asked the man at the other end of the line if he'd heard about the nuclear submarine explosion.

"No, sir. We don't listen to the radio while working."

"Well it *did*!"

"What?"

"Go *off*!"

"An explosion?"

"A *nuclear* bomb, for God's sake!"

"Right. So you had a question about your bill?"

"Don't you *care*?"

There was a pause, then the man from the power company said, "Look, Mister Wolfekow, I've got about fifty people on my call list today. Do you want to talk about your bill or not?"

"I'm sorry, but I just can't believe you don't care that a nuclear bomb just went off."

"Mr. Wolfekow?"

"Okay, okay. Yes, my bill was about twice what it normally is."

"Well, Mr. Wolfekow, I see that you have a remote meter monitor."

"Yes. They installed it a few months ago."

"They're very accurate; we take readings directly. Have you recently installed a new appliance? Maybe a dishwasher or clothes dryer?"

"No, nothing's changed. Maybe your monitor thing broke."

"They don't break, Mr. Wolfekow."

"What? They're, like, maybe as reliable as the Navy's nuclear submarine missiles?"

Again, there was a pause. "I can send a man out to take a manual reading if you like."

"Yeah, but how do I know the electric meter itself isn't screwed up?"

"Mr. Wolfekow, they—"

"I know, I know. They never screw up. Okay, just send the guy out."

Gabe hung up the phone. He walked to the window. There was no orange glow in the sky, just the leaves of the Eucalyptus trees in the canyon glinting in the morning sun. The birds chattered away like every other morning. Maybe the world wasn't going to end after all.

He picked up the electric bill still lying on the table. He could feel the tension seething inside him. Why did he have to be such a wimp when it came to conflict? Hell, this was just some jerk from the power company.

Gabe suspected that his mom had, unintentionally, taught him to be. He'd been born when she was just eighteen, and they'd lived with his grandmother here in her house. He didn't even know who his father was. When he was five, his mother went on a vacation without him and never returned. Even now, he didn't know if she was dead or alive. She'd been a terrible mom during her short career. Gabe remembered only two extremes: either cuddling and cooing, or yelling and throwing things. His uncle had called her manic-depressive, but his grandmother had said she was just a spoiled brat who never grew up.

But still he missed her.

His grandmother had been his salvation, his day-to-day mom. When she'd died a few years before, the old house seemed unbearably empty. He missed his mom in a whimsical way, like he missed his childhood. The loss he felt towards his grandmother, however, was an acute ache, a tearing grief.

At twenty-four, Gabe still felt like a lost little boy.

The static was annoying, so Gabe shut off the radio. The coffee was ready, so he sat down at the table, and Punky whined to jump up on his lap. "No," he said, waving him off. "Give it a rest, you pest." At this attention Punky began jumping around hysterically, so Gabe made room and helped him up. Punky walked two circles, nearly falling off the precarious ledge, and then settled down to snooze.

Gabe drank his coffee and slapped at another silver ant. He missed, and it scurried away around the edge of the table. The phone rang again. He gently laid Punky, growling in his sleep, on the floor, and picked up the phone. "Hello."

"Gabe, did I wake you?" a female said.

The voice was familiar. He knew he knew her, but how? "Uh, no, not at all."

How the hell did he know her?

"Gabe, this is Christie."

Like her voice, the name tickled recognition but evaded identification. "Hey . . . Christie. How are you?"

There was a pause. "You don't remember me, do you?"

"Sure I do." Gabe tossed the contents of his mind's filing drawers around randomly, frantically searching for remembrance.

Another pause. "Raige Aige?"

A woman's face clicked into place. "Christie! Yeah! How are you?"

They'd spent a night together about a year ago. He'd gone to a CD release party for a local band that he despised. He didn't so much despise the band, as the droning monotony of their metal-grunge music. She'd come to the party with Brent, the guitar player, but he'd been busy getting drunk and making an ass out of himself, so she'd sat and talked with Gabe. They hit it off, and he ended up driving her home and staying the night. It had been the most blissful night of his short life. He hadn't seen her since.

"I guess you're surprised to hear from me," she said. "I hope we can put the past behind us."

Gabe was indeed surprised to hear from Christie. He thought she'd never talk to him again.

"Uh, sure," he agreed. "No hard feelings?"

She was silent a moment. "Of course not," she finally said, not too convincingly.

He could hear it in her voice. It had been a year, and he knew she was still mad at him. So, why was she calling? "It's good to hear from you, Christie. I never had a chance to explain—"

"There's nothing to explain," she said quickly. "That's history. No need to dwell on it."

Not dwelling sounded fine to Gabe. Christie had been with Brent for six months. She'd fallen for his good looks, stage charisma, and the fact that he was abusive. Christie's father was a mean drunk. She left home when she was sixteen, and an attraction to abusive men followed along. She'd told Gabe that a part of her despised Brent, but she hadn't been able to break away.

She'd found something different in Gabe, and she'd reached her hand out with the hope of escaping her cycle of abuse. When Brent had pounded on her apartment door the next morning shouting murder, Gabe and Christie climbed out the back window. They had both run from Christie's abuse. Her hope in Gabe had been ill-founded. If he hadn't been able to face her demon, how could he help her? She didn't return his calls, and he'd given up after a week.

"How have you been?" he asked. "Still going to school?"

"Just two classes. I'm working as a waitress. You know, getting by."

"I know how it is. I finished two years, but I don't have money to continue."

"You were majoring in math."

"Good memory."

Gabe winced. It also meant that she'd really been listening—had really cared—that night a year ago. "Jobs for two-year math majors are few and far between," he explained.

"You still play in a band, though."

And that's why she's calling, he thought. She'd obviously seen the ad he'd placed in the paper for a vocalist.

"Yeah," he said. "Still with the same guys. I've been carrying all the vocals, and the audience is starting to bring tomatoes in their pockets. We've changed the name of the band to *Jump Start*. It's a take-off from the jump-blues of the fifties."

"I guessed as much. The ad mentioned that you were looking for someone who could sing like Ann Cole. I had to do some research—she recorded *Got my Mojo Working* in 1957."

"On the button. Have you heard that version?"

"That took even more research, but yeah. It gives me goosebumps. She's a high bar to climb over."

"She has the same effect on me. So . . . I guess you'd like to try out for the band?"

"If it's okay"

"Sure. Uh, do you have any experience?"

He felt silly asking this kind of question of a woman he'd slept with.

"I only started a few months ago, but I've been working on it. I sang for a while with Raige Aige, but Brent couldn't stand to see guys looking at me on stage."

Well, there it was.

"So, I guess you're still with . . ."

"Brent?"

"Yeah—"

"No," she cut in immediately. ". . . well, yes. No!"

Nothing's changed, Gabe thought. "Sounds complicated."

"It is. It's complicated. But, the short answer is that we're not together now."

"Now?"

"I'm taking a break. He's supposed to be thinking about the whole thing. Last I heard, he broke up Raige Aige and disappeared. He does this every couple of years."

"I see . . ."

"But this has nothing to do with that."

"Of course. You're just another candidate trying out for my band."

Christie was silent a moment. "Is there a problem with that?"

"No. No problem. No reason we can't be friends."

There was silence at the other end of the line.

". . . or business associates," Gabe finally added, "band co-members."

"Business associates," she repeated.

Gabe thought he heard regret in her voice, but decided that it was just skepticism.

"I've never known a local band that made enough money to consider themselves a business," she countered.

Gabe laughed. "You're right. It's a labor of love. No fame, no fortune, but an endless supply of hope."

Christie asked about the audition, and Gabe gave her two songs to learn: *Summertime*, the old Gershwin song recorded by Janis Joplin, and the very same Ann Cole song they'd already talked about, *Got my Mojo Working*. The band had a gig the next night, and he invited her to come along and try out. She hesitated. He understood why. It was difficult enough auditioning, let alone in front of an audience. He was going to suggest something else, but she agreed before he had a chance.

They said their goodbyes and Gabe hung up the phone. He sat staring at his coffee. Talking to her had conjured forgotten images. Christie was a petite woman, but not skinny. Gabe imagined her as a mini-sized version of a super-model. He distinctly recalled her curly, chestnut hair falling softly over her shoulders . . .

Ouch! No sense torturing himself.

Mrs. Jones strolled nonchalantly through the room, pretending that she didn't see them. Mrs. Jones was a cat for whom Gabe had pet-sat for some time until her owner, old Tom Heinke, had died. Tom's wife had never wanted anything to do with Mrs. Jones, so Gabe adopted her. Tom had named her after the seventies Billy Paul song: *"Me and Mrs. Jones, we got a thing goin' on, we both know it's wrong."*

"Come here, you flirt," Gabe said.

Mrs. Jones' aimless stroll serendipitously managed to bring her past Gabe's chair, and he reached down and scratched her behind the ear. She continued her casual meandering, but now confined it to circles around his chair. Punky growled under his breath, opened one eye, and growled more earnestly. Punky and Mrs. Jones got along amiably enough, except when they were around Gabe and Punky became jealous. The jealousy bursting in Mrs. Jones' chest was indiscernible.

"Family hug's over," Gabe declared, standing up and placing the reluctant Punky back on the floor. "If I don't get to work, we'll all starve."

Every day Gabe made the rounds, caring for other's pets while their owners were away. He visited some of his clients only occasionally when they left for vacation; others he visited every workday to walk their dog. He had never actively initiated this career. He had looked after a neighbor's dog years ago in high school, and word slowly spread until he now got calls from people who were referred by people that he didn't even remember.

Punky trotted behind him to the car. Mrs. Jones bade her farewell by rubbing herself against the door post. In a moment of career ambition he'd ordered a magnetic sign, which he'd slapped onto his car door. It read:

Gabe's Pet Sitting
The Only Friend Your Pet Will Ever Need.

This was the only advertising he'd ever managed to muster. He thought the plastic sign looked cheap and dorky clinging to his Sentra, but he'd paid eighty bucks, and for that kind of money, he could swallow his pride.

Gabe reviewed the day's schedule. As his clients called for his services, he wrote their names at the top of the appropriate sheet of his daily calendar book. Now, as he did each morning, he re-ordered them to create the day's route. The rounds took him anywhere from one to four hours to complete. His income barely paid for his food, gas, and car insurance, but the hours were flexible, and he had plenty of time for the band. It also provided plenty of time for college, except that there wasn't money left over for that. There were seven clients today. He figured he'd be back home in time for Oprah.

His first stop was a new client, a Doberman. Gabe got out of the car and shut the door before Punky could escape. The poodle's face bobbed up and down on the other side of the window, and he could hear the muffled yapping from inside.

"You know the routine," he called through the glass. "First time, I go alone. You'd be dessert for this big guy."

He pulled his ID rag from his pocket and headed up the walk. "Hell," he muttered to himself, "some day *I'll* end up as cheesecake for one of these canine monsters."

His ID rag was simply an old T-shirt that he never washed. He made a point to visit each new client before they left on vacation and he gave their dog a good whiff of the sweaty shirt, hoping the beast would remember his smiling face later when he came around again. As he came up to the large, expensive door to this large, expensive house, he could hear the frantic barks of the Doberman inside swearing up and down that he was going to rip open Gabe's throat if he could just get to him. He flipped through his large key ring, looking for the one with the number he'd assigned to this client. His job seemed easy to his friends, but it was times like this that he truly earned his money.

He found the key and unlocked the door. From inside, the Doberman's barks took on a new level of murderous intent. Gabe took a deep breath and opened the door a crack. A black muzzle immediately appeared, growling and pushing to get out. Gabe leaned against the door to keep the Doberman from slipping through. He held his ID rag up to the muzzle. Quick as a flash, sharp teeth grabbed the cloth from his hand and pulled it through. Gabe heard snarling and biting, then silence. He put his ear to the crack and heard sniffing. Once again, the stink of his sweat had come to the rescue.

Gabe opened the door another inch and put his closed fist up to the opening. He could lose a finger with an open hand if the Doberman decided he wasn't going to fall for the old rag-trick. It had happened to others. The muzzle appeared and sniffed his hand. Gabe slowly opened the door to reveal eighty pounds of sleek muscle: the perfect watch-dog. The Doberman stood tensely, growling under his breath. He recognized Gabe, but wasn't necessarily going to like him. Gabe took a cautious step forward. The Doberman's growl notched up in pitch. It appeared as though he wasn't quite home free yet. He slowly reached down and retrieved the stink-rag. Maybe the monster needed a refresher about Gabe's association with the shirt. He held it out for the dog to smell again. With one quick snap, the Doberman grabbed the end of the shirt. The growls now issued through clenched teeth.

It was a standoff, as Gabe didn't want to let go of the shirt since it seemed to be occupying the part of the dog he most wanted to avoid. He gave it an experimental tug. The dog tugged back. Maybe he just wanted to play. The growls, though, implied that Gabe was the preferred chew-toy.

He took a tentative step through the door. As he did, the shirt became slack and the Doberman took the opportunity to advance his grip and move his hold closer to Gabe's hand. Gabe instinctively stepped to the side, into the hallway of the house. The growling was a steady drone, like a lawnmower in the distance. The dog's eyes stared into Gabe's. *One wrong move*, they said, *and you're minced-meat, mister.*

He took a step backward, towards the kitchen. The dog followed, keeping a steady pull on the shirt. Step-by-step, man and dog inched through the house—a dance of two species. Gabe didn't see the kitchen doorway jam behind him and stumbled, almost falling. The dog's growl became excited at this unexpected development. Gabe froze until the Doberman settled back to a steady drone.

Gabe glanced to the side and saw a note hanging on the refrigerator. With one hand, he reached over and pulled it off. He read:

Mr. Wolfekow,

Hello! I hope Toodles wasn't scared of you—he's such a sensitive animal, I hate to leave him alone. Just a reminder: his food is under the sink. Don't forget his water. He'd love it if you played with him a while. He's probably lonely.

Thanks again,

Joan

Gabe laid the note on the counter and shook his head.

"Okay, Toodles. Easy does it," Gabe said in a tone he hoped was reassuring. "You're just overcompensating for feelings of emasculation."

With one hand hanging on to the shirt, Gabe used the other to get the bag of food out and pour some into the dog's bowl. An equal amount spilled onto the floor. Gabe then filled the water bowl, spilling half of that over the dog food already on the floor. "Ho-boy," Gabe said to the dog, "that's going to make a mess." As he leaned over to set the water bowl down, the dog decided to have some fun and gave the shirt a tug. Caught off-balance, Gabe did some fancy footwork to keep from falling backwards. As he shuffled around, he felt things crunching under his feet. He looked down and saw that he'd stepped all over the spilled food and water. It looked like the two of them had had a food fight.

Gabe contemplated the situation. He reached down, picked up the dog dish, and dumped the contents back into the bag, and then closed the cabinet door.

"Okay, funny-dog," Gabe said, nodding towards the strewn mess on the floor, "there's your lunch and dinner. Clean it up."

Gabe and the dog waddled their way back to the front door. He knew he might as well let the damn dog have the shirt, but Gabe was feeling spiteful. He stepped through the doorway, and then with his free hand he snapped his fingers above the dog's head. When the dog let go of the cloth to bite at this new target, Gabe snatched the shirt away and slammed the door shut. He heard mad barking and thumping as the angry dog threw himself against the door.

Gabe stood there listening. "Okay, maybe that wasn't such a good idea," he called to the dog.

He had to come back tomorrow.

When Gabe got back in the car he said to Punky, "He's a very friendly dog, maybe a little shy. Tomorrow you can go in first and surprise him."

Gabe could still hear the barking from inside the car.

He checked his route. He could cut ten minutes if he used Mission Canyon Road. He took a deep breath and looked at Punky. "Wadda'ya say? You wanna to visit your old stomping grounds?"

Three streets down Gabe turned onto a tree-lined street. He'd always enjoyed this stretch. It wound along the side of the canyon before jumping across to Pacific Boulevard. Tree-shade is a luxury in San Diego, and the canyon growth provided an exotic feel. He hadn't been along this way since . . . well, since he'd kidnapped Punky.

"You stay down, out of sight," he said sideways to Punky.

The dog peered around with keen interest. He seemed to recognize the area, and gave an excited little bark.

"You stay low. That's all we need is for old Crabnuckle to see you."

Hearing the name of his former owner, Punky started jumping around the front seat, barking.

"Hey! You sound like you *want* to see her!"

Punky wasn't listening. He was busy making as much ruckus as he could.

"*Cut it out!*" Gabe yelled.

Punky froze, surprised by Gabe's outburst.

This was a mistake. Gabe felt guilty about taking the dog from the elderly woman, and it was setting him on edge. He knew Punky was better off with him, but, after all, he *had* kidnapped him. "Stay down," he said gently. "What's done, is done."

Punky continued peering around, but kept quiet.

They came around a wide turn, and there was Crabnuckle's house on the left. Gabe was relieved to see that she wasn't outside.

Upon seeing his old home, Punky started barking again.

"No you don't," Gabe said, leaning over to hold him down.

He had to divide his attention between the road and the dog, and Gabe didn't see the car backing out from the driveway just beyond Crabnuckle's until almost too late. He slammed on the brakes, screeching to a stop. Punky tumbled forward onto the floor. A man's head appeared out of the driver's window and looked back at Gabe. He was swarthy, with black, curly hair. His sunglasses stared at Gabe for a second. Gabe waved sheepishly. The head pulled back inside, and the car took off.

Gabe saw motion out of the corner of his eye. It was Mrs. Crabnuckle! She'd been bending down behind the shrubs, working in her yard, and had now stood up, curious about the commotion. She looked right at him, a slightly puzzled expression pinching her plump face.

"Oh shit," Gabe whispered. He turned his sheepish wave now to her, simultaneously tightening his grip on Punky out of sight on the seat next to him. Punky wasn't used to such rough being handled by Gabe, and he nipped him.

"Yeow!" Gabe cried.

Suddenly Punky was on his lap, barking away at the windshield where a bee buzzed, tapping against the glass. Punky had been stung once by a bee and had sworn eternal vengeance.

Gabe glanced over at Crabnuckle. Her face had changed from puzzlement to suspicion. He saw recognition spread.

"Pinksty! Oh my Pinksty!" she cried, running forward and waving her gardening tools. Punky looked at her and his barking turned to a low growl.

"*Now* you decide you don't like her," Gabe said, putting the car in gear and taking off.

In his rearview mirror he saw Crabnuckle run out into the road.

"I knew it was you, Gabriel!" she yelled. "I *knew* it! I'm going to call the police!"

Gabe took the next turn doing fifty, and the yells faded behind them. He looked down at Punky. "You finally remembered, eh? She dressed you up like a clown. Then she tortured you when you didn't behave like a trained little monkey. Remember?"

Okay, tortured was maybe extreme, but Gabe just couldn't stand to see her snap her finger against Punky's little snout whenever he didn't behave right. He *knew* that hurt like hell—he saw it in Punky's eyes.

Oh well, he thought, she was bound to find out eventually. He suspected that she never really believed that Punky had run away like he told her.

Gabe looked down at Punky and grinned. "Oh *Pink*-sty," he said, in a mocking tone. "What a *cute* little doggy!"

Punky barked once and then ignored Gabe.

Changing his name from Pinksty to Punky was the first thing Gabe had done.

What the hell kind of name was Pinksty, anyway?

Ж Ж Ж

Back home after finishing his rounds, he found a message on the answering machine from Mrs. Crabnuckle. She promised to sue him for everything he had, and then see that he was thrown in jail for life.

"That doesn't sound so bad," Gabe said, giving Punky a good rubdown. "Someone can feed *me* for a change."

Chapter 2

Wednesday morning

Gabe heard his name. It was the same gravely voice he'd fabricated as a kid by swallowing air and then burping out words. He assumed he was dreaming, but it seemed too real. He opened his eyes. The raccoon's face was inches away. "Gabe," it said again.

This was too much. He sat up and cried out, holding his face in his hands. When he looked down, the raccoon was gone.

Too, too real. He took a deep breath. His heart was pounding. Damn! Why had he let Derrick talk him into trying that LSD? Shit! Was he going to have to live with flashbacks forever?

On the other hand, these raccoon hallucinations didn't have that feel. LSD flashbacks took you back to what you were *feeling* when you tripped. He didn't think a flashback would include actual hallucinations, particularly since his trips hadn't even starred any raccoons.

And he hadn't drunk that much the night before. Okay, maybe he had, but those threats from Mrs. Crabnuckle had gotten to him.

As if on cue, Punky came trotting in. He froze, staring at the open French doors. Gabe used his grandmother's sitting room as his bedroom, and the doors opened to a small deck. He never closed them completely, even in winter when the temperature fell into the forties at night. Punky's ears stood at attention and his legs were spread wide, as though he was posing at a show. Suddenly he barked and ran through the open doors. Outside, Punky continued barking frantically. It was a daily routine. The ground squirrel that lived under the deck teased Punky, and the fool fell for it every time.

"Shut up, you worthless mutt!" Gabe yelled. "You're going to wake the neighbors!"

He looked at the clock. It was 9:40. Well, maybe not.

Gabe was climbing out of bed when he thought he heard someone outside say, "Back, mutt!" in that same raspy voice of his flashback. Punky gave out a painful yelp. Gabe went to the French doors to investigate, but was met by a whimpering Punky hightailing it back inside. Once safely behind Gabe, the miniature dog turned and started barking again. Gabe looked outside. The morning marine layer cast a diffused light across the small yard, but nothing moved other than birds flitting from one bush to another.

"Leave the poor squirrel alone, you bully," Gabe scolded.

Punky divided his attention between Gabe and the open doors, as though expecting someone to come through.

Gabe saw a wet gleam on the dog's nose. He reached down and picked him up. "It looks like you got too close to Mr. Squirrel," he said, touching his finger lightly against the wetness. It was a drop of blood from a small scratch. "You'd better stick to the food I put in your dish, big boy. It doesn't fight back."

He took Punky to the bathroom and dabbed the blood off, and then tried to apply an antiseptic, but the wiggling ball of muscle squirmed out of his arms. "I hope the police come to take you away, you worthless parasite!" Gabe called to the dog as he scampered off. "It'll serve you right."

Gabe went to the kitchen and started coffee. He turned on the radio. Through the static, he heard ongoing reports on the explosion in the Pacific the day before. Radiation readings confirmed that it was nuclear, and no contact had been made with the submarine. The pentagon had as good as admitted that the explosion had indeed been the sub. Authorities downplayed the dangers of fallout, pointing out that the winds were easterly at the site, carrying whatever radioactive debris there might be farther out to sea. As a precaution—simply as a precaution—they were advising people in Acapulco, a couple of hundred miles northwest of the explosion, to stay indoors for a few of days.

"Like when the Soviets told the cleanup crew at Chernobyl that they'd be okay if they just kept a scarf over their noses," Gabe told himself.

Every last one of the first crew on the scene had died within a week.

The constant static made the carefully worded news seem even more dire. He reached over and switched it off. Static was replaced by sounds of birds chirping outside and the coffee bubbling through the filter.

ж ж ж

Gabe and Punky made the rounds for the day, avoiding Mission Canyon Road with a wide margin. As he pulled back into his driveway, Gabe noticed an old, blue Buick LeSabre parked on the street in front of his house. He got out and saw a man in the driver's seat on the gray side of middle age watching him. At first he thought that Mikhail Gorbachev had come to visit, for there was a birthmark the size and shape of a frog on the man's bald forehead. Thinking that the guy might need directions, Gabe walked over, but Mikhail started the car and drove away.

"Good luck," he said to the receding rear bumper.

Inside, he found that two male candidates had left messages in response to his ad for a vocalist. Three more plus a woman called later in the afternoon. He asked each to send a demo tape, explaining that he'd call after listening to it. He reminded himself that he hadn't asked Christie for a tape. Well, he never claimed to be an equal opportunity employer.

He arrived at the bar that evening at 7:30. They weren't due to start until 9:00, but it took nearly an hour to set up the equipment, and he liked to relax and have a bite to eat before starting. Derrick and Randy generally showed up at the last minute and tangled each other in cords as they scrambled to be ready on time.

This was the second time they were playing this bar. It had originally been a house, and the owner had knocked out an inner wall and added an extension on the front. It still looked like a house though, making the gigs feel like a high school party. The band set up in a tiny alcove that used to be the pantry. They were hidden off in a corner, and the people in the bar had to crane their necks to see them, at least those that even bothered to check out the band. Although the front door was only about ten steps from the pantry cum band-stage, the bar owner insisted that they bring the equipment all the way through the kitchen in the back. No sense risking disrupting a long line of people that might, for the very first time, queue up out front to get in.

Gabe pulled into the back parking lot. His car was crammed from floor to roof. There was barely room for him to squeeze in. It was a Rubik Cube puzzle packing it all. After six trips through the kitchen he had the boxes, amps, and speaker cabinets strewn around the small pantry, and he began the task of arranging and wiring it all up to produce a working band stage. From the time he began packing the gear at his house until he arrived back home and had it all stored away again, he would put in a full eight-hour work day. All for twenty-five dollars in pay—a labor of love for sure.

Gabe gave the waitress an order of fish tacos and was testing the microphones when he looked up to find Christie standing there, smiling. His memory had not enhanced her one bit; in fact, if anything she was even more attractive than he'd remembered. Her smile warmed a happy spot in his chest that he hadn't felt in some time.

"Hello, Gabe," she said. "It's good to see you again."

Considering that she'd refused to return his calls a year ago, he assumed she meant that is was good to be auditioning.

"Hey, Christie," he said in greeting, stepping off the six-inch stage. Uncertain what to do next, he extended his hand, and Christie shook it. Her hand was warm and soft—a tactile extension of her smile.

"Ready to sing some tunes?" he asked.

"No. But if I wait any longer, I'll be too nervous to even try."

Gabe grinned and swept his hand around at the rabble that was filling the place. "Not exactly a tough crowd. If they listen at all, they'll just be glad I'm not singing."

"It's not the audience I'm nervous about," she said, blushing.

Right. He had control of her destiny with the band. He would decide whether she was given the opportunity to tour the dingy little bars of the back streets of San Diego for roughly three dollars an hour.

Gabe's fish tacos arrived. He abandoned the microphone checks, and sat with Christie at a sticky table. "You're looking great," he said.

She raised an eyebrow. "Compared to what?"

Gabe didn't know what to say. He wasn't sure if she was implying that he probably didn't have many girlfriends, or to the fact that he'd only ever seen her in one other outfit. In either case, she wasn't exactly going out of her way to draw him in.

"I'm sorry," she finally said, obviously sensing his consternation. "That probably sounded rude. I didn't mean it that way."

This really was awkward. Was she being careful because she liked him, or because she wanted to get in the band?

"No problem," he said. He changed the subject. "Hey, how about that nuclear explosion?"

She seemed relieved to be on safer ground. "I *know*! I can't believe people are so blasé about it. It's as though they don't really know what's happened."

He shrugged. "Maybe they don't. News has become just another type of entertainment. The world's troubles are one big show, paid for with a cable subscription. The only time people get upset is when the local news drums up some fabricated scare about poison in the water, or invisible radiation from their cell phones."

Christie gave him a quick conspiratorial smile. "The media cries, 'Wolf!' and the sheep go 'Baaa!' "

Gabe returned her grin and offered her one of his tacos. He wished to God he'd never crawled out of that rear window in her apartment a year ago. Where would he be now if he'd just stayed and stood up to Brent?

Probably in a wheelchair, he decided.

Derrick pulled in at 8:20, and Gabe went out to help him carry in the fiberglass drum cases. Right on cue, Randy pulled up behind him and struggled to extract his massive bass amp from his Volkswagen bug. Nine o'clock arrived, and Derrick and Randy were still fiddling with their setups. Gabe took his place and waited patiently. He'd learned long ago that there was no point in making a fuss before or during the gig. The key was to keep everybody relaxed and grooving (to borrow a term from his grandmother). He would remind them at the next practice, but he knew he didn't have much leverage; they were practically volunteering their time as it was.

They finally kicked off their first set. Christie sat at a front-side table, and Gabe found himself quite pleased to have her there. It made all the difference having someone to play to. Everyone else in the joint carried on their conversations, albeit at an increased yell volume. In fact, the owner came over after a couple of songs and, following ritual, asked Gabe to turn down. It happened at every job. The problem was the drums. They had no volume control. Derrick could try to play lighter, of course, but it killed his spirit. Gabe understood this, so they continually tussled with bar owners, tying to find the maximum acceptable level.

Forty minutes later it was Christie's turn. They'd decided that she'd come up and do her two songs at the end of the first set. Even though Gabe didn't really know her all that well, he could see how nervous she was. She thanked the band, introduced herself and the song, and they were off into *Summertime*. Gabe realized only as they were playing, how difficult this piece was for a vocalist. The popular version has a pace that's so slow it feels almost like a dirge. The singer must hold on to every third and fifth syllable, carrying the note so that it hangs there in the air for all to see. The slightest drift from true pitch is painfully obvious, a test for even a seasoned professional. The fact that Christie didn't fall flat on her face was encouraging. That's not to say that her delivery was worth preserving. A forgiving critic, as Gabe knew he was, might have described it as a "mixed" success. It was hands and feet above what he had been feeding the bar, however, and more than a few in the audience paused in their conversations to watch her. The room filled with applause when they finished, the first time that night.

Before the clapping faded away, Gabe launched the two-four riff of *Got my Mojo Working*. Derrick and Randy joined in with the heavy back-beat, and Christie took the microphone from its stand and burst forth with the impassioned title line. The dusty corners of the bar reverberated with the infectious foot-stomping beat as Christie implored the audience with sincere entreaty to please, please explain why her mojo "just won't work on you." Like the gospel-trained Ann Cole, Christie's words impaled the audience with the heartrending frustration of unrequited love. Gabe saw people grinning with unabashed joy. He felt the hairs rise at the base of his own neck.

Hot damn! This girl could *sing!*

They crescendoed the song through the final chord, and the room flooded with applause. Gabe saw the owner standing at the back, clapping and smiling. He put down his guitar, took the mic from Christie, and announced that the band would take a break, but the applause and whistling just thundered on. Christie was blushed and grinning from ear to ear. Gabe knew the feeling. There'd be no turning back for her now.

The applause finally died away, and as Derrick passed by, he casually said to Christie, "You're hired." She looked at Gabe, and he just shrugged.

Gabe went off to the bathroom and left Christie with Randy at the band table. When he returned, he found that Randy had gone off to another table to visit with some friends, and two guys he'd seen lounging at the bar had come over and sat down with Christie. One of them, wearing just a denim vest in order to show off his construction-worker muscles, had his arm around the back of Christie's chair and was leaning in close, talking to her. She did not appear to be enjoying his company.

Gabe stood for a moment studying the situation. The last thing he wanted was a confrontation, particularly with a couple of testosterone-infused construction studs. He considered calling in the bar owner to explain that the table was reserved for the band, but decided against this, firstly, because it was a pretty wimpy thing to do, and secondly, and perhaps more importantly, the "band table" was a concept completely fabricated by the band.

There was only one course. Gabe strode over, feeling the blood pounding in his temples.

"Sorry, guys," he said louder than he'd intended, "this table is reserved for the band."

Christie looked up with relief. Vest-guy turned a deliberate, slow glare on him. He then turned with mock perplexity to the two remaining empty chairs. "I don't think there's a problem here, pal. Seems to be room for everybody."

No use beating around the bush. "I don't think Christie wants to be bothered."

Vest-guy held Gabe in a cold stare. " 'You don't think'—that about sums it up."

How do you argue with pure belligerence?

You don't, Gabe decided; you simply stand your ground. "Leave her alone," he demanded, wishing it had sounded more authoritative, rather than like a plea.

Vest-guy grinned. "Let's ask the lady—"

"Yes, let's," Christie cut in. "You can either go back to the bar and scope out some other victim, or have this beer poured down the front of you. Your choice."

She held up her half-full glass to demonstrate.

Vest-guy was taken by surprise, and leaned back, holding his hands up in protest. "All right! All right! All you have to do is ask."

He got up and turned back to the bar, but uttered, "*Bitch!*" just loud enough for them to hear.

"Hey!" Gabe yelled before his brain had a chance to process the wisdom.

Vest-guy stopped and turned to Gabe. He looked at him a moment then spat, "Faggot!" and walked away, gesturing for his friend to follow.

Gabe watched them take their place back at the bar. "Want to get some fresh air?" he asked.

"Sounds good," Christie replied, then added in a loud voice, "*The stink lingers!*"

Vest-guy glanced over, but immediately turned away.

They went out the front door into the cool California night and sat down together on a low cement retaining wall next to the building.

"Thanks for coming to my rescue," she said.

"It seems like you did most of the rescuing."

She smiled. "It's easy to be brash when you have the cavalry standing next to you."

"Cavalry? More like a crowd heckler. I'm a faggot you know."

She gave him a quick look, and then laughed. "That's right, and I'm a bitch."

"The definition of which is any woman who won't go to bed with the jerk. Are you sure you want to spend your free evenings crooning to these kinds of guys?"

She pretended to think deeply about this. "I guess it's the price I have to pay for fame and fortune. I'll manage as long as I've got you guys to protect my honor."

She was silent a moment, then added quietly, "It sounds like maybe I passed the audition."

He nodded slowly. "Technically we have to agree on it, but Derrick already cast his vote, so it looks like a majority."

Gabe spread his arms behind him and leaned back. His left arm was behind Christie, and she sat back against it, using it like the back of a chair. It seemed a cozy thing to do, and Gabe considered wrapping his arm around her shoulder, but figured he'd better not push it.

Instead, he decided to demonstrate that he too had been listening a year before. "As I recall, you ran away from home when you were sixteen."

"Not so much ran as just walked out the door. My mom wanted me to come back, but not enough to dump Dad."

He looked at her. "That was your condition?"

She nodded. "Yeah. My mom kept telling me she was going to, but she could never pull the hooks out."

"Are they still alive?"

"My mom is. She lives with my sister in Chicago. My dad died three years ago in a car accident. He was drunk, of course."

Her brow furrowed with concern, or maybe pain.

"I'm sorry," he said.

She looked at him, puzzled. "About my dad? Don't be. His death was my freedom. No, the tragedy is that he also took the life of a little boy in the other car."

The carefree voices of happy people spilled from the open door. They seemed far away.

"Well then, I'm sorry for the little boy," Gabe corrected. "You really hated your father? That much?"

"I really hated him."

The period at the end of that sentence didn't sound very solid. He looked at her.

"He was my dad," she finally added. "Did I love him? I don't know. I *needed* him . . . but I also hated him. That's for sure."

"Needing something you hate. Boy, sounds like hell."

She took a deep breath, as though expelling for the thousandth time a lung-full of bad air. "How about your parents? Was your father a bastard too?"

Gabe lifted his shoulders. "I never knew him. I don't even know who he is."

Christie nodded. "I remember, you told me that. Your mom left you."

"That was *my* freedom. I didn't know it at the time. I just felt abandoned in a way that very few people can even imagine. After a while, though, my grandma became my real mom."

Christie looked up at the stars and smiled. "We're both just lost puppies looking for a safe home."

He wanted to wrap his arms around her, but Randy called from the open door. It was time to start. Gabe stood up and stretched, and they headed back into the light and the drone of garbled bar conversations.

Ж Ж Ж

Christie sat alone at the band table. Gabe thought the second set was working up to be one of the best they'd ever done. He knew that pretty eyes watching him skewed his perception, but he floated on the joy of it anyway.

Towards the end of the set, a tall man with serious intent appeared in the crowd. He looked around, searching, and Gabe recognized him. He had cut his hair short and traded in the outlandish uniform of a rock band priest for a full-length black leather bad-ass coat, but Gabe would never forget that face.

Brent had arrived.

Gabe's solo faltered, and his heart stopped as time stood still. Brent's eyes scanned the room and locked on Christie. He strode over and took a seat next to her. Gabe tried to concentrate on finishing the song, but couldn't take his eyes off the two of them. He tried to read her face. Did it speak welcome? She seemed initially irritated, or maybe confused, but as Brent sat close and talked into her ear she was soon nodding reluctantly, perhaps in resignation. Several times Brent glared up at Gabe.

The second set dragged to an end, and Christie came up to him before he even had a chance to take off his guitar.

"I've got to go," she told him, watching his face.

He shrugged. "Right," he said, trying to sound nonchalant.

He pretended to concentrate on adjusting his strap. Christie stood there, seemingly uncertain what to do. "He wants to talk," she finally explained.

He looked over at Brent. The handsome man sat waiting, impassive.

"Sure," Gabe agreed.

What *could* he say? That he wanted her to tell Brent to go to hell? Beg her to come home with him so that he could make passionate love to her?

"I understand," he mumbled.

But he didn't understand. From his mouth came the words, "I had the idea you were through with him."

"I was . . . I am. He just wants to talk."

"To talk," Gabe repeated. He didn't know what else to say.

Christie sighed. "He claims he's changed."

"That sounds familiar."

"I know, he's said that before. But I think it's true this time."

"Oh yeah? What's changed?"

"He seems more . . . serious. More settled."

"Of course. He realized what he was losing."

Gabe was surprised to hear himself say that.

Christie put her hand on his arm. "I've got to go, Gabe. I'll call you tomorrow."

"Okay," he said, turning away to unplug his guitar. "Talk to you tomorrow." He tried to sound uncaring.

He could sense her standing and watching him. When he looked, she was walking off, and Brent stood up to take her away.

Gabe took off his guitar and sat down at the empty band table. He stared at the people getting drunk around him. Nothing ever worked out. It was his own fault for letting his guard down, for allowing hope to seep through. He considered getting soaked himself. As part of their compensation—potentially a majority portion—the band's drinks were half-price.

He shook his head. Getting drunk was something you should do for fun. Start drowning his sorrows and it could become a habit.

Derrick and Randy wandered back, and they started the third set. The band table looked abandoned and forlorn.

During the break before the last set, Gabe stepped out the back door through the kitchen for some fresh air. After a few minutes Derrick joined him.

"I've got something to cheer you up," Derrick consoled.

The guys obviously guessed what was going on.

"News that Brent is wanted by the FBI?"

"Not quite so useful, but the FBI would probably be interested."

Uh, oh. He could guess what it was. This was Derrick, after all. "What kind of drugs tonight?"

His friend gave him a hurt look. "My honor is wounded. I don't *always* have drugs."

He looked at the drummer in surprise. "I apologize for jumping to conclusions. What, then, pray tell, do you have to lift my spirits?"

Derrick pulled a small wad of crumpled tin foil from his jacket pocket.

"Hash?" Gabe asked, perplexed.

"From Morocco," Derrick replied, carefully unwrapping the packet and pulling a small pipe from his pocket.

"I thought you didn't have drugs?"

Derrick threw him a querulous glance. "Hash isn't a drug."

"Oh, it's not? What do you think our FBI friends would call it?"

Derrick waved off the idea. "They call everything a drug. If I smelled glue, they'd call it a drug."

He raised one eyebrow and looked at his friend, giving him a moment to think about this. Derrick was giving his full attention to lighting the pipe, so Gabe said, "Der, I think in that case, the glue *would* be considered a drug."

"You're cracked. Glue's glue. Drugs are drugs. Here," he said, coughing as he handed the lit pipe to Gabe.

What the hell, Gabe thought. He took the pipe and inhaled deeply. Instantly, memories of all the other times he'd smoked the sweet pot-derivative came rushing back. He wasn't even high yet and his mind was taking off. The hash was brown and dense and crackled wickedly as they drew deep tokes. By the time the last tiny ember extinguished, Gabe was good and high.

Derrick was right. He was happy. No, not happy. He still hurt somewhere inside, but that place was tucked away. Now he lived in the moment, second-by-second, and each second had a life of its own. After one amazing second passed, the next seemed even more amazing, and the previous one part of history, long, long ago.

ж ж ж

The last set lasted about six hours, although Gabe's watch claimed that only the standard forty-five minutes had passed. He played beautifully, his notes ascending dizzying heights of thundercloud updrafts, to be flung through the stratosphere on spinning trajectories of pure esthetic intent. Gabe knew this, felt this, as he stood transfixed in a transcendental shaft of inspired light on the six-inch stage in a bar that used to be a house and was now home to all the local soaks who, by the last set, could marginally manage to command their hands to produce a weary clap and their mouths to call out in slurred words, "Shmoke aaawwwn the Waaater!"

Gabe wasn't fooling himself. He knew that had they recorded this set, upon later listening he'd find that the device had only captured one dimension of the beautiful creation he now heard. He knew that the recording would sound for all the world like his normal playing, only more sloppy.

It took him a long time to pack up the gear as he attempted, over and over, to fit it all into his car. Each time he tried, there, on the pavement, would sit two or three pieces after the car was full. The speaker cabinets had apparently found food and gotten fat. He finally drove off with an amp head on his lap, and found his way home on streets that he knew intimately, but tonight were simultaneously familiar and eerily strange.

He pulled the car into the garage and was surprised when Punky didn't greet him at the kitchen door. "Where's the Punkster?" he called out.

He thought he heard a whimper in the living room, and found the dog cowering under the sofa. "Punky! What's the matter, big boy?"

His little companion refused to come out.

He wasn't going to try to understand. Not tonight. Not sky-high on hash. He was immensely sleepy. This was the last mile of the hash trip. His brain had toured all the rides at the carnival, and now it was time to lay down on the backseat of his grandmother's car for the ride home and drop off to sleep. He wasn't sure he could make it to his bed. He began stripping off his clothes as he staggered towards his bedroom.

When he saw the raccoon sitting on the chair, he assumed that it was a trick of the shadows, as only the hallway light illuminated his room. He flipped on the light, but the raccoon remained. It said, "Hello Gabe," in the now familiar gravelly voice. "Please don't yell."

Gabe was incapable of yelling. He could do nothing but stand with his shirt in hand, staring at the apparition.

"We need to talk, Gabe," the apparition said.

Gabe blinked hard. He had, on one or two other occasions, hallucinated on hash, but they had been transitory and mild. When he'd accepted the pipe from Derrick, he hadn't thought about the possibility that he might re-invoke serious LSD flashbacks.

It looked like he'd made a bad mistake.

"Gabe, can you understand me?" The raccoon's mouth moved in a most unnatural way when it spoke, as though manipulated by sophisticated computer graphics.

Some part of him rebelled at conversing with an hallucination. That was the last phase of the druggies who'd crossed over the line. But this creation of his mind insisted that he respond. He compromised by simply nodding his head.

"Good. Gabe, I need your help, and you are probably wondering what I am."

Maybe that had also been a mistake. It only encouraged his imagination to continue the charade. He dropped the shirt, turned off the light, and fell into bed. Maybe it would disappear if he ignored it.

"Gabe, are you still listening?" he heard the raspy voice say.

He pulled the pillow over his head and wrapped his arm around it to block out the world. He could still hear the muffled words of the raccoon, sounding eerily like Louis Armstrong, but he wrapped his arm tighter and let the hash carry out its final task. Disturbing thoughts about the raccoon hallucination evaporated, and Gabe drifted off to blissful sleep.

Chapter 3

Thursday morning

Gabe woke the next morning feeling vaguely melancholy. The memory of Christie leaving with Brent floated up through the remnant hash fog. Gabe's melancholy slumped into sadness.

It served him right for setting himself up.

He opened his eyes, threw away the covers, and rolled over onto his back.

"*Oh shit!*" he said. The raccoon was still sitting there in the chair. It didn't say anything; it just sat watching him. Gabe searched for some explanation. Perhaps this was a normal, albeit bold, raccoon, and he'd only imagined its linguistic abilities. His theory was weakened by a small metal pendant hanging from the Raccoon's neck. It wasn't even a pendant, more like a small version of the talk-boxes he'd seen throat-cancer victims wear.

Like a bad nightmare whose inevitable conclusion is already sensed, the raccoon's mouth moved and words blared forth. "GOOD MORNING, GABE!"

Gabe sat up, but that was all his brain could muster.

"CAN YOU HEAR ME NOW?"

Could he hear him? The question was: could he trust his own sanity?

Punky began barking from the living room, and Gabe heard the patter of feet as the dog galloped down the hall. Punky came dashing into the room and slid to a stop with one shocked yelp. Instantly he spun around and ran back out, whimpering.

There was no getting around it, this flesh-and-blood Disney creation was real.

"Okay, I surrender," Gabe said, feeling more than a little foolish. "Who or what the hell are you?"

The raccoon smiled. This only advanced the surreal sense of the situation, since Raccoons aren't meant to smile. They aren't built for it. The effect was vaguely grotesque.

"A RACCOON," came the reply. The words boomed crackly and distorted as though amplified through a faulty bullhorn.

Gabe closed his eyes and took a deep breath. When he opened them, the raccoon was still there, but it had thankfully relaxed the bizarre smile. "That is obvious," Gabe said, trying to be reasonable. "How can you talk?"

"ALTHOUGH NOT NEARLY AS FLEXIBLE AS HUMAN VOCAL CORDS, A RACCOON'S LARYNX CAN MANAGE SPEECH. IT MUST BE FORCED, THOUGH, AND PAINS THE ANIMAL IF DONE TOO LONG."

Gabe raised his eyebrows and pointed at the metal pendant.

"THAT IS MERELY AN AMPLIFIER. I HAD THE IDEA THAT YOU COULDN'T HEAR ME LAST NIGHT."

Gabe nodded. "Can you turn it off? I heard you, I just didn't believe in you."

The raccoon reached up with its paw and pulled it away. "Can you still hear me?"

"Just fine. I'm still not sure I believe in you."

Gabe squinted at the animal. No, he didn't feel any lingering effects of the hash. He shrugged. "But I can play along for now. You refer to yourself—to the raccoon—in the third person."

The guest sat motionless, staring at him. When it finally spoke, Gabe had the sense that it—something—had been thinking about what it would said. "You mean that you surmise that there is more to the intelligence speaking to you than the animal's brain?"

Gabe raised one eyebrow. "I couldn't have worded it better."

"That's correct."

Gabe was irked. Wait . . . was it referring to his reply or . . . "Do you mean, correct that I couldn't have worded it better, or correct that you're some other intelligence?"

The raccoon paused in thought again, but for only a moment. "Correct that I am a separate intelligence. Possibly correct to both."

"Okay, brutal honesty it is then."

"Have I offended you? I assumed you would value honesty."

"No, I do. I'm just not used to honesty that hasn't been politically sanitized."

The raccoon sat silent for several seconds. The "intelligence" was apparently chewing on the metaphor. "I find this the hardest part of my task," it finally said. "Nuances of human interactions are almost beyond comprehension."

Gabe smiled. "I didn't realize we were so complex."

"You're not. All intelligent beings have their singularly evolved interactive complexities."

Gabe bit his tongue. He decided he would just going to ignore the insults. "You say 'all intelligent beings' as though you travel the galaxy . . . look, who the hell are you?"

"A visitor."

Gabe shrugged. "What kind?"

"Friendly."

Gabe sighed. "Well, that's good to know . . . from where?"

"A place distant from here."

Gabe felt as though he was playing twenty questions. "How distant?"

The raccoon paused a moment in thought. "Sixteen light-years."

Gabe snorted. "So, you're a space alien?" he scoffed.

"I had hoped to avoid that term."

"Why?"

"It seems to hold derogatory connotations."

"So, you're telling me that you *are*? A *space* alien?"

"Correct."

A hundred questions clamored for attention. He needed a handle of some sort. "Do you have a name?"

"Ronald."

"Ronald?"

"Correct."

"You're kidding."

"I'm not joking. Why would you think that?"

"Ronald? It's just so . . . I don't know, American."

"That was the intent."

"What's your real name?"

"You mean the label I use when communicating with my own kind?"

"Yes, of course."

The raccoon stared at him through another thought-pause. "I don't know how to pronounce it in words."

"You mean, you can't pronounce it in English, or in any words?"

This thought-pause seemed to last longer. "I can't pronounce it in English," the raccoon finally replied.

"So, let's hear it in your own language."

This thought-pause seemed even longer still. Maybe it was hurting the raccoon's throat too much. "It can't be vocalized by the raccoon."

Gabe had been feeling intimidated by the extraordinary circumstances. It felt good somehow to be pressing an issue. "Come on, give it a try."

The raccoon sat silent for so long, Gabe thought that the alien spirit had departed. Finally it said, "There are a myriad ways to which I am referred. One could be, 'Ambassador.'"

"That's no surprise." *And not much help, either*, Gabe thought.

He could understand that an alien culture might have fundamentally different structures of thought and communication, but a name seemed so, well, fundamental. Gabe had the sense that the alien was hiding something. Maybe he didn't want to reveal his true name, like Rumplestiltskin.

"So, how did you come up with Ronald?" Gabe asked.

"I wanted a name that you would feel good about."

"Why would I feel good about Ronald?"

"My full name is Ronald Reagan."

The raccoon sat staring at him.

Gabe burst out laughing. "You *are* kidding."

After a short thought-pause the raccoon said, "I believe I have perhaps misjudged this."

"Why, in God's name, would you call yourself Ronald Reagan?"

"I had the idea that you often name your children after people you hold in honor. I thought that Ronald Reagan was perhaps the most honored man in recent time."

Gabe shook his head. This was too bizarre. "I might get that impression from watching Fox news."

He suddenly had an epiphany. "That's how you got your information, isn't it? The TV?"

"And radio, and news on the Internet."

"The Internet?"

"Easy access."

"Okay. Well, Ronny, you're either the manifestation of a troubled mind, or the most important thing to happen to Earth since the asteroid wiped out the dinosaurs."

" 'Ronny'? "

"It's a nickname for Ronald."

"I see."

Gabe jumped when the doorbell rang. He felt disoriented at this interruption from the sane world. He wasn't ready to meld the two together. He hadn't even decided yet what he thought about this talking raccoon named Ronald Reagan.

"Is that someone at your door?" Ronny asked.

"I guess it is."

Gabe felt paralyzed.

"Are you going to let them in?"

"I guess so."

Gabe crawled off the bed and walked out of the room. "Stay here," he said as he closed the bedroom door. He was swinging the front door open when he realized he was only wearing his boxer shorts.

Christie was standing there.

"Hi Gabe," she said and looked down at his bare legs.

"Oh! Hi, Christie. Uh, how are you?"

She grinned. "I'm fine. You look comfortable."

"Oh, yeah. I, uh, just got out of bed."

Christie's grin faded. "Am I interrupting something?"

Gabe looked at her blankly. He felt dazed, as though still high on the hash, even though he knew he wasn't. "No! Of course not! Why would you say that?"

She searched his eyes. "You seem . . . distracted."

"I'm not distracted. I just woke up."

"I see," Christie said, although she didn't seem to. Her tone had turned formal. "Well, I just came by to apologize for leaving so suddenly last night." She waited a moment, then said, "Goodbye, Gabe," and turned and started walking away.

She thinks I brought a girl home last night. The thought hovered there, like a flashing road sign.

"Wait! Christie!" he called.

She turned.

"I'm alone . . . sort of."

She raised one eyebrow.

"Look," he said, "come inside, okay?"

She looked at him skeptically. "Are you sure?"

She didn't believe him. "Yes, I'm sure. I have something to show you."

The words were out before he had a chance to think about them. He held the door open, and she came back and walked into the house. He closed the door behind them and said, "You're not going to believe what you're about to see, or hear."

"Try me."

She seemed cautious, holding her judgment.

"I can't explain it," he said going to the bedroom door. "It just showed up."

He paused a moment letting her catch up, then swung the door open.

The chair was empty.

"Shit!" Gabe exclaimed. "He must have left."

Christie glanced around the messy room. "He?"

Gabe stood with his hands on his hips. "I assume it's a he," Gabe said distractedly. "He talks like a man, but they may not have the same sexes as us."

He looked at Christie. She was staring at him with obvious surprise. "Sex?" she said.

What a mess. "The raccoon."

Christie looked at him in disbelief.

Gabe shook his head. "No, no! I didn't have sex with a raccoon. I didn't have sex with anybody—with any-*thing*. Oh, jeez, look there was a really weird raccoon here this morning . . ."

Gabe realized he was going to sound totally insane. He couldn't tell her the truth. "It was tame. It may have been somebody's pet that got away. It must have come in during the night."

Christie was still giving him the look. "And he could talk?"

"Not really talk, but it sort of sounded like it. The owners must have taught him some tricks."

Gabe had always thought that if you're going to lie, you should drag the truth along as far as you can.

Christie finally looked somewhat satisfied. She walked back out to the hall, picked up the shirt he'd discarded the night before, and smelled it. "You were smoking pot last night?" she said.

"Hash," he replied.

"Uh-huh. How much?"

She was giving him an out. "A few grams, I guess. Moroccan."

"Do you do it often?"

"Hardly ever. Derrick had some, and after you left I was feeling . . ."

She blushed.

Gabe took a deep breath. "Listen, Christie, I have to do my rounds later. Maybe you'd like to come along and we could listen to some more of the band's songs."

"Rounds?"

"My pet-sitting business."

She nodded, thought a moment, and then shrugged. "Okay, that sounds fine."

"About noon?"

"Okay. So . . . this means I have the job?"

Gabe nodded. "Yeah." He nodded harder. "Yeah, you have the job."

She grinned ear-to-ear. "See you at noon, then," she said, walking to the door.

The question swelled from somewhere deep within and overwhelmed him.

"Christie . . ."

She stopped at the door and turned.

"Did you . . . and Brent . . ."

"Sleep together? No. I told you, he just wanted to talk."

Gabe was hungry to know what the outcome of *that* was, but he sensed where the line was. "Great! I mean, okay . . . see you later."

Christie smiled and walked out.

Gabe stood looking at the door. Was he setting himself up yet again?

Of course. But, what the hell.

ж ж ж

Gabe walked back to the bedroom. "Ronny, baby! You can come out now," he called to the empty room. Only the birds answered through open French doors.

Oh well, he thought. Good riddance. Maybe it *was* just a lingering combination of hash and LSD legacy.

Ronny's head appeared from around the edge of one of the French doors. "Is she gone?" he asked.

Gabe sighed. "Yes, but you're not."

The raccoon stared at him through one of those thought-pauses. "Why would you say that? It seems obvious."

"It's called sarcasm, probably another singularly evolved interactive complexity."

"I know what sarcasm is. Was that also sarcasm?"

"I guess that's for you to decide."

Another thought-pause. "Somewhat."

Gabe rolled his eyes. "Somewhat that it was sarcasm? Or somewhat that sarcasm is a unique human complexity?"

"The two are exclusive, aren't they?"

"Somewhat."

Thought-pause. "That was sarcasm also? Repeating the use of the word somewhat?"

"This could go on all day. Maybe I'll just avoid using sarcasm altogether."

"No. Please, I could use the practice."

"Great," Gabe grumbled. "I can see my place in history. Louis and Clarke had Sacagawea to guide them through the wild American frontier; Ronny-the-alien had Gabe to help him master sarcasm."

"This is your hope?"

Gabe just looked at the raccoon's head in the doorway.

After some seconds Ronny said, "That was sarcasm again, wasn't it?"

Gabe nodded slowly.

"Okay, I agree. Let's leave the sarcasm for later."

"Agreed. If you hang out on the deck my neighbors are going to start asking questions."

Ronny waddled in on his four paws and climbed back up on the chair.

"I have a thousand questions," Gabe said.

"I have time, but I'm surprised that you've enumerated so many already."

"That was hyperbole."

"I see. That's different from sarcasm, but not by much."

"Ronny, where are you?"

Thought-pause. "Gabe, I'm right here in the chair. I suspect I don't understand your question."

"I know the raccoon is here, but where are *you*, the part that's thinking about the difference between sarcasm and hyperbole. I doubt the raccoon's brain is up to it."

"That is difficult to answer, although you are right, I am not using the raccoon's brain to think."

Ronny sat silent for a moment—yet another think-pause. "Let me say that I am in association with the animal. I can see and feel what it does, and can control its movements."

"Invasion of the raccoon snatchers."

Think-pause. "I don't understand."

"Never mind. So, where *are* you?"

Think-pause. "I am simultaneously with the raccoon and with my colleagues."

"And, where would that be?"

"I am sorry Gabe, but I cannot tell you that."

Gabe noticed there was no think-pause for that answer. "Fair enough, for now. So, there's no actual physical connection with the raccoon?"

Think-pause. "That is correct."

"Does that mean that you could take control of me as well?"

A long think-pause. Gabe didn't like the delay. "No."

"Why not? If there's no physical connection, then what would stop you from just flying your spirit into me?"

"You are not compatible."

"Not compatible?"

"Correct."

"How? How am I any different from a raccoon?"

"You are super-sentient, meaning that although the raccoon is also sentient to a degree, you—a human—have a developed intelligence which works easily with abstractions."

Gabe waited, but apparently Ronny thought that this was explanation enough. "And this is why you couldn't control me?"

"Correct."

"Because I can understand abstractions?"

"Correct."

Gabe looked at the raccoon a moment. "Ronny, are you trying to be sarcastic with me?"

"No, Gabe. Why? Does it seem so to you?"

"Never mind. Let's get to the bottom line. Why are you here? I mean, why are your people on Earth? And why did you choose to contact me?"

"We've come to save the human race."

Gabe sat down on the bed. "Ronny, no more sarcasm, right?"

"I'm not being sarcastic, Gabe. We've come to save you."

"From what? Ourselves?"

Gabe had a vision of Klaatu walking down the ramp of his flying saucer onto the mall in Washington in 1953 with Gort, the laser-eye robot, behind him. How would the movie have turned out if Klaatu had been a raccoon? Gort would be zapping hunters with his heat-ray as their hound-dogs chase Klaatu up a tree.

"Not from yourselves," Ronny said. "From the Demon-zombies."

Gabe sat staring at Ronny. "Demon-zombies," he repeated.

"Correct."

"Ronny, are we on Candid Camera?"

"The TV show?"

"Yeah."

"No . . . I see. You think I'm joking. I'm not joking, Gabe."

"You're telling me that the human race is in danger from beings called Demon-zombies. Wait, you had to make up that name. They wouldn't have a name that's pronounceable either."

Think-pause. "Correct."

"You *chose* to call them Demon-zombies."

"Correct."

"Why?"

Think-pause. "The words seemed to describe them. They are parasitic beings who depend on other living organisms for their existence. More importantly, they have no sense of the individual. Like ants or bees, each unit only exists to further the hive."

Gabe found himself alarmed for the first time since meeting Ronny. "So, they'd place no importance on an individual human life."

"They put no importance on anything other than the hive. They put no importance on the entire human species."

"They want to wipe us out?" Gabe was on his feet now.

A long think-pause. "Possibly. They don't come with that specific intention, but they might decide this if they think you're getting in the way."

"Of what?"

"The expansion of the hive. Akin to bees swarming."

"Why the zombie part?"

"They can take control of human individuals."

"Like you did to this raccoon?"

Think-pause. "It's not the same."

"Why?"

"I do this to help you. They do it to conquer you."

"That's a difference in intent, not in method."

Long think-pause. "Perhaps. But nevertheless, the difference remains, and I think it's important."

"It is, I agree. But, Christ! I can't believe this is happening."

"It is indeed a dire situation. You need our help."

Gabe sat back down on the bed. "What's in it for you?"

Think-pause. "Satisfying our altruistic fundamentals."

"Somehow that sounds a little too politically correct."

Think-pause. "It does not sound credible?"

" 'Correct,' as you like to say."

Long think-pause. "We also want to stop their expansion."

"That's more like it."

Gabe felt an undercurrent of unease that he had to pry the real reason from Ronny. "Tell me, why do you have to operate through a raccoon? Why couldn't you contact me directly?"

"A raccoon has prehensile hands, is a reasonable size, does not generally alarm people, and has a marginal ability to speak."

"That explains the choice of animal, but still, why don't you talk to me directly?"

"That would be difficult."

Gabe waited, but Ronny didn't elaborate. "Why?"

"You might find me offensive and distracting."

"Where are your companions? Where is your spaceship?"

"Gabe, I think you can understand that I can't reveal that to you."

"You don't trust me."

Think-pause. "I trust you, Gabe. My companions must be careful. Surely you understand that there are people around you that may not be as trustworthy as yourself."

Gabe smiled ruefully. "Like Brent," he muttered to himself. "The bastard."

Think-pause. "This is the Brent you mentioned when talking with Christie?"

Gabe's eyes widened. "You were eves-dropping?"

"Not intentionally. I heard your conversation, though."

Gabe shrugged. "Yeah, that's Brent."

"He is not a friend of yours?"

Gabe laughed. "Oh no, quite the opposite."

"I see."

Gabe studied Ronny. "Okay, fair enough. I won't press you for the location of your ship. So, when will these Zombie-demons arrive?"

"They're called Demon-zombies, and the full force of the invasion will begin soon."

"Full force? It's already started?"

"The advance scouts are already here. We don't have much time."

"They're *here?*" Gabe was on his feet again.

"Just a few. Many more may follow soon. These advance agents have already tested your technology."

Gabe imagined slimy worm-beings holding cell phones to their antennae and asking whether they could be heard *now*. "How?"

"These scouts have detonated a small nuclear bomb—"

"The submarine explosion!"

"Affirmative."

"Jesus! Do you know where they are? Are there any here in California?"

"Some."

Gabe glanced out the window, as though he might find them lurking in the bushes. "Are there any in San Diego?"

"Yes, but not in the immediate vicinity."

"What do they look like?"

"I explained. They take over a human body."

"Right. The zombie part. Do you have pictures? How will I recognize them?"

Long think-pause. "You don't need a picture."

"Why?"

"You know one of them."

"*What*! Who? *Who*, for God's sake?"

Think-pause. "Brent."

Gabe put his hand to his mouth. "No way!"

"Way."

Gabe shook his head in disbelief. "No. That's ridiculous. I saw Brent just last night. He wasn't a zombie."

"How would you know?"

Gabe remembered Christie saying that Brent had changed since she'd last seen him. A thought came to Gabe which set his neck hairs on end. "What about . . . Christie?"

"You mean, is she a zombie?"

"Yes. *Yes*!"

Think-pause.

"*Well*? Yes or no, for God's sake! Its' a simple question!"

"No, she's not a zombie."

Gabe took a deep breath. He felt relief wash through him. Close behind, though, was a nagging doubt. It seemed too . . . connected. Gabe rewound the previous couple of minutes. Yes, he was pretty sure he'd brought up the subject of Brent before Ronny revealed him as a zombie.

Quite a coincidence. "Are there other zombies around?"

Think-pause. "Yes."

The doorbell rang again. Both Gabe and Ronny jumped. They froze, staring at each other. "Somebody's apparently at the door," Ronny finally observed.

Gabe nodded and padded in his bare feet to the front door. He looked through the peep-hole and breathed a sigh of relief when he saw the badge on the man's shirt. He trotted back to the bedroom. "It's just the electric man."

"Electric man?" Ronny squawked. He sounded almost alarmed.

"Yeah, he works for the electric company. He's come out to figure out why they've been overcharging me. They claim I'm using twice as much electricity as normal."

Without a word, Ronny jumped off the chair and scampered out the French doors.

"He won't be coming in here!" Gabe called, but the raccoon was already gone.

It was the first time Gabe had a view of the back of the raccoon, and he saw a distinct lump on the back of the animal's neck. He didn't have a chance to think about it, as the doorbell rang again, more insistently. He hurried to the front door and let the utility man in.

"Sorry to bother you, Mr. Wolfekow," the middle-aged man explained, "but your records shows that your meter is not accessible from outside."

Gabe rolled his eyes. "That's a whole other problem with you guys. That's because my grandmother used to keep a dog out back where the meter is. The dog's been dead for eight years. I've called about five times, but they can't seem to get that information updated."

"Sorry, sir," the man said, looking at his clip-board and not sounding sorry at all. "Can you show me the meter?"

Gabe took him back outside and around the side of the house. Gabe was opening the backyard gate when he noticed movement above. He looked up and caught the flash of dark fur. It was Ronny's tail disappearing above the roof. They had probably caught him by surprise. He doubted the utility man, or anybody else, would think twice about seeing a raccoon in the neighborhood. He realized that Ronny had chosen a good subject after all.

Gabe walked through the gate, but noticed that the utility man wasn't following. He turned around and the man just pointed past him, into the back yard. Gabe looked where he was indicating. Charlemagne, the big, dumb mongrel from next door, was lying there gnawing on one of Punky's chew toys.

"This is the dog that's been dead for eight years?" the utility man asked dryly.

"That's my neighbor's dog. He always comes over to visit."

The utility man gave Gabe a smug look that said that he, and the entire utility company, were now totally vindicated.

"It's not my dog!" Gabe repeated. To hell with it. He clapped his hands. "Charlemagne! Get out of here!"

The dog barked and started running around in circles. Gabe yelled and chased him, and the dog finally bounded easily over the three-foot yard fence. *What a dumb mutt*, he thought.

The utility man had found the meter while Gabe was running around chasing Charlemagne. He wrote down the readings, then put the pencil behind his ear and started walking away.

"That's it?" Gabe asked.

The man turned around, surprised. "Yeah."

"That's all you came to do? Read the meter?"

The man shrugged. "What else did you think?"

"I thought you were going to investigate why I've been using . . . er, why you've been overcharging me."

The man looked annoyed. Gabe was just another in a long line of irate and, in his eyes, misguided homeowners. "I'm not an engineer. I read meters. I do what's on the ticket," he said, holding up a green slip of paper for Gabe to see.

"Fine," Gabe responded curtly. He had at least as much reason to be annoyed as this guy. "Maybe I'll just stop paying my bill until this is straightened out."

"I wouldn't recommend that," the man cautioned, walking away. "They'll just cut off your service."

The man was nearly gone around the corner of the house. "Did you ever see *Fun with Dick and Jane?*" Gabe called to the man, but he either didn't hear him, or, more likely, chose to ignore the threat.

Gabe was still dressed in just his boxer shorts, but the San Diego sun had broken through the morning marine layer, and the outfit was now appropriate—at least, for around the house. He walked to the side of the house and called quietly up to Ronny. He waited a moment, but there was no response. Gabe went around to the front of the house, and back in to his bedroom. He was half expecting Ronny to be waiting for him, but the chair was empty. The room felt sort of empty as well.

Gabe remembered the lump on the back of Ronny's neck. It was clearly something which Ronny—Ronny the alien—had implanted. It was probably how he was controlling the raccoon. Ronny had said that there was no physical connection. It was possible that Ronny had misunderstood, but it seemed more likely that he had simply lied to him.

This wasn't good, Gabe decided. Not good at all.

Chapter 4

Thursday, late morning

Gabe stepped out of the shower as Christie arrived. She was early. He looked at the clock-radio next to his bed. Nope, she was right on time. With a towel wrapped around his waist, he let her in and sat her down in the living room to wait while he finished getting ready. When he returned, Mrs. Jones was sitting on Christie's lap and Punky lay curled up beside her. They weren't fighting. This was almost more amazing than Ronny the Talking Raccoon.

Gabe grabbed the song tape containing original versions of songs on the band's play-list. He could explain any unusual arrangements, and they could work out harmonies as they made the pet-rounds. When they got into his car, Punky curled up in Christie's lap as though this was automatically the new routine.

The very first stop was the killer Doberman. Gabe related his previous encounter and told Christie to stay in the car with Punky. "If I'm not back in fifteen minutes," he instructed, "contact the authorities."

"Let me go with you," Christie suggested.

"You don't understand. This dog hates humans."

"No dog hates all humans. You probably didn't develop a rapport."

That would be a woman's approach to a man-eating monster: develop a rapport. Maybe sit a hungry tiger down and explain how it is destructive behavior to eat those who care for you. But Christie's beautiful, trusting eyes were impossible to resist.

"Okay," Gabe said, "but don't be mad if you get killed."

Christie was holding Punky when she got out of the car.

"Are you planning on tossing him in for an appetizer, or do you think his life just won't be worth living alone after we're eaten?"

Christie gave him a reproving side-glance. "You probably didn't even let the Doberman meet Punky, Mr. Smart-alec."

"What do you mean?" Gabe asked, following her up the walk.

"Punky's scent is all over you."

"Yeah . . ."

"How did you expect the Doberman to accept you, when you didn't give him a complete picture of you?"

Gabe unlocked the front door, while inside, the Doberman again roared threats of mutilation and dismemberment from the depths of hell.

"What would you do," she continued, "if you were told to guard property and somebody showed up with a blanket thrown over them and just the barrel of a gun poking out?"

Gabe looked down at Punky. "If this guy is a gun, then his bullets are made of cork."

"The Doberman wouldn't be able to tell the size of Punky just from his smell, silly. As far as he knows, Punky could be Hulk-Dog: wrestler of grizzly bears."

Christie knelt down in front of the door, holding Punky tight. "Now, open the door just a couple of inches. Don't let him out."

These were totally superfluous words. He eased the door a crack and instantly the black and brown snout poked through, barking and snapping. Christie had to hold Punky back, as he was also snarling, begging Christie to let him go so that he could show this overgrown braggart who was boss. Christie held Punky for a second, letting the Doberman get a good look at him, and then carried Punky back and put him in the car. She returned and squatted down in front of the Doberman. She held her hand out so that he could smell her. The Doberman continued to bark, but paused periodically to smell her hand.

She sat back on her haunches and said, "Okay, open the door."

Gabe stared at her. He obviously hadn't heard her correctly.

She looked up at him. "Go ahead. Open it."

Those eyes. He couldn't argue with those beautiful eyes. He didn't want to look as he opened the door. The dog pounced forward and stood barking at Christie who sat staring him in the eye. Although the Doberman's bark was loud and nervous, Gabe noticed that the dog was no longer growling. Christie slowly lifted her hand and the Doberman stopped to sniff it again. He barked once, and then stood panting and looking at her. His tail began to wag.

Christie got up and walked in. The Doberman followed, whimpering for attention.

ж ж ж

Five minutes later they were back in the car and on their way.

"Where did you learn that?" Gabe asked.

"There's nothing to learn," she replied. "I just put myself in his place. If you're nervous, it makes him nervous. He doesn't know what it is, but there must be *something* that's making you frightened."

Gabe chuckled. "I always thought it was the most ridiculous advice: 'He won't hurt you if you're not afraid of him.' It's like telling me, 'Don't visualize a tomato. Whatever you do, just don't imagine a tomato.' Or, telling a person on the electric chair, 'Don't be scared and it won't hurt as much.'"

Christie smiled at him and shrugged. "It's still true, though."

Gabe shook his head. "Do you really think it's possible to logically convince myself not to be scared?"

Maybe if I had one of Ronny's lumps stuck on my neck, he told himself.

The thought of Ronny sobered Gabe. With Christie, he almost forgot the whole incredible business about aliens and zombies. It seemed like the lingering echoes of a bad dream. He hadn't decided just how much of it he was buying, but he was sure that at least Ronny—the intelligence behind the talking raccoon—was real. Either that, or he had to find somebody to watch after Punky and Mrs. Jones while he checked himself into a hospital.

Should he tell Christie? He wanted to. It would be a relief to share the burden, but he sensed that it wasn't time. She was probably still checking him out.

His musings were interrupted when the radio announcer began an update on the nuclear explosion in the Pacific.

"I guess it was bound to happen eventually," Christie said. "No matter how safe they think things are, in the end, something blows up."

If only you knew, Gabe thought.

Demon-zombies. And this was Ronny's best descriptive name.

Ж Ж Ж

They continued the rounds, and at every stop, the cat, or dog, or Vietnamese Potbellied Pig greeted Christie like a familiar old friend. Between stops they sang along to the song tape. Although Gabe's voice was sadly lacking for lead vocals, it served well enough for background harmonies, and people on the sidewalks paused and then smiled as they drove past, a Louis Prima or Ruth Brown tune sailing out of the open car windows.

Gabe thought that he could be happy if he did nothing else for the rest of his life. Contented satisfaction lulled him into broaching a subject that he'd been ignoring. "How long had it been since you'd seen Brent—I mean, before last night?"

Christie looked out her side window for a moment, as though she too had, for a while, forgotten about him. "Three, maybe four months. I told him I wanted to take a break, get some perspective. Within days he broke up Raige Aige and disappeared. We've been through this dance together before. As soon as I think I've had enough, he backs off. If he begged me to stay, I'd probably have let him go for good. But it's like he knows instinctively what to do to keep me roped in. He pulls away, and I panic. It's twisted logic. If somebody can reject me, they must be valuable. Or, if they reject me, they're probably the one person in the whole world who can save me."

"Because," Gabe said, offering the obvious, "this is what the most important man in your life did when you were a kid."

He was sorry he'd broached the whole subject. Christie was basically describing how she could never be deeply attracted to him.

Christie shrugged as if accepting her fate and stared out her side window.

"It sounds like you've had some therapy," Gabe said.

She turned and smiled at him now. "Oh yeah. Many hours with Dr. Phil."

He laughed. "You probably watch Oprah too."

"Who doesn't?"

"Only the poor sods who have nine-to-five jobs and don't know what they're missing."

Gabe drove on in silence for a while. She left him to his thoughts.

"Christie," he finally said, "do you realize that you describe your attractions to guys like Brent in the present tense?"

She shrugged again, that submission to destiny. "I'm not going to instantly change my emotional drives just by understanding them."

Gabe glanced over at her. She was watching him.

"It's a first step," she explained. "And, just because I have attractions doesn't mean I have to act on them. A recovering alcoholic doesn't stop drinking because he loses the taste for whiskey."

Neither said anything for a while.

Gabe finally broke the meditation with a last thought, which sat burning in his chest. "Resisting an unhealthy attraction is one thing, but developing a healthy one isn't something you can necessarily control either."

There, he'd said it, and now he wished he could take it back.

"That's true," she said. "The best I can do is to make sure I put myself in positions that allow the possibility."

Gabe glanced over at her and their eyes met. Words were superfluous.

As they drove towards their last stop for the day, Gabe thought, *But, Brent is a zombie.*

If he told her this, how else could she take it but a desperate attempt to dissuade her?

He'd tell her when the time was right.

Ж Ж Ж

After they'd finished the rounds, Gabe asked Christie if she'd like to get a cup of coffee. He didn't want coffee; he just didn't want to let her go. She said that'd be great. He picked up Nimitz Boulevard to Rosecrans Street and found a parking spot a block from The Koffee Klutch, a popular hangout for UCSD students living around Shelter Island. Gabe came here sometimes, since he could sit with Punky outside on a large porch, which wrapped around three sides of the old house. A lot of the regulars knew him by name. Some of them knew Gabe's name as well.

They were walking along the sidewalk when Gabe saw something which made him stop dead. There, on the side-porch, was Brent, the zombie, reading a newspaper.

"Come on," Gabe said low and terse, turning back. "Let's go."

"Why?" Christie asked, concerned.

"I'll explain in the car. Let's go."

He made the mistake of taking one last look. Christie followed his gaze. "It's Brent!"

"Come *on*," Gabe insisted, "before he sees us."

He took her hand and tried to walk away, but Christie held her ground.

"What's this all about?" she asked, looking both concerned and irritated.

"I told you, I'll explain in the car."

"What are you afraid of? Brent won't hurt you. He knows I'm in the band now."

"I'm not afraid of Brent . . . okay, yes I am, but I have a good reason."

Christie studied him, as though seeing him life-sized for the first time and maybe not liking the size.

"Look," he said, "I just want you to stay away from him for now. I can explain everything in good time."

"I'm not going to run from Brent," she said levelly. She didn't add, *like we did a year ago.*

She turned to walk towards the coffee shop.

"What about all that talk in the car?" he asked.

She turned back and he could see that she was getting angry. "What about it?"

He knew he should let it go, but the fool in him insisted on getting a few words in. "This doesn't seem like breaking-away behavior."

Her eyes flashed and she poked a finger into his chest. "Who the hell are you to tell me how to live my life? You act all wise and understanding, but you're just looking out for your own interests. Then when the chips are down, you can't take the heat."

She pulled her finger dagger back and shook her head as though disappointed. "At least Brent stands up for himself."

And with that, she turned on her heel and strode off towards the coffee shop.

Gabe wanted to run and grab her and explain everything, but he couldn't let Brent see Christie with him. The zombie might be checking out Gabe because he'd been talking with Ronny. No sense drawing any more attention to his connection with her.

Gabe walked back to his car and sat staring at nothing. Punky tried to cheer him up with his tongue, but Gabe just pushed him away. It had happened so fast. One minute he was walking through the Garden of Eden, and the next he was an outcast. Instead of a snake, though, he'd been betrayed by an alien zombie. A Demon-zombie.

Ж Ж Ж

After many minutes of self ass-kicking, Gabe finally started the car and drove home. When he arrived, he saw the same Buick LeSabre parked in front of his house as the day before. Skipping a heartbeat, it occurred to him that this might be one of Ronny's Demon-zombies. He pulled into his driveway and tried to think. What should he do? He wished Ronny was here. On the other hand, the raccoon weighed fifteen pounds at most. What could it do? Gnaw on the zombie's ankle? Maybe Ronny had instilled superhuman strength. Not likely. In spite of whatever advanced technologies Ronny used to control the Raccoon, the bones and muscles were still those of a raccoon.

Well, in any case, Ronny wasn't here. He was on his own. So what to do?

Nothing *to* do, he decided, but face it. "You stay here, you saliva monster," he said to Punky, then opened the door, and got out.

Gabe saw that it was the same man with the Gorbachev birthmark, and he was pointing some sort of instrument at him through the open window. Instinctively Gabe dove for the ground. He lay with his nose in the grass. Nothing happened. He looked up. The man had put the instrument down and was looking at Gabe in astonishment. The man shrugged and aimed the instrument again. Gabe saw now that it was a camera. The man was taking pictures of him!

He jumped up and walked over, but, like the previous day, the man drove away. Gabe watched the rear of the LeSabre until it turned the corner at the end of the street. He realized that he'd failed to get the license number.

Gabe sighed and walked back to let Punky out of the car. A bee had gotten in through an open window, and Punky was jumping frantically around trying to bite the poor, trapped fellow. Punky *really* hated bees. Gabe picked him up and dropped the squirming ball to the floor once inside the house. When Gabe walked into his bedroom, there was Ronny waiting for him on the chair.

"How long have you been here?" Gabe asked.

"Around three and a half hours."

"Didn't you see that guy in the car out front?"

Think-pause. "No."

"I think he's been stalking me. He was taking pictures. What do you think?"

Think-pause. "I don't understand what you're asking."

"You don't understand . . . what's there to understand? What do you think about this guy?"

Think-pause. "I'm sorry, Gabe. I still don't understand what you're asking."

Gabe rolled his eyes. "Do you think this guy is maybe a zombie?"

Think-pause. "Yes."

"Really?"

"Yes."

Gabe had been thinking of Ronny as a male, but maybe "he" was really a "she." Gabe had stumbled through this sort of conversation with girlfriends before.

"What do you base that conclusion on?" he challenged.

Think-pause. "Please describe this man."

"I only saw his head through the window of his car. He's maybe fifty, half-bald. He's got a mark on his forehead that looks like a frog. He was wearing a dark T-shirt. He looked unconcerned—bored, actually."

"Yes."

" 'Yes' what?"

"Yes, he is a zombie."

"Really? You know that for sure?"

Think-pause. "No. I can't know for sure, but it is highly likely."

"Why is he stalking me?" He was beginning to sound a bit hysterical.

Long think-pause. "Gabe, perhaps we should continue our conversation from this morning. That might help you understand the situation."

Gabe shrugged and sat down on the bed. "Shoot."

Think-pause. "Do you mean proceed?"

Gabe rolled his eyes again. "Yes, 'shoot' means proceed."

"The Demon-zombie scouts exploded the nuclear missile aboard the submarine in order to analyze human weapons technology—"

"They blew up a submarine to see if our bombs *work*?"

"Essentially, yes."

Gabe shook his head. "That's *crazy*! What, they thought that maybe the hundreds of thousands of nuclear bombs are all bluffs?"

Think-pause. "Not exactly."

"Maybe they never saw a nuclear bomb before?"

Think-pause. "Of course they have. They wanted to investigate the details of your implementation."

Gabe understood the basic operation of an atom bomb. You take radioactive material and force it into a shape and density that's above its critical mass, and it explodes—in a really big way. The basic principle is almost simplistic. The original atom bomb dropped on Hiroshima was nothing more than two chunks of uranium slammed together with TNT.

It seemed to Gabe that there was more technical sophistication in a cell-phone. "I don't see the point."

Long think-pause. "They wanted to analyze the quality of your plutonium and the lithium-6 deuteride used in the secondary detonation of the fusion portion of—"

"Okay. I got it. The alien Demon-zombies are setting off nuclear bombs like firecrackers in order to hear the bang. Here's the question that's been nagging me all day, though: why me?"

Think-pause. "Do you mean, why am I contacting you?"

Gabe sighed. "Yes," he said with exaggerated weariness.

"I need your help."

Gabe raised his eyebrows. "*My* help? You're an interstellar traveler who can make a puppet out of a living raccoon. How can I help *you*?"

"You are human."

Gabe remembered the beautiful alien women that inevitably fell in love with Captain Kirk, unable to resist his charm. Was Ronny indeed maybe a female?

"That's right," Gabe agreed. "I am human, along with five billion other people on Earth."

Think-pause. "Do you mean, why did I choose you over other people?"

Gabe closed his eyes a moment in exasperation. "Yeah."

"I believe that you are in a position, and contain the qualities, to aid me."

"Okay, explain."

"First of all, you are a friend of animals."

"Who's not? How am I different?"

"You advertise this on your car. 'The Only Friend Your Pet Will Ever Need.' Also, Punky chose to live with you instead of Mrs. Crabnuckle."

Gabe eyed his alien guest. "Punky didn't *choose* to live with me, I *kidnapped* him!"

Think-pause. Ronny shrugged. At least, Gabe interpreted the spastic lifting and dropping of the raccoon's shoulders as a shrug. It looked like the beginnings of a seizure. It was alien and distracting.

"So, why is that important?" Gabe asked.

"In order to explain that, I must expand the scope and describe our plan for thwarting the Demon-zombies. Let me add that you are the only human that knows of our presence."

Gabe waited a moment, and then waved his hands, palms up, indicating he was impatient to hear more.

"We can intercept the Demon-zombies as they arrive," Ronny went on, "but we will need the full cooperation of your people—"

"How do they arrive?"

Think-pause. "That's not important now, what is important is that we have humanity's cooperation."

"Okay, where do I come in? You understand, by the way, that I'm not the President."

"Of course. That seems obvious, Gabe."

"Humor, Ronny. Humor."

"Right. It was important that you are a friend to animals so that you wouldn't kill me."

"You think the average person *would?*"

"The evidence seems to indicate that."

The essence of that sunk in. "You're not the first raccoon, are you?"

"The first raccoon, yes. The first host animal, no."

"The other ones were killed . . . by people?"

"Correct."

Gabe leaned back on his arms and contemplated that a moment. "Frankly, it *was* pretty scary waking up to find you talking to me."

"I was afraid at first that you were indeed going to kill me—and you are a friend of animals."

"Sorry about that. Remember, I'm treading new ground here. What were the other hosts?"

"Rats."

"*Rats?*"

"Correct."

"Well, jeez-louise, no *wonder!* People *hate* rats. We kill them any chance we get. I'm surprised you didn't try cockroaches."

"We considered many possible hosts. A cockroach's visual acuity is poor, and they are somewhat small for our purposes."

"Ronny, I was joking."

"Right. Humor."

"Okay, so I didn't kill you. That was one reason to pick me."

"We also need your help convincing people that we are not a threat, that we are, in fact, friends."

Gabe stood up. "Okay. I'll go tell them." He started for the door.

"Gabe," Ronny said.

He stopped at the door and turned back, pretending to be surprised. "Yes?"

"I don't think that this is the best course. Further, I suspect that you are again joking with me."

"Congratulations!"

Think-pause. "You continue to joke."

"You're catching on, my friend. Where were we? I like animals and didn't kill you, and I'm going to help convince the world that you're a bunch of cute Disney characters that have come to help us beat back the Demon-zombies."

Think-pause. "Correct . . . I think."

"So, why me?"

"You have the key to Mrs. Crabnuckle's house."

Gabe stared at Ronny. He blinked once. Ronny blinked back. "What's special about Mrs. Crabnuckle's house?" Gabe finally asked.

Think-pause. "She lives next to terrorists."

Gabe took a deep breath and let it out slowly. "I'd better sit down."

Instead, he began pacing the room. "Do you mean Demon-zombies?"

"No, I mean terrorists—individuals who use violence in order to create shock and draw attention to their cause."

Gabe stopped and sat on the floor so that he was now looking up at Ronny on the chair. "Look, just tell me the whole story. This spoon-feeding is driving me nuts."

Ronny attempted another shrug. It went better this time, appearing as though he was stretching a cramp in his back. "Jihad terrorists have taken residence in a house next to Mrs. Crabnuckle and have been assembling a crude nuclear fission bomb—"

"*You're kidding!*"

Think-pause. "I'm not. The enriched uranium U235 was developed in North Korea. The detonation mechanism is crude, but effective. Details are readily available from various web-sites. This small nuclear bomb will be detonated in two days—"

"*Two days!*"

"Yes, when the British Prime Minister will be here attending the wedding of his niece."

There had been a fair amount of media hoopla about this since she was marrying a Hollywood movie star. The wedding was going to be held at the historic Presidio Mission and would be small and very private, with the whole world watching from a hundred feet away. Mrs. Crabnuckle's house sat maybe a half-mile across the canyon. The mission would get the full blast. Gabe's house was a couple of miles away on the other side of a hill. He wondered if it would still be standing.

"I didn't know the Prime Minister was going to attend," he managed, although his throat seemed to be wrapped tight in baling wire.

"This hasn't been made public. It will not be announced until tomorrow, for obvious reasons."

Gabe shook his head, trying to clear the fog. "How do you know all this?"

Think-pause. "Our expertise is information technology."

"You picked it all up on the Internet?"

"Almost anything communicated electronically is available to us. Although your governments take great care to protect their secrets, at some point everything is transmitted across publicly accessible networks. Their encoding provides an unjustified sense of security."

Gabe massaged his face. "Why don't we contact the FBI?" he asked, putting his hands down. "Just the fact that you've figured all this out will make you instant heroes."

"No. That would be a mistake. For one, your government would intercept the terrorists, but the public would never learn of it. This has happened multiple times already in the last decade. Second, they wouldn't believe about us. You would be interrogated and held until they discovered what they thought was the truth behind your ties with this terror organization, which, of course, they never would, so you would be held indefinitely."

"You'd be with me to tell them the truth."

Ronny turned his head slowly from side to side. Gabe saw that he was trying to shake his head. "They still wouldn't believe you. I would be killed and dissected and they would never understand the truth."

Gabe shuddered at the thought. "You predict human behavior with a lot of confidence, considering you don't even catch our common metaphors."

"Individual human behavior—motivation and reaction—is fairly straightforward. The intricate complexities of evolved human interactions, on the other hand, such as negotiations, social positioning, and metaphors, are almost beyond comprehension. Also, government operation is far removed from individual human behavior, and is predictable almost to a percentile of confidence."

"Well, I can't argue that government isn't human," Gabe muttered. "Okay, I get the picture. So, what's my role?"

"I need your help getting to the bomb. We need to place a device within a few feet before it goes off."

"How can *I* help?"

"You're human."

"We established that, but how does that help?"

"As a raccoon, I cannot get near the bomb."

"Have you already tried?"

"Not I, but others."

"Right—the rats. What happened?"

"The terrorists keep a guard posted around the clock. They hate rodents. They shoot at them with a pellet-gun for target practice. I think that they may hate all animals."

"And how will I, a human, do better?"

Think-pause. "I'm hoping you will have some ideas."

Gabe rolled his eyes. "Okay, assuming I'm able to come up with something and we actually place this device near the bomb, what do we do then?"

"We let the bomb go off."

Gabe sighed in resignation. He was almost beyond reacting. "Yup. That should convince them. How could they possibly question your existence after that?"

Think-pause. "Was that sarcasm?"

"Yes. I'm sorry, Ronny. I'm afraid I'm in overload."

"I understand. Perhaps I should let you absorb all this. But first, let me explain that, although we would allow the bomb to go off, we would also contain the explosion so that it does little damage beyond the terrorist's house. In this way we will demonstrate technology that is beyond human capabilities, and, simultaneously, show that we are your friends."

"Friends of America, not the Jihad."

Think-pause. "Correct. I don't think the Jihad would be very useful in warding off the Demon-zombies."

"What will happen when you 'contain' the explosion?"

"We cannot eliminate the energy released, of course, so the basement of the terrorist's house will contain a glowing ball which will radiate a moderate amount of heat and light well beyond your lifetime."

Gabe smiled ruefully. "No more heating bills for the terrorists. What about Crabnuckle's house?"

"It will be undamaged . . . other than the high probability that the government will confiscate it afterwards for its convenient proximity."

"Well," Gabe concluded, getting up, "at least there's that advantage. With any luck, Crabnuckle will end up homeless on the street."

Gabe glanced at Ronny. He seemed to be in the throes of a seizure. The raccoon's eyes rolled up until Gabe could see practically all white, then rolled to one side and settled back in place.

"Nice try, Ronny," Gabe said. "You need to practice it until you can do it a lot faster, and you should add an expression of impatience."

"Yes, Teacher."

Gabe winked.

Chapter 5

Thursday afternooon

Gabe took Punky for a walk. There was a lot to think about. Ronny had told him that the bomb would go off in two days at around two o'clock in the afternoon, half way through the wedding ceremony. Strolling along under the neighborhood fruit and palm trees, with birds chirping, and backyard dogs yapping for attention, it was hard to believe that a terrorist nuclear bomb was just two miles away, or that alien Demon-zombies were establishing a foothold on Earth.

In a way, though, it was too fantastic *not* to be real. If nothing else, Ronny's displays of imperfection—his clumsy attempts to mimic Gabe's expressions, for example—seemed a good clue that it wasn't all an extended hallucination. Gabe was confident he didn't have the imagination to fabricate something so bizarre.

But there was something about Ronny that nagged at Gabe. It was that lump on the back of his neck. It might seem trivial in this grand, bizarre new world he was facing, but, regardless, that lump seemed out of place. It bothered him.

His thoughts were disrupted by Charlemagne galloping down the sidewalk. Gabe wondered if the dumb brute spent *any* time at his own home. The routine was always the same. For a few minutes Punky growled and barked with an intensity implying that Charlemagne had unforgivably insulted his mother. The big mutt just waited patiently for the tirade to finish. It would, and then the two would be pals until they met again.

"Not today, gentlemen," Gabe said, picking up Punky who scratched his arms trying to get at Charlemagne. "We have serious business with Demon-zombies and talking raccoons to deal with."

When Gabe returned to the house, he found Ronny's tail sticking out from one of the kitchen cabinets. "Are you trying to hide?" Gabe asked. "Or has Mrs. Jones been giving you a hard time?"

The tail backed out, and Ronny's head appeared. "I think I'm hungry."

"You *think* you're hungry?"

"I find unbidden images of crawfish and discarded food appearing. It's distracting."

"Don't you *know* when you're hungry?"

Think-pause. "There are many adjustment to living in this animal."

"I can well imagine, but I'd think hunger would be pretty basic. When was the last time you ate?"

"I don't know. Not in the four days since I merged sentience."

Merged Sentience. A handy euphemism, Gabe decided, for brain-jacking.

"Ronny, if you haven't eaten in four days, believe me, you're beyond hunger and deep into famished. I'm surprised your little raccoon brain isn't flashing images of eating Punky."

Think-pause. "I hope you weren't being sarcastic, Gabe."

"Why?"

"I was."

"You were thinking about eating *Punky*?"

Think-pause. "Please understand, Gabe. These thoughts belong to this animal, not to me. I can't help them."

Gabe raised an eyebrow. "No problem, but I think we'd better feed you before your little raccoon brain mutinies and goes for my leg."

He decided to feed his entire extended family. He set two bowls on the kitchen floor, and filled one for Punky with his dry food, and the other with Mrs. Jones' canned Tuna Delight. But what to feed Ronny? He knew that raccoons ate fish. He opened another can of tuna cat food, dished it into a third dish, and held it out for Ronny to smell. "What do you think?"

Ronny sniffed it. "I find an overwhelming desire to eat this."

Gabe wasn't sure what to do with the dish. It seemed degrading to have someone probably more intelligent than himself eating on the floor. On the other hand, how would Ronny manage if he set a place at the table? Would he balance himself on a pile of pillows?

Ronny broke his pondering. "Gabe, now that this animal has smelled that food, it's most anxious to get at it. I find myself in conflict trying to maintain control, and it's disturbing."

"Chow down," Gabe invited, setting the bowl on the floor.

Ronny pounced on it, and Gabe found the resulting gnashing and smacking embarrassing. If it embarrassed Ronny, he didn't let on. Mrs. Jones, Punky, and Ronny sat on their haunches in a row contentedly dining.

After a couple of minutes, Punky leaned over to investigate what Ronny was eating. Instantly, Ronny turned to Punky and growled and snapped at him. Punky jumped back, surprised. Ronny turned his head around to look at Gabe. "I'm sorry. That was an instinctual response that surprised me."

Gabe smiled and shook his head. "You don't need to apologize to me. I wasn't the one getting nosey about your lunch."

Punky was apparently humiliated, though, for he now insisted on tasting Ronny's food, even though he'd never been interested in Mrs. Jones' Tuna Delight. Ronny, or his pesky instinct, was equally determined to save every last morsel for himself. The two of them barked and growled at each other, while Mrs. Jones continued taking dainty little bites as if this sort of thing happened every meal.

Gabe crossed his arms and marveled: an interstellar alien, fighting with a toy poodle over some cat food.

Between growls and barks, Ronny managed to clean his bowl. He peered over at Mrs. Jones. "Gabe, do you think she's going to finish all of that?" Ronny asked.

Gabe laughed. "Mrs. Jones seems passive, but trust me, once she's riled up, Punky is a kitten in comparison. Besides, if you eat too much, you might puke it back up."

"Really? I feel nothing but this consuming hunger."

"I'll tell you what, let that settle for a while, and then if you think you're still hungry, I'll open another can."

"Very well." Ronny continued to lick his empty bowl.

The afternoon sun caught a glint in the fur at Ronny's neck. That damned lump. It *really* bothered Gabe. Casually, he said, "I guess your association with the raccoon must be pretty close."

"Yes," Ronny said, smacking his mouth.

"But, not physical."

Think-pause. "No."

Gabe pointed at Ronny's neck. "Then, what's that lump?"

Long think-pause. "I don't know. Perhaps some sort of tumor."

"Like a cancer?"

Think-pause. "Perhaps."

"Then, why is it metallic?"

Long think-pause. Ronny reached around and felt with his tiny fingers. Another long think-pause. "I see. The skin has parted."

"Okay, Ronny, what's up with this?"

Long think-pause. "This is my connection."

"I thought you said your connection wasn't physical?"

Long think-pause. "I obviously misunderstood you, Gabe."

Gabe took his own think-pause. "I don't see how the words 'physical connection' could be misinterpreted."

"By physical connection, I thought you meant a physical connection from a remote location."

"You mean, you thought I was talking about wires connected from the raccoon, through the window, and across the neighborhoods of San Diego to your spaceship?"

Long think-pause. "In a sense."

"That's *ludicrous*! How could I possibly think that?"

Long think-pause. "I obviously don't understand the subtle workings of the human mind."

"*Subtle* workings? I'd have to be an imbecile to think that!"

Think-pause. "I understand that now, Gabe. I'm sorry if I insulted you somehow."

Gabe studied the raccoon who sat watching him with equal steadiness. Had Ronny been outright lying? Or was it really just a misunderstanding?

Ronny broke the mutual trance. "I'm truly sorry, Gabe. I find regret that you're probably doubting my sincerity. I hope you understand that this is a most difficult situation for me."

Gabe sighed. He wasn't sure he believed Ronny, but he didn't have much choice. "Don't worry about it. Let's just try to be up front from now on."

Ronny watched Gabe a moment. "Gabe," he finally said, "you probably don't understand, but this is a lonely position I'm in."

Ronny was right. How *could* he understand? On the other hand, perhaps loneliness was a universal curse. "You're cut off from your kind?"

Long think-pause. "In a way, yes."

"What is your connection, I mean between your spaceship and the raccoon?"

Think-pause. "I'm sorry, Gabe. I can't talk about that."

Gabe met the raccoon's eyes and slowly nodded. "Fair enough. It's better than lying."

Ronny nodded in return. It seemed quite natural.

ж ж ж

"That's just nuts," Gabe scoffed.

He and Ronny were on their way to Crabnuckle's to scope out the terrorist location. Gabe had left Punky behind, for reasons obvious. They needed a plan to place the alien nuclear-containment device within five feet of the bomb's control mechanism. Ronny had suggested that Gabe pose as a terrorist cell leader.

"Let me see if I can find some holes in that plan," Gabe continued. "Hmm, for one, I don't speak Farsi, or Arabic, or whatever country these terrorists come from. Second, I don't look middle-eastern. My mother is Irish, for God's sake. Third . . . I don't speak their language."

"The first and third are the same reason," Ronny pointed out.

"No shit, Dick Tracy. That would be the fourth and fifth reasons as well."

Think-pause. "I think I understand. You feel that the fact that you don't naturally speak their language is worth the weight of multiple reasons. The Dick comment I assume is merely sarcastic."

"I'm glad to see we're at least communicating okay."

"Let me explain that you would be wearing a device in your ear so that I could talk to you. I'd tell you what to say."

"You speak their language?"

"Of course. It's no more difficult than English."

Gabe was still amazed that Ronny had learned English just a couple of weeks before. How many Earth languages did he know by now?

"I repeat—that's nuts. They'd recognize my accent, or complete lack of one, in an instant. They'd shoot me before I had a chance to apologize for mispronouncing my own name."

Think-pause. "I'd be pronouncing the words very precisely, directly into your ear. You'd only have to accurately repeat what I say."

" 'Accurately' is the key word there. Even with days of practice, there's no way in hell I could convince them that their language is native to me."

This was the sort of assumption that convinced Gabe, more than Ronny's ability to commandeer a raccoon's body or learn multiple languages in a matter of hours, that he was not from Earth. On the other hand, the lack of comprehending the obvious nuances of pronunciation implied that everybody on Ronny's planet spoke the same language. Maybe they had TV longer.

"Besides," Gabe continued, "they've probably already seen me on their surveillance camera. In fact, that guy backing out of the driveway when Crabnuckle caught me with Punky probably saw me."

"Perhaps we should mull on it awhile," Ronny suggested.

"Yeah, I'll mull it, but we'd better have a plan-B ready."

They came to Crabnuckle's block and Gabe slowed down. Nobody was around outside either her or the terrorists' houses. Mrs. Crabnuckle had surprised him the day before, though, and Gabe wasn't taking any chances. He pulled over a hundred feet before her house, just beyond which they could see the old, two-story house of the terrorists.

"The nuclear bomb is located in the attached garage," Ronny explained. "The garage windows are covered, and they keep the outside door locked at all times. They never leave the house unguarded."

Gabe peered at the house through binoculars. "Don't they worry about radiation?"

"The uranium won't arrive until the day after tomorrow, the morning of the day it will be set off. They carry it in a shielded container—mostly to hide it from detection. Remember that they don't place the same level of concern for their safety as you would."

"How do you know all this?"

"They talk on telephones."

"If you could tap their phones, so could the FBI. Why don't they know all about this?"

"They would if they knew where to look."

"How did *you* know where to look?"

Think-pause. "We can monitor many more lines than the FBI, and we don't wait for a court warrant."

Gabe absorbed this. Ronny's crew had discovered the terrorist plot by randomly monitoring hundreds of thousands, maybe millions, of phone conversations. It was staggering to think about. Of course, they wouldn't necessarily have been listening themselves. They probably used some sort of sophisticated computer system . . . wouldn't they? Gabe knew Ronny wouldn't tell him those kind of details.

"Okay," Gabe said, "since we're not going to use your hare-brained scheme, then—"

"*I knew you'd be back!*" screeched Mrs. Crabnuckle's voice from somewhere.

Gabe looked in the rearview mirror and saw her coming up from behind, waving a stick. She'd either been out for a walk, or had been hiding in wait for him. Before he could put the car in gear and pull away, she was at the open driver-side window.

"*What are you after now? My fish?*" she shrieked.

"Calm down, Mrs. Crabnuckle," he said.

She bent over and leaned into the window. "Where'd he steal you from, you poor animal?" she asked, looking at Ronny.

Gabe panicked for a moment, thinking that Ronny might reply, but he just sat there, looking like a raccoon.

"I didn't steal him from anybody," Gabe said. "He just showed up. He was hungry."

"We've got our eyes on you, young man," she said, her face inches from Gabe's. "We're going to find out where you're hiding my Pinksty."

Gabe wasn't listening. He'd noticed that a camera mounted above the front door of the terrorists' house was in motion, turning away from them. Gabe guessed that it automatically swept back and forth through 180 degrees. It would be pointing back towards them in a dozen seconds.

"Uh, I have to go, Mrs. Crabnuckle," he said and reached to put the car into gear.

"Oh, no you don't," she commanded as she leaned in and grabbed the steering wheel.

"Mrs. Crabnuckle, please," Gabe pleaded, trying to pry her hands loose.

"You're not going to get away with this. You're probably torturing poor Pinksty."

She kept one hand locked on the wheel, and used the other to try to open the car door.

"Mrs. Crabnuckle *please*! Look, let's go in your house and talk about this." Gabe was watching the camera and saw it beginning its return sweep.

She paused, still gripping the steering wheel. "You won't try to steal my fish?"

"No, Mrs. Crabnuckle, I promise."

Gabe felt something scratching him. He looked down and saw that Ronny had reached out and placed a paw on his leg. The alien had grabbed a handful of pants, and the little Raccoon claws were pinching him. "Ouch!" Gabe yelled. "Cut it out!"

Mrs. Crabnuckle leaned in farther and peered at Ronny. "Aggressive little beast, isn't he?" she said.

Ronny bared his teeth and hissed.

Mrs. Crabnuckle jumped back in surprise. Gabe jammed the car in gear and pulled away.

"*We'll get you, young man! You just wait and see!*" she yelled from behind them.

Gabe drove past the terrorists' house and around the curve. "Why'd you do that?" Gabe asked. "Did you see the camera? I just wanted to get out of the car and away from its view."

"I saw the camera," Ronny replied. "I didn't want it to view you entering Mrs. Crabnuckle's house."

"Why? Is she a zombie or something?" It would explain a lot about her.

Think-pause. "Yes."

Gabe looked at Ronny in surprise. "No way!"

"Way."

"I can't *believe* this!" Gabe looked at Ronny again. "Mrs. *Crabnuckle?*"

Ronny nodded his head up and down slowly.

"Jesus! This is like the Invasion of the Body Snatchers! Who *isn't* a zombie?"

Think-pause. "Was that a rhetorical question?"

"Huh?" Gabe was hardly listening. "Yeah, rhetorical. I guess that's why she said, 'we.'"

Think-pause. "I don't understand."

"Mrs. Crabnuckle. She referred to herself as 'we.' She said, 'We're watching you.'"

"Actually, what she said was, 'We've got our eyes on you, young man.'"

Although spoken in a gravely little raccoon voice, Ronny's inflections of Crabnuckle's speech were eerily accurate.

Gabe glanced over. "Thanks for that critical correction. It completely clarifies the meaning."

Think-pause. "Sarcasm?"

"Sorry. I think it's genetically bred into me. Anyway, she must have been referring to the fact that she's part of the integrated zombie group. Don't you think?"

Think-pause. "Presumably."

Gabe took a deep breath. He let it puff out his cheeks as he exhaled and shook his head. "Look, shouldn't we call the FBI? Or the CIA? Or NSA, or Secret Service, or maybe even the Border Patrol?"

"We've been through this, Gabe. We have to demonstrate our abilities and intentions first."

All those government agencies brimming with guns and nary a bullet to spare. He nodded in resignation. "We have to get that nuclear-containment thing planted."

"Exactly."

Ronny lifted his shoulders in a clumsy shrug.

ж ж ж

When they arrived back home, Punky was ecstatic to see them, dancing around like a circus show-dog. Every time Gabe left, even for ten minutes, Punky acted like it was a miracle of providence that he returned at all. It could be annoying, but Gabe had to admit that it wasn't bad having someone overjoyed just to have you around.

Why couldn't women throw themselves at his legs when he walked in?

Gabe still felt bad that he'd deprived Mrs. Crabnuckle of this. He consoled himself by imagining Punky cowering under a chair rather than hopping for joy. But he knew that, twisted as she was, she truly missed Punky.

Gabe stopped in his tracks at that thought. That wasn't the behavior of an alien Demon-zombie. That was normal, mean old Mrs. Crabnuckle.

"Ronny," he said, "you're sure Mrs. Crabnuckle is a zombie."

Ronny had crawled up onto a kitchen chair to get away from Punky's hysterics. He was trying to shoo the dog away with his paw. "Correct," he replied.

Gabe raised one eyebrow. "Her behavior didn't seem like a zombie."

Think-pause. "What would you expect a zombie to act like?"

"Not like that."

Ronny lifted his little shoulders again in a shrug.

"In fact, I don't believe it," Gabe added.

Long think-pause. "We should talk about a plan to place the nuclear-container."

"Don't try to change the subject. I don't think Mrs. Crabnuckle is a zombie."

Ronny stared at Gabe. "You'll just have to trust me."

Gabe stared back. "No I don't."

"You're narrowing your eyes, Gabe. What are you going to do?"

Gabe strode over the phone on the kitchen wall. "I'll just give her a call."

Think-pause. "Gabe, don't do that."

"Why?" he asked, running his finger down the list of numbers hanging next to the phone.

"You'll put us in danger."

"I'm betting not," Gabe said, dialing the phone.

"Gabe—"

"Mrs. Crabnuckle?" Gabe said into the phone when he heard it pick up. "This is Gabe. Listen, I'm sorry about driving away like that. I have a question—are you a Demon-zombie?"

"You're bluffing," Ronny said.

Gabe held out the handset, and the shrill sound of Mrs. Crabnuckle's yells could be clearly heard. He put the handset back to his ear. "Mrs. Crabnuckle . . . I know—hold on, that's not all. That raccoon that was in my car? That wasn't really—"

"Gabe!"

"Hold on, Mrs. Crabnuckle." Gabe put his hand over the mouthpiece. "Do you have something to tell me?"

Long think-pause.

Gabe put the phone back to his ear. "I was saying, Mrs. Crabnuckle, that the raccoon in the car was actually an alien—"

"Gabe, okay. I admit that she's not a zombie."

Gabe continued into the phone. "Mrs. Crabnuckle? I think I dialed the wrong number. Sorry."

He hung up the handset and sat down at the kitchen table with Ronny. "Okay, spill the beans."

Think-pause. "A metaphor for 'provide the details'?"

Gabe nodded.

"I was not truthful about Mrs. Crabnuckle."

Gabe nodded again. "I think we've established that. Why?"

"We may want to use her house as a staging area. I didn't want to draw their attention to it."

Gabe replayed the sequence and wagged his head. "Uh-uh. We'd already driven away. In fact, as I recall, it was me who suggested she might be a zombie—as a joke! You agreed."

Long think-pause.

"Stop thinking about it and just tell me the truth," Gabe insisted.

"I decided that if you thought Mrs. Crabnuckle was a zombie, you wouldn't be tempted to continue to talk to her and draw their attention."

Gabe locked Ronny's eyes and slowly shook his head. "That's an awfully flimsy reason, Ronny. If you'd lie about something as unimportant as that, how can I trust you about *anything?*"

Ronny returned his gaze a moment. "You're not joking, are you Gabe?"

Gabe just shook his head again.

"I'm sorry, Gabe. I'm distressed that I've weakened your trust in me. It leaves me feeling more abandoned. Can we talk about the plan to plant the nuclear-container?"

Gabe wrinkled his brow. "I don't think so, buddy." He stood up and picked up his wallet and keys. "See you later."

"Where are you going?"

"You haven't earned the right to that answer," Gabe replied, heading for the door.

Before walking out, he turned and looked back. The raccoon's head was waving slowly back and forth, mimicking Gabe. It looked kind of pathetic.

Gabe watched impassively, and then walked out, closing the door behind him.

ж ж ж

Gabe sat in the lobby of the San Diego FBI offices. He told the receptionist only that he wanted to report suspicious activity near his home. He was now waiting to talk to an agent.

He'd debated during the entire twenty-minute drive whether he was doing the right thing. In the end he just let the momentum of his decision in the kitchen carry him to this seat. He couldn't shake the feeling that he was betraying Ronny, but he reminded himself that Ronny had lied to him. He just couldn't trust him anymore.

Ronny had said that he was distressed that he'd broken Gabe's trust. It left him feeling more abandoned. *More* abandoned? What was that about? In fact, this was the first time Gabe remembered Ronny talking about any feelings he had. Maybe he really *was* remorseful.

Gabe's thoughts were interrupted when the receptionist called his name. He looked around and saw a middle-aged man in a shirt and tie looking at him. Gabe always thought of FBI agents as trim men in dark suits and thin black ties. This guy looked like the manager of the bowling alley on Clairemont Boulevard.

"Mr. Wolfekow?" the man asked.

Gabe stood up and shook his hand.

"I'm agent Paul Weston. Let's go to my office," the man said, turning and walking through the inner doors without waiting for a reply.

Beyond the doors Gabe followed Weston through a maze of partitioned cubicles. They stopped at one that was just large enough to hold a desk and two chairs. This was apparently the agent's "office". Gabe could clearly hear the conversations in the "offices" around them.

"You have suspicious activity to report?" Weston said, flopping down in one chair, and indicating the other for Gabe.

Gabe sat down. He found that he had to sit sideways in order to avoid bumping knees with Weston. "Not so much suspicious as . . . well, it's sort of hard to believe."

Weston smiled. "Don't worry, son. We've heard all the strange stories here. Just give it to me straight."

Weston looked bored, like he was just pretending to be interested in what Gabe had to say.

"Okay," Gabe started, "there are terrorists that have an atom bomb here in San Diego. They're planning to set it off tomorrow afternoon at two o'clock when the British Prime Minister is here."

Gabe watched Weston's eyes initially go large, then narrow to suspicion. The agent drummed a pencil against the plastic arm of his chair. "Terrorists, you say," he finally said.

Gabe tried to find a comfortable position. It didn't seem possible. "Yes. Over on Mission Canyon Road."

Weston nodded, watching his pencil bounce up and down. "You even know the location."

"Yes," Gabe replied. "They're next to Mrs. Crabnuckle. I could give you her address."

"That'd be handy. Mrs. Crabnuckle . . . did she tell you that terrorists were living there?"

Gabe's wished the guy would stop with the pencil. "No, I don't think she knows that they're terrorists."

"I see. How do you know?"

Gabe found it impossible to speak the words. "I'm afraid that if I tell you, you won't believe me."

He realized that the agent probably didn't believe him already.

Weston bounced the pencil and followed it with his eyes. He acted as though he was anticipating everything Gabe was telling him. "I hadn't heard that the Prime Minister was going to be in town. I'd have thought this would've made the news."

"They're keeping it a secret until the last minute."

Weston nodded as though this was, of course, obvious. "But you know about it, even though the FBI doesn't. Tell me, Gabe, what do you do—for a living?"

He sighed. "I'm a musician and pet-sitter."

Weston raised his eyebrows and nodded appreciatively. "San Diego Symphony?"

He knows damn well I don't play in the symphony, Gabe thought. "Blues band—fifties jump-blues, some forties hop."

"You probably have access to a lot of drugs, eh?"

Gabe just looked at the agent. How the hell was he supposed to answer something like that? He could feel that he was getting red in the face. It looked like Ronny had this pegged after all.

Gabe stood up. "I'll be leaving now."

Weston held his hands up as if to say, *I'm not stopping you.*

Gabe walked to the end of the aisle and realized he didn't remember how to get to the front doors. He found his way back to Weston's cubicle. "Uh, excuse me," he said to Weston's back, "could you show me how to get out?"

Weston turned and gave him a big smirk, then stood up and led the way out.

Gabe wanted to give him one right in the kisser. He imagined the agent talking to some cute intern at the coffee pot: "You should've heard the crack-pot I talked to today . . ."

On the way home, Gabe tossed around his options. Only one came anywhere near the top. He'd have to trust Ronny for the time being. How did Ronny's namesake put it? Trust, but verify?

Chapter 6

Thursday evening

Ronny was gone when Gabe got back. This was fine; he didn't want to talk to him right now. It was time to go to band practice anyway.

He grabbed his guitar and Blues Junior amp, tossed them in the car, and drove to Derrick's house. Years ago Derrick had covered the inside of his garage with heavy insulation to deaden sound, and it was their de facto studio. Gabe wasn't sure if Christie would be there. He didn't know if she was going to kiss off the whole band, in addition to him. He pulled into Derrick's driveway and heard voices coming from the garage, one of which was Christie's.

This was going to be awkward.

Gabe got his equipment from the car, and when he walked into the garage he found Derrick and Christie sitting together on the old sofa Derrick had dragged in from a yard sale. They were laughing, and Christie slapped Derrick's leg in playful reprimand. Derrick had probably just told her one of the hundred or so ribald jokes he kept filed in his head.

"Hey! The Gabester's here!" Derrick called out.

Christie glanced over at Gabe. The smile on her face from Derrick's joke didn't change. She could have been looking at a cat that had wandered in. She turned back to Derrick. "You *really* drove all the way home naked on your motorcycle?"

Derrick raised one hand in oath. "Swear. It was dark, though, and I kept to the side streets as much as possible. I heard about it on the news when I got home—a traffic alert on the Five, north. Right up there with the occasional stray cow or kitchen sink."

Gabe remembered that one. It was true. Derrick had been sitting in a hot tub with a woman when her husband came home unexpectedly. He'd made the mistake of leaving all his clothes in the house, and had to crawl over the back fence with just a towel wrapped around his waist. The wind blew it off as soon as he drove away.

This was Derrick, the stereotypical drummer. He was a total, unabashed womanizer, and the fact that he made no bones about it seemed to be attractive to a lot of women who wouldn't otherwise give the time of day to slick two-timers.

Gabe found the situation now unsettling. He hadn't considered the Derrick-factor. Gabe liked Derrick. A lot. His honest, unassuming, devil-take-care approach to life was refreshing. Gabe just didn't want him dating his sister . . . or Christie.

Gabe plugged in his amp and tuned his guitar. Randy walked in and took his bass guitar from its case. Randy had two bass amps, and kept one at Derrick's for practice. This was handy, since his amps were a lot heavier than Gabe's guitar amps, and it was always a project getting them in and out of Randy's VW bug. This was another band stereotype: bass players, who had the largest amplifiers, always drove the smallest cars.

Gabe thought he should at least say something to Christie, but he didn't know where to begin. Instead, he addressed the band as a whole and suggested a few songs he and Christie had gone over during the pet rounds. Randy and Derrick nodded agreement, and Christie looked on as though this was a routine they'd been through a thousand times. In fact, they ran through the tunes flawlessly.

She really was amazing.

After they'd gone through all the songs he and Christie had already reviewed, they started in on the others. This went slower, as they listened to the original recordings first before working out harmony parts. Still, by 9:30—the unofficial neighborhood band curfew, established through a series of visits from the police—they had one full set of solid material.

Gabe and Randy put their guitars away, while Derrick handed cans of beer around. The following night, Friday, would be

Christie's big debut. They were playing The Schooner, a large tourist bar in Mission Bay beach that always packed an enthusiastic crowd. It was their best gig, sort of the Ying, balancing the Yang of all the smelly little joints. They would share the night with the headline band, warming up the place with the first two sets. Gabe decided to have Christie come up and finish out the last half of each. This way they could spread her dozen or so numbers across the show.

They were ready to leave, and Derrick asked Christie if she needed a ride. She said yes, and then for the first time since Gabe had arrived, glanced at him as someone more than just another member of the band.

"I'm going that way," Gabe blurted. "I'll take her."

Derrick looked from Christie to Gabe and smiled. "No necking on the way."

Christie blushed and Gabe guessed that he was too.

Once in Gabe's car, though, Christie made it clear that all wasn't forgotten. She corralled the conversation to matters of the band, and refused even to smile at Gabe's attempts at humor, a sure sign a woman is wielding a grudge-club. Maybe he'd misinterpreted her look back at Derrick's garage.

"I could swing by my place and give you more tapes to listen to," he finally said, deciding to test the water.

"Okay," she agreed, looking out the window, taking his words at face value.

Gabe wished he knew what she was thinking. This was work. It was easier talking to Ronny, and as far as Gabe knew, he might not even have an actual mouth.

When they got to Gabe's house, Punky greeted Christie as though she was his long-lost sister. Gabe asked her if she'd like a cup of tea, and, happily, she casually accepted. He heated water and was pouring it over the teabags when Ronny came ambling around the corner from the bedroom. Gabe froze. Didn't the alien realize that Christie was here?

"Gabe!" Christie cried. "It's that raccoon you were talking about, the one that you thought could talk."

Gabe wasn't sure if he should panic at having Ronny about to be exposed, or be happy that Christie's wall had, at least for the moment, come down.

Ronny veered over towards Christie, much the way Mrs. Jones might tour around the room. Perhaps Ronny had taken some lessons from her. Christie slid out of her chair and sat on the floor with her legs under her. Ronny walked right up to her.

"Can I pet him?" Christie asked.

"He hasn't bitten me yet," Gabe replied.

He realized that he'd never touched Ronny. Even getting in and out of the car, Ronny crawled up and down by himself.

Christie scratched Ronny under his chin and down his neck. Ronny lifted his head to give her a better angle, and Gabe would have sworn the space traveler was enjoying it. What the hell was he up to?

"Has he been hanging around much?" she asked.

"He thinks he lives here," Gabe replied. Ronny moved his eyes to look at Gabe. "They're natural scavengers, you know—basically, opportunistic beggars of the wild."

"Well, I think he's a cutie-pie. Aren't you?" she cooed as she gave his whole head a rub. "You should give him a name."

"I have."

"Don't tell me you've named him Rocky."

Gabe smiled. "No, actually, it's Ronny."

"*Ronny?* What kind of name is that for a raccoon? Everybody's going to think of Ronald Reagan, for God's sake. They'll try to run him over."

Gabe looked at Ronny and nodded. *See?* he was saying. *I told you so.*

It suddenly came to Gabe what Ronny was probably up to. The little schemer was trying to cuddle up and rebuild Gabe's trust. If that was the case, Gabe thought, he was cuddling up to the wrong person.

Or was he? Maybe Ronny understood more about human psychology than he let on. Maybe he understood that the door to Gabe's heart lay through Christie. Ronny was using Christie to gain Gabe's trust, while he himself was trying to regain trust with *her.*

Sheeshh! It was like social chess.

Gabe finished preparing the tea and set the cup on the table next to her.

"Can I use your bathroom?" she asked, standing up.

"Around the corner, to the right. Either close your eyes or don't turn on the light. My yearly cleaning is overdue."

Gabe waited until he heard the bathroom door close and the fan come on before he knelt down in front of Ronny. "I know what you're up to," he whispered.

Think-pause. "I don't understand," Ronny said in a reduced volume version of his normal, raspy voice.

"Shhh! Whisper! You're trying to suck up to me, aren't you?"

Think-pause. Ronny made an unintelligible whistling sound by blowing air as he moved his mouth.

"You can't whisper, can you?" Gabe said.

Ronny waved his head back and forth.

Gabe looked at Ronny and shook his head in sad resignation.

"I think I heard someone at the front door," Ronny said.

Gabe stood up in alarm. He went through the living room and opened the front door. Nobody was there, just one of the neighbors pulling away in their car. That must have been what Ronny had heard.

When Gabe returned to the kitchen, Ronny was standing on Christie's chair with his front paws on the table. He was peering into her cup of tea. He looked at Gabe and jumped back down onto the floor.

Gabe bent down over Ronny. "What are you up to?" he whispered.

"I was curious about tea."

Just then Gabe heard the bathroom fan stop, and the door open. Christie came around the corner. "Who are you talking to?" she asked.

Gabe looked at her, dumbstruck. "The telephone . . . it was a wrong number."

"It sounded like you were trying to imitate a frog."

"Ha!" he laughed. "Yeah. I was goofing with them."

She gave him a funny look. "With a wrong number?"

He lifted his hands and shoulders in one long shrug, thinking madly. "It was actually a friend," he finally said. "He punched in the wrong button on his cell."

Christie nodded and sat down at the table.

Gabe gave a silent sigh of relief and shot Ronny a hard glance. The raccoon stared back without emotion.

Gabe picked up his cup and sat at the table across from Christie.

"You know, Gabe," Christie said, stirring her tea and giving him a sidelong glance. "I think it's wonderful that you're so good with animals."

Gabe smiled. He was happy to do something wonderful in her eyes. "They have lower standards than people."

She looked at him critically.

"I'm joking," he said. "Listen, Christie, I'm sorry about this afternoon. I . . . don't know how it got so twisted."

She took a sip and placed the cup carefully down on the table. It was apparent that she wasn't ready to put the incident completely behind her.

"How did it go with Brent?" As soon as he said this, Gabe realized it was a mistake.

Anger flashed briefly across Christie's face. "Fine."

Gabe shook his head. "I'm sorry. I shouldn't have said anything. It's not my business."

In fact, he wanted desperately to know how it had gone with Brent, but he wasn't a total fool.

Christie took another sip of tea. "No, it's not . . ." She had a perplexed look on her face.

"What's the matter?"

She stuck out her tongue and delicately picked something off with her fingertips. "Sand in the tea," she explained, looking at the grain on the end of her finger.

Gabe leaned over. "Let me see."

She tipped it into his palm.

He held it up to the light. It had a familiar silvery glint. "Sorry about that. I think it's actually an ant."

She wrinkled her brow. "It seemed hard for an ant. I think I swallowed a couple. Anyway, I have to finish things with Brent. I can't just cut it off without any transition."

Gabe saw Ronny ambling off towards the bedroom. "I understand," he lied.

The worst of it was that it wasn't even Brent anymore who she was trying to break away from. Who knew what happened to the original Brent? Gabe thought that the Demon-zombies must be very sophisticated to be able to fool Christie into thinking that Brent was still Brent.

"It will end," she said.

He knew he was about to make more trouble, but he couldn't risk letting Christie have any more contact with the Demon-zombies. "I really would like you to stay away from Brent, just for the next couple of days."

Christie's face became stone. "Why? *Why*, Gabe?"

He had to tell her. He had to drag Ronny out from the bedroom and make him tell her in his own little frog-voice. Gabe remembered agent Weston's smirk. No, he couldn't tell her. Ronny probably wouldn't cooperate, and she'd end up thinking the same thing as Weston—that he was harmonizing along to a loony-tune.

"I can't tell you . . . not yet, anyway."

"Well then, let me tell *you* the reason," Christie fumed. "It's because you're insecure. Gabe," she said, looking at him levelly, "I need security. I'm sorry that's the way it is, but more than anything, I need that."

Gabe took a deep breath. No, he just couldn't tell her.

Christie suddenly stood up and carried her empty cup to the sink. "I think it's time to go," she said curtly.

Gabe wordlessly picked up his keys and walked towards the door. It was going to be a frosty ride to her apartment.

ж ж ж

When Gabe returned forty minutes later, Ronny was curled up on the living room sofa waiting for him.

"So, what was all that about?" Gabe asked him.

"I know where you went this afternoon," Ronny said, lifting his head from the sofa.

"I went to see the FBI."

"I know."

"How?"

"I've told you, information is our specialty."

"What information?"

"In this case, the information agent Weston logged about your visit. Fortunately, he thinks you're a crackpot. That is a proper term, isn't it?"

"I'm trying to figure that out myself."

"Gabe, that was a dangerous move. I can't allow you to try something like that again."

"You can't *allow* me?" Gabe exclaimed, pacing back and forth. "What the hell is that supposed to mean?"

Think-pause. "I believe the meaning is clear."

Gabe threw up his hands. "Oh, yeah! The meaning is clear all right, and I don't like what it implies. Not one bit."

He shook his finger at the reclined raccoon. "Look fella', I'm going out on a limb here. Christie thinks I'm not secure, the FBI thinks I'm a crackpot, and Mrs. Crabnuckle thinks I'm harassing her and has probably called the police. If anybody needs to watch their step, it's you, buster."

Long think-pause. "I must repeat, Gabe. Don't act without consulting me from now on."

"Or WHAT?" Gabe challenged, yelling now.

Think-pause. "I could make you unhappy."

Gabe stopped. He could barely control himself. "You know what? I'll tell you what I'm going to do. The FBI don't give a shit, why should I? Tomorrow morning I'm going to pack a bag and go visit my friend in LA for a couple of days. I'll be sitting in his house drinking a beer and watching the news when they report the terrorist bomb that just went off in San Diego."

Gabe stormed off to his bedroom without giving Ronny a chance to respond. He slammed the door, pulled the French doors closed for the first time in ages, and peeled off his clothes. Climbing under the covers and turning the light off, Gabe thought, *I might just do it. I might.*

He rolled over and tried to go to sleep.

Chapter 7

Friday morning

Gabe woke. He must have fallen asleep after all. By 2:30 a.m. he had decided he was probably going to be up all night. He looked at the clock. It was 8:45.

He'd made his decision. He was going to go and get Christie, even if he had to carry her over his shoulder. Then, before heading north to LA, he was going to swing around and tell Mrs. Crabnuckle that there were terrorists with an atom bomb next to her. She was a mean old bat, but didn't deserve to be atomized. Once in LA, he'd call everybody he knew in San Diego and tell them to head to the mountains to watch the fireworks. Wearing proper protective dark glasses, of course. He was also going to call the Union Tribune. Like the FBI, they were surely going to discount him as a lunatic, but he wanted to ensure his peace of mind afterwards. They'd all have twenty-four hours notice. Their fates would rest on their own fool heads.

He pulled on his jeans and walked out to the kitchen. Ronny was lying on the table.

"No animals on the table," Gabe barked. "Mrs. Jones isn't allowed up there, and neither are you."

He poured water in the glass carafe for coffee. "Particularly any lying animals," he added.

Ronny stood up and crawled down onto one of the chairs. "Gabe I'm very sorry."

"I'll say you are."

Long think-pause.

Gabe sighed. "That's a pun."

"Right. Gabe, I think I can explain."

Gabe poured the water into the coffee maker and took the bag of ground beans from the cupboard. "You have five minutes. As soon as I have some coffee, I'm dumping you outside and I never want to see you again. I would do it now, but I might lock myself out."

Think-pause. "Gabe, I'm a trained liar."

Gabe paused, and then continued measuring the ground coffee. "Good start. I have no argument with that."

Think-pause. "My colleagues are incapable of lying. This has evolved over a very great period of time. Long ago our predecessors were like you. We were like all other first-stage intelligent beings—"

" 'First-stage'?"

"We have found that intelligent life tends to evolve through three stages. First, comes the raw newborns who, like humans, are products of niches filled in a natural environment—in your case, hunter-gatherer scavengers—"

"Our anthropologists seem to downplay the scavenger part," Gabe said dryly.

Think-pause. "I suspect they have chosen to de-emphasize this since most people view it as unsavory. In the second stage, the unpolished, naturally-evolved species takes control of its own evolution and moves towards a form that is specifically adapted for an existence where survival is dependant on cooperative co-existence. This is necessary, for example, to avoid annihilation from larger natural threats, such as mega-ton asteroid impacts, or escape from stellar systems whose nearby suns are in the final stages prior to going super-nova."

Gabe had poured fresh coffee into his cup and sat down across from Ronny. "Something tells me that both of these happened to your ancestors."

Think-pause. "Very astute, Gabe."

"Sucking up won't help. What about the third stage?"

"This one is not so easy to explain—"

"You mean to a raw and wild, naturally-evolved animal like myself."

"Correct." Think-pause. "I see, you were being facetious."

Gabe waved it off.

"The third stage," Ronny continued, "is more or less the culmination of intelligence, sort of the final form of the universe."

Gabe swallowed and sat looking at Ronny. "You're right," he finally agreed. "I'm not sure I understand that."

"It seems pretty clear that the universe was created to develop intelligence. It is, in a sense, a womb for sentience."

Gabe smiled. "So, there is a God after all?"

Think-pause. "I'd hesitate to call the creator of the universe God. That implies a being in some way similar to you . . . to ourselves. You are intelligent to a degree—"

"Gee, thanks."

Think-pause. "Pardon my bluntness, but I'm trying to be more honest."

Gabe nodded. "My apologies. Please proceed."

"No matter how advanced and sophisticated the intelligence of our universe develops, I doubt that it will resemble that which created this universe. Intelligence cannot conceive of anything transcending its own intelligence."

Gabe took a sip of coffee. "In that case, how do you know this creator exists at all?"

"To us, a stage-two intelligence, the evidence is blinding."

"Maybe he's shining a flashlight in your eyes, aiming to stomp on you like a cockroach."

Think-pause. "I assume that was a joke, and I will proceed. To presume this universe occurred by random processes is unsupportable. It would require an unacceptable amount of coincidence."

"That it occurred at all?"

"That it occurred in its present form. The universe has flowered since the big bang in ways that very specifically provides an amenable home for intelligence to form. You marvel at the wonders that biological evolution has created around you, but you take for granted the sun, the stars, and the galaxies. The very essence of the matter of this universe can only be explained as a specific medium for intelligence to develop, from the precise amount of balancing nuclear forces which allows atoms to exist, to the unimaginably far-flung web of galaxy-wide gravity that causes stellar systems to form."

"A veritable galaxy-sized ant-farm." Before Ronny had a chance to finish the think-pause this initiated, Gabe continued. "You started to explain the third stage of intelligence."

"Yes, we believe that this is the purpose—the destiny—of this universe, the development of one grand, final intelligence."

Gabe took another sip of coffee and set the cup down. "Why? What will the creator do with it?"

Ronny lifted his shoulders in a raccoon-shrug. "I doubt that this will be known before the end."

Before the end. Gabe found that unsettling, but he decided not to probe that path. "One final intelligence, eh? So, who's it going to be? You, or the Demon-zombies? I'm guessing we raw humans aren't in the running."

Think-pause. "That is a difficult question to answer. I don't believe that the final intelligence necessarily means the exclusion of all others. I suspect that multiple evolving sentient paths may choose to merge together. Perhaps millions or billions of individual instances of intelligence in the universe will combine to form one vast super-intelligence."

"The ultimate big-brain."

"I very much doubt that these advanced intelligence entities will actually use brain matter as—"

"Ronny, I was kidding. So, you claim to be second-phase—"

"Second-stage."

"Excuse me, second-*stage*. What about the Demon-zombies?"

Think-pause. "Unfortunately, second stage as well."

"Will you two merge on your way to the super-brain convention?"

Think-pause. "I assume that not all second stage intelligence will make it to third-stage, just as only a fraction of first-stage ever progress to second-stage."

Gabe smiled. "You two are duking it out for the spot?"

Think-pause. "In a manner of speaking, I guess. Perhaps it's more accurate to say that the Demon-zombies wish to be the only third-stage intelligence."

Gabe sat back in his chair. This gave his stomach more room to absorb it all. "Before we got side-tracked with our metaphysical discussion, you started to explain how you're a trained liar."

"Yes. Painting that larger picture was necessary in order to understand the nature of my people. For millennia we have been evolving in a mode of cooperative enterprise. This cannot proceed very far in the context of mistrust. Indeed, the very concept of deceit has been but an abstraction for us for as long as there have been records. Dishonesty is naturally weeded out at its infrequent inception. It is simply not tolerated by the whole."

Gabe laced his finger behind his head. "I think I see where you're going here. You had to learn to lie because you're dealing with people who themselves lie."

"Correct. Indeed, people who lie naturally, spontaneously, exuberantly."

"Cut it out, you're making me blush."

Think-pause. "Joke?"

"Correct."

"Please don't construe my assessment as judgmental. Lying is a universal attribute of stage-one intelligence. You see, it's what spear-headed the evolution of your brains in the first place."

Gabe raised an eyebrow. "I was designed to lie?"

"Correct. Lying is part of the complex social maneuvering that made your hunter-gatherer lives so demanding of an expanding intelligence. The art of negotiation is nothing more than high-level lying under a cloak of group purpose."

Gabe could see the truth in this. "The person who is willing to lie has the advantage over one with incurable honesty—at least in the short term."

"Correct."

Gabe mulled this. "We don't all lie all the time, though, do we?"

Think-pause. "Correct."

"That's part of the magic of the whole business of being human—knowing when someone is lying to you."

Think-pause. "Correct."

Gabe hadn't thought about it this way before. "It all comes down to trust, knowing *who* you can trust."

"Correct."

"A little piece of advice: saying 'correct' all the time gets annoying after a while."

Think-pause. "Understood."

Gabe laid his hands out on the table, palms down. "It looks like we've come around full-circle. I can't trust you, and so I'm tossing you out."

"I have a suggestion."

"Shoot."

"I will carry your questions to my companions who will answer them through me."

Gabe shrugged. "What does this achieve?"

"Gabe, I just explained that they are not able to lie. They can only answer your question with the truth."

Gabe laughed. "But, you're a liar! How do I know you'll relate their answer correctly?"

Think-pause. "They can put it in written form."

"They understand and write English?"

"Of course."

Gabe thought about it. "How do I know *you're* not writing the answer yourself?"

Think-pause. "Gabe, at some point, you'll have to trust me with something. We have to establish some baseline."

"How do I even know you're telling the truth about your people not being able to lie?"

Ronny sat back and lifted his paws in an imitation of a human submission gesture. This left him unbalanced, and he barely caught himself before falling forward onto the kitchen floor.

Gabe stood up and began pacing the kitchen. "I don't know. I've had nothing but trouble since I met you. You tell me yourself that you're a professional liar. Why *shouldn't* I just head off to LA for a couple of days?"

"We're trying to stop the Demon-zombies. They could destroy the Earth."

Gabe glanced over at him. "I thought you said they wanted to use the Earth as an expansion post? What good would it do them if they destroyed it?"

Think-pause. "Yes. I meant that they could destroy all humans."

Gabe stopped and looked at Ronny. "You were trying to tell a lie just there, weren't you?"

Long think-pause. "Yes."

"In order to try to influence my decision, right?"

Long think-pause. "Yes."

"Why would you *do* that, for Christ's sake? We just got done talking about . . ." Gabe shook his head. "This is ridiculous! I can't believe *anything* you say!"

"It's because this is so important, Gabe. They could destroy all humans."

"If that's the truth, you could have just said that. That's plenty scary all by itself."

Think-pause.

"And, why do you hesitate with these pauses sometimes before answering?" Gabe asked. "You're thinking about what to say, aren't you?"

Think-pause.

"ANSWER ME!"

"Yes."

"You're probably thinking through your lie, right?"

Think-pause.

"ANSWER ME!"

"Yes, but only sometimes."

"No more lies, no more hesitation. Got it?"

"Yes, Gabe. I will not tell you any more lies."

"Promise?"

"I promise, Gabe."

"Humph. Do you even know what a promise is?"

"It is true that the concept is foreign to my companions, since a promise essentially implies a guarantee that you're not lying, but, since I can lie, I can understand the essence of a promise."

"Do you understand what happens when a promise is broken?"

Think-pause.

"NO MORE HESITATION! REMEMBER?"

"I'm sorry Gabe. I wasn't thinking through a lie. I was honestly trying to formulate an answer to your question. I do not know what will happen if I break this promise."

"It will provide absolute proof that I cannot trust you. One more lie will instantly and irrevocably end my association with you."

"I understand, Gabe. Does this mean you'll help me?"

Gabe took a deep breath. "I don't know."

"A lot of people will die if that bomb goes off, Gabe."

"I *know!* Okay, look, I'll at least come up with some questions for your people. We can take it from there."

Gabe sat down at the table and began writing on a piece of paper.

"Gabe, you can just tell me. I have perfect memory."

Gabe looked at Ronny, and then slid the paper aside. "Very well, here goes. One: how many of your kind are on Earth? Two: is Ronny the only liar? Three: where are you from. I mean, where is your home—"

"Gabe," Ronny cut in, "I can't carry that question to them. I think you can understand that."

"Right. Okay. Three: uh, is there really a terrorist bomb next to Mrs. Crabnuckle's house that's supposed to go off tomorrow afternoon? And, four: does Ronny really want to plant a nuclear containment device there?"

"That's it?"

"Hmm, yeah—no, wait. Five is 'Why are the Demon-zombies stalking me?' "

"Any more?"

"No. That'll do for now." Gabe stood up and stretched. "I'm going for a walk. I need to think."

"Gabe, could I ask a favor?"

"What's that, liar?"

"Could you feed me?"

Gabe smiled. "You *think* you're hungry?"

"Now that I've experienced the satisfaction of relieving hunger, I find the sensation very demanding."

Gabe laughed. "Welcome to the world of mammals."

Ж Ж Ж

Gabe walked along Chester Avenue, hands in pockets, three blocks uphill from his house. He often came here because he could get glimpses of the Pacific Ocean through the palm trees. He didn't notice now, though, as he was deep in thought. He should have taken more time coming up with questions. For example, he could have asked more about the Demon-zombies. Well, he, decided, he could always send Ronny back with more.

He smiled to himself. He hadn't thought about Christie for at least an hour. He really must be distracted.

He heard an engine behind him. He glanced back and saw an old blue car pulling over to the curb. He forced himself to continue walking. His heart was pounding. He remembered seeing a blue car pull over to the curb on the previous street. It was obviously following him. He visualized it in his mind. It was the same LeSabre that had parked in front of his house.

It was the Demon-zombie!

He told himself to remain calm. Don't let the zombie know he was on to him.

Gabe turned the corner and walked quickly until he was confident that the first house blocked the view. He stopped, turned around, and knelt down, pretending to tie his shoe. The LeSabre turned the corner slowly. The zombie apparently didn't see Gabe, for he started up the street, still driving slowly. The car was next to Gabe when the zombie finally looked over and saw him. Their eyes met. It was the same man . . . or at least, the same hijacked body. The brown frog birthmark clung to his forehead. Gabe quickly forced his attention back to his shoelace. His hands shook. He heard another car come up the street, and the LeSabre was forced to reluctantly move on.

Gabe stood up and walked back the way he'd come. It took all his willpower to keep from looking behind him. He turned the corner, and after an eternal ten steps, finally looked back. The same house hid his view, now from this direction. Gabe sprinted off down the street.

Think! What to do? Maybe the zombie was trying to catch him alone. He had to get away, back to Ronny. Ronny would know.

Gabe came to a path that led between two houses, up the hill to an open-space park. The path connected with a hiking trail about a hundred yards above. Gabe started up.

He quickly realized that this was a mistake. The hill above was just open, scattered shrubs with no place to hide. The zombie would see him before he could get over the top and away. To the left and right were the backyards of the houses. They were empty. The owners were probably away at work. The house on the left had a tool shed close to the path. Perfect. Gabe crossed the thirty feet of dirt and crouched behind the shed. He peeked around the corner and could see a slice of the street on each side of the house.

He was wrong, though, about the people not being home. He now heard a radio playing in the kitchen just across the back patio. Somebody opened the back door from inside, and a news announcer's voice came through clearly. The British Prime Minister was arriving that evening on a surprise visit to San Diego. The trip was described as a personal vacation, and there'd been no other details.

"Holy shit!" Gabe whispered.

A little girl, about four, came out through the back doorway. She walked purposefully to the tool shed and right around back until she was standing in front of Gabe, crouched before her. She'd obviously seen him approach.

"Who you hiding from?" she asked.

Their eyes were almost level. "I'm, uh, resting," he said, trying to sound casual.

"Why don't you come and sit in a chair?" she invited, pointing to the patio furniture.

Gabe smiled. "Thanks, I'm okay here."

"*Marcy! Who are you talking to?*" her mother called from the house.

"A man. He's resting."

Gabe peeked around the corner of the tool shed and saw the mother standing at the back door. She also saw him, and ran out and across the patio. Beyond the house, the blue LeSabre was coming slowly along the street. It disappeared behind the house—it would reappear in a matter of seconds.

The mother was suddenly standing above him. "Who are you?" she asked a little shrilly, pulling the girl back and wrapping her arms around her.

"Hi," he said, standing up. "I'm Gabe, Gabe Wolfekow. I'm a neighbor—I live over on Oleander."

"What are you doing sneaking around our property?"

The LeSabre appeared from behind the house. He could see the zombie driver's bald head. "Truthfully? I'm hiding from somebody."

The woman's eyes morphed from caution to fright. "Look—Gabe—I called the police. You'd better leave before they get here."

Gabe knew she hadn't. At least not yet. It was the sort of bluff you always try in this situation. In other words, she'd lied. Ronny was right, people lie at the drop of a hat.

She would probably call the police, though, and he'd already given her his name and street. He should have lied.

He saw that the LeSabre had passed on down the street and was turning the corner at the intersection. Gabe stood up. "I'm sorry ma'am, I shouldn't have come on your property. I actually didn't know anybody was home, and I didn't think I was doing any harm back here behind the shed. I'll leave."

Gabe strode away, back to the path, and turned down towards the street. He looked back and saw the woman watching him warily, holding fast to the little girl. As Gabe hit the sidewalk, he heard the mother railing her daughter for talking to strange men.

ж ж ж

Ten minutes later Gabe burst through the door of his house. He was relieved that the police weren't waiting for him.

"Ronny!" he called, holding Punky off with his foot. "You here?"

Gabe heard the familiar tapping of raccoon nails on the hardwood floor of the bedroom hall. "I just heard the news about the British Prime—"

He saw that Ronny was carrying something in his mouth. "What's that?" he asked.

It looked like a small scrap of the shiny inside of a snack food bag.

Ronny stopped in front of him and took the film in his paw. "Your answers," he replied, holding it out to him.

Gabe took it between his thumb and finger. It did have the color and consistency of a potato chip bag, like thin Mylar. It was about the size of the paper slip in a Chinese fortune cookie. Gabe saw that there was some sort of design imprinted in very thin, black lines. He realized that it wasn't a design, but writing—very tiny writing.

"This is it!" Gabe exclaimed.

Somehow holding this tiny film made by space aliens seemed almost more fantastic—more out-of-this-world—than a talking, lying raccoon.

"Correct."

Gabe held it close. He could just barely make out the words. They'd probably made it small so that Ronny could carry it without drawing attention.

Wait a second . . . "Hey! Your spaceship must be close by."

"Why do you say that?"

Gabe gave him a look that said, *Do you think I'm an idiot?* "Can you maybe fly?"

"No, Gabe . . . that seems obvious."

"I mean, it's only been a half-hour. How far can you go in ten minutes?"

Think-pause.

"Ronny!" Gabe reprimanded.

"Sorry, I was thinking how to explain. First of all, you're apparently assuming that I had to physically carry the questions to my companions. Second, you're assuming that I had to physically go to retrieve the response."

"Neither of which are true, I take it?"

"Gabe, I won't make up any more lies, but there are some things I won't be able to tell you, like hints about my companions' location."

"Fair enough. Let's see if I can make out this spider scrawl."

Gabe held the note under the oven light and was able to see the writing:

1. 287 entities.

2. Ronny is the only currently active liar.

3. There is a terrorist nuclear bomb next to Mrs. Crabnuckle's house. The plan is that it will go off tomorrow afternoon.

4. Ronny does want to plant a nuclear control device at the bomb.

5. We cannot answer that; a Demon-zombie would perhaps want to get information about your pet.

"This is amazing," Gabe gushed, holding the note out before him. "Actual space aliens wrote these words."

"I'm also a space alien," Ronny reminded.

Gabe glanced over and laughed. "Don't be jealous. You just don't seem like an alien. More like an overdone genetic experiment. So, what's this 287 entities?"

"Gabe, that's the answer to your first question."

"I know that. I forgot what my questions were—see? I knew I should have written them down."

"Your first question was, 'How many of your kind are on Earth?' "

"287! Jeez-louise! Your space ship must be as big as a destroyer! Where could you hide it?"

Ronny just sat looking up at him.

"Right," Gabe agreed. "You can't tell me anything about that."

He peered again at the note. "You're the only 'current' liar."

He looked at Ronny.

"I already explained that there were previous ones that were killed by the terrorists."

"Right. Third: there really is a bomb. Okay, fine. Fourth: you do want to plant the device. And last...."

Gabe looked at Ronny, perplexed. "The Zombies may be trying to get information about my 'pet'?"

"I'm pretending to be your pet."

"What was the question again?"

" 'Why are the Demon-zombies stalking me?' "

"Ah, I see. They're trying to get to *you*. Of course, if you're only pretending, then maybe I don't have to feed you."

"I assume you're joking, Gabe."

He looked at the raccoon and laughed. "Don't worry, I'll keep the tuna fish coming."

"Can we talk about the plan?"

"To place your containment device?"

"Yes."

"I haven't agreed to help you."

"I see. I thought that if—"

"Okay, I won't make you beg. Do you have any ideas?"

"I would like to revisit the idea that you pretend to be their cell leader."

"You weren't listening, were you?"

"Of course I was. I said 'You could pretend to be their terrorist cell leader,' and then you replied, 'Let me see if I can find some holes in that plan—' "

"Okay, I got it. You were listening. You're just insane."

"Again, you're joking?"

"How would I even *know* what a sane space alien acts like? Yes, I'm joking—but not about your idea. That wouldn't even get us through the front door. What all do you know about these terrorists?"

"There are three that live in the house. Abdul-Baari is here on a work visa, Nabeeh is a student at UCSD, and Isaam is here illegally and incognito, and he is the leader here in San Diego. He's thirty, and has already killed two Israeli soldiers."

"They're Palestinian?"

"Not exactly. Isaam was born in the occupied Palestinian area, but one parent is Syrian. Abdul-Baari is Arabian, and Nabeeh is Kuwaiti."

"Kuwaiti? They're our allies! We saved their country in the first Gulf War!"

"Gabe, I don't think any middle-eastern country, other than Israel, is America's ally. In any case, terrorists are rarely associated with any one government, so from which country they hail is not necessarily relevant. The second worst terrorist act in America was implemented by Americans."

Gabe shrugged. "You're probably right. Anything else?"

"Perhaps you could be specific. What do you want to know about them? Otherwise this could take a long time if I just relate everything I know."

"How *do* you know all this?"

"As I've said, we're specialists—"

"In information technology, I know. If you ever need a job, you could work for the NSA. Okay, what about their habits? You know, their daily routines?"

"Nabeeh usually rises first in the morning. He's the most devout and takes his sunrise prayers seriously. Isaam rises next. He always makes the breakfast tea and often complains that the others don't do their part. Abdul-Baari is the youngest, and does not rise until Isaam—"

"Uh, you're right. This could take all day. Can you filter out just the stuff that might be useful?"

Think-pause.

"Ronny?"

"I'm sorry, Gabe. I was analyzing that. The problem is that knowing specifically those things that are useful implies that we already have a plan, which we don't. Not since you rejected mine, at least."

"Get over it, Ronny. I see your point, though. Okay, do they ever leave the house unattended?"

"Never. This is a firm rule."

"Do they have guns?"

"Of course."

"Of course?"

"They're terrorists, Gabe."

"Right. They must leave *sometime*. Is there ever just one of them there?"

"Yes. On Friday nights Isaam and Abdul-Baari go to night-clubs. Nabeeh, being devout, stays and guards the bomb."

"That's tonight! Now we're getting somewhere. We can do it after the gig. Can we monitor the house? Can we tell where Nabeeh is at any time?"

"Yes."

"Wow! You must have the whole house bugged."

"I can't discuss that, Gabe."

"I'll take that as a yes."

Ronny just sat and looked at him.

"Hey!" Gabe exclaimed. "If you're able to get in to bug their whole house, why can't you manage to get the nuclear containment device planted?"

Ronny said nothing.

"I get it, I get it. I'm treading forbidden territory. Okay, so we have a house with just Nabeeh inside, and you can tell at all times where he is. Well, my friend, I don't mean to sound trifling, but this seems trifling. The guy has to go to the bathroom sometime. When he does, I'll sneak in and plant the device."

"Let's review this, Gabe. Your new plan is essentially to just walk in and plant the device."

"Yeah. Timing is everything."

"It sure is."

"You sound skeptical."

"That's because I am. What if he happens to catch you?"

Gabe shrugged. "I run."

"First of all, he has a gun. You can't run faster than a bullet. Second, even if you manage to plant the device and happen to avoid his bullets, the whole venture is virtually useless if they suspect anything, for they'll then be suspicious and likely find the device."

Gabe shrugged again. "That's the best I can come up with."

Ronny looked at him a moment. "We only have one device. We only have one chance."

Gabe just shrugged.

"Are you sure you don't want to pretend to be their new cell leader? I could coach you every step of the way."

Gabe just looked at Ronny.

"Very well. We risk everything with a simple-ass plan."

Gabe's eyes went wide in shock. "My, my. I believe I just heard both sarcasm and a crude colloquialism all in one sentence."

"It seemed that emphasis was appropriate."

Gabe grinned at him.

"Gabe," Ronny said.

"Yes?"

"I'm sure you understand that you have an advantage since we need you, but I can tell you that I would be lonely if our association ended. As a liar, I can no longer expect the same close association with my colleagues as before."

"You'd mentioned earlier that they don't tolerate dishonesty."

"I can translate the name they use for me: Ronny the Liar."

Gabe smiled warmly at the raccoon. "You're more like us than them, huh?"

"In many ways, yes. Gabe, do you realize that most humor relies on lying?"

Gabe raised one eyebrow.

"Think about it," Ronny said. "For you, lying is so natural that you take it for granted, but almost all humor relies on a twist of reality, if not a complete fabrication. Sarcasm uses an opposite meaning to mock. Irony, almost the same. A pun uses an unintended meaning of a word—again, a divergence from the truth. Jokes are made-up stories; cartoons, gross exaggerations of reality. Anything that's funny is rarely an honest and accurate detailing of the truth. Believe me, Gabe, my companions find human humor inexplicable. So did I, until I learned to lie."

Gabe raised both eyebrows. "By that definition, novels are nothing but lies."

"So, what's your point?"

Gabe chuckled. "Did you intend that to be funny, or did you just get lucky?"

"Does a bear shit in the woods?"

Gabe laughed out loud and sat down, cross-legged, in front of Ronny. "You've got a ways to go before you're ready for stand-up, but you're getting the hang of it," he said, scratching Ronny's chin. "You may be right about humor requiring an understanding of lying, but humor can also reveal truths as well."

"Humor is sometimes truth wearing a silly hat," Ronny quipped.

"Where did you hear that?"

"I made it up."

Ronny turned his head so that Gabe could scratch his neck. "Gabe," he said, "you called me your friend earlier. Was that just a meaningless expression, like when you refer to Punky as Saliva Monster, or did you mean it?"

Gabe expanded the scratching until he was massaging Ronny's shoulders and neck. "I meant it, Ronny the Liar," he said, shoving him so that Ronny slid sideways across the kitchen linoleum. "But don't let it go to your head."

Chapter 8

Friday evening

Gabe jammed the last piece of band equipment into his car and opened the passenger door for Ronny. The raccoon climbed in, and Gabe slammed the door behind him and ran around to his own side. They were running late due to a near-disaster during the pet rounds. There had been a miscommunication, and he'd accidentally let a young cat escape from a client's house. Mr. Berdowski had bought the kitten just a few days before, and there hadn't been time for it to associate the house with "home". Luckily, the cat headed straight for the nearest tree instead of taking off for Timbuktu. The new pet sat on the lowest branch of the huge oak, about fifteen feet above Gabe, gazing down at him.

The cat would eventually come down when it got hungry, but Gabe would have to be there waiting, otherwise it would wander off. He couldn't leave until the cat was safely back inside the house.

He had waited out of sight, but after a half-hour he gave up. He had no idea how long before the cat decided that tree-time was up. And even if it did come down, it was just as likely to scamper up another tree when Gabe tried to grab it. He'd have to move on to proactive action.

Gabe found a stepladder in Mr. Berdowski's garage, but despite his best efforts at a slow and non-threatening climb, the cat simply moved to the next higher limb as soon as Gabe's hand came within a foot.

What a pickle. Gabe noticed that Ronny was sitting next to him looking up at the cat as well. "Go up and get him," Gabe told him.

Ronny looked at Gabe as though unsure if Gabe was actually talking to him. "You want me to climb the tree and retrieve the cat?" Ronny asked.

"That's right," Gabe replied.

"Are you joking?" Ronny asked.

"No. Go up and get him."

Ronny looked up again. "I could fall and get hurt."

"You're a raccoon," Gabe reminded him. "Raccoons climb trees."

Ronny looked up at the cat. "It will probably fight and scratch me. It could, for example, damage one of my eyes."

Gabe sighed. "Look, climb up the trunk on the other side from the cat. Then just come back down on its side. It'll be forced down as it tries to stay away from you."

Ronny had studied the situation a minute, and then without another word, walked around the tree and started climbing. The cat guessed something up, but held to its spot. From about forty feet up, Ronny called down, "Is this far enough?"

"Yeah!" Gabe called back. "Look mean."

Ronny paused a moment to think. "Raccoon-mean, or human-mean?"

Gabe considered. "Let's try raccoon-mean."

Ronny proceeded down the tree head first, arms splayed to each side, emitting a low growl with teeth bared. The cat waited patiently until Ronny was less than a foot away, and then suddenly decided it was time for an active defense, raising its fur and hissing.

This took Ronny completely by surprise, and he held up one paw and yelled, "Hey! Stop that!"

It was the cat's turn to be surprised, and it scampered down into Gabe's arms.

Back on the ground, Ronny said, "It appears that human-mean was the ticket."

But, now they were late for the gig, and Gabe hated to be late, particularly for this, their best job. The usual Friday evening traffic slowed him further, and Ronny learned the proper inflection of a few of Gabe's crustier colloquialisms. Gabe pulled into the Schooner's tiny back lot just as Derrick was starting to unload his drums. Ronny stayed in the car while Gabe dragged the gear from his car and through the loading door. Gabe came out from one trip to find a dog barking wildly into the half-open passenger window. Ronny was inside, sitting up on his haunches, shooing the dog with his paw and calling, "Down, Rover! Down!"

Gabe chased the dog away and wound up the window. "Somebody could have heard you!" he scolded.

"Raccoon-mean wasn't working," Ronny replied.

Gabe looked around. Tourists and locals milled by on Mission Boulevard down the alley. "Come on, I can't leave you out here alone. You're just like a little kid."

Ronny sat at the back of the stage watching while Gabe set up the equipment. Gabe had to explain to nearly everyone in the club that he was watching a client's pet. At one point while Gabe was bending down to pick up a monitor next to Ronny, the raccoon said into his ear, "Lying is the fabric of your lives."

Although he tried to ignore it, Gabe could feel a tightening in his stomach at the anticipation of Christie's arrival. He hadn't talked to her since he'd dropped her off at her apartment the previous night when she jumped out of the car with hardly a good-bye.

Gabe finished setting up the PA, and turned to his guitar amplifier. One of the advantages of playing a larger room like the Schooner was an opportunity to use his vintage Fender Showman amp head. At 100 Watts, it was far too loud to crank in the smaller clubs.

He looked up and saw that Christie had arrived. She was stunning. The band had talked it over and had decided to at least take a nod at the clothes styles of the forties and fifties jazz musicians. That meant no blue-jeans, baggy T-shirts, or running shoes. Gabe had settled for a flower-print shirt and a pair of Dockers pleated pants. Christie was wearing a silky, cream-colored, knee-length dress. A fake pearl necklace lay coy and elegant against her sun-tanned chest. Gabe's heart thrummed an enthusiastic overture.

"Hey, Christie!" he called when he caught her eye.

She smiled and gave him a little wave.

Either she'd softened since last night, or she was simply giddy with nervousness. The gig was even more significant for her since she'd worked here as a waitress until two months ago. Most of the employees knew her well, and Gabe imagined that this must seem like a modern-day Cinderella scene for her.

One of the waitresses—Gabe remembered her name as Melinda—came over and gave Christie a big hug. They started talking, so Gabe finished the band set-up. He helped Randy lug in his bass amp and as they manhandled it into position, he heard Christie behind him cooing greetings to Ronny. She carried the raccoon to the front of the stage, scratching his neck.

"You two have become inseparable," she said to Gabe.

"Yeah," he replied, handing Randy his instrument cord, "he's like a tick that you're afraid to pull out because it might leave its head still embedded in your skin."

It seemed to Gabe that Ronny raised one eyebrow slightly.

"Don't say that," Christie reprimanded, pretending to give Ronny a kiss on the side of his snout, "he can understand you."

Gabe shot her glance, but she was hugging the raccoon to her neck. She'd obviously been kidding.

The manager came over. "Hi, Christie," he said. "All set for your big debut?" Then, before she even had a chance to answer he said to Gabe, "You just about ready?"

Gabe looked at his watch. It was already 8:40. They were supposed to have started at 8:30. "You bet."

Christie took the side stairs down to the dance floor. Unlike most of the bars they played, the Schooner had a stage that was more than something you might accidentally trip over. She sat, still holding Ronny, at the band table—a bona fide band table—off to the left. Gabe hastily tuned his guitar, and they launched into their signature theme song, an instrumental version of *Chicken Shack Boogie.* They hadn't had a chance to do a sound check, and Gabe thought the bass was too low, so he walked over and turned up Randy's amp a couple of notches. Not that it mattered, really, since the place didn't really start filling up until nine o'clock. This was the dues you paid being the lowly warm-up band; you played your first set to a largely empty house in order to attract the attention of the people passing by outside.

They finished the first song, and Christie and Melinda clapped wildly. He had learned long ago that, although highlighting just how *few* people were listening, one or two people applauding, was nevertheless encouraging.

Christie joined them for the fourth song, and Gabe thought she did okay, considering how nervous she obviously was. She'd sung this tune a lot better at practice, but it wasn't so bad, and judging by the wildly enthusiastic applause from both Melinda *and* the manager, her friends at least liked it.

She seemed more relaxed with each song, until, by the last tune of the forty-five-minute set, she was belting away as good as Gabe had heard her. Perhaps a dozen people in the audience clapped—a relatively smashing end to a warm-up band's first set.

Gabe took off his guitar and set it on its stand, then adjusted the PA settings before joining the other three at the band table. Christie was holding Ronny again, and she looked flushed with the rush of the performance.

"Quite a thrill, isn't it?" Gabe asked.

She nodded vigorously. She seemed too adrenaline-charged to even talk.

"Wait until there's people actually *listening*."

Gabe wasn't sure from her face if the thought elicited euphoria or fear.

Gabe, Derrick, and Randy dove into the burgers they'd ordered before the set, while Christie snuggled Ronny and seemed to catch her breath. They made small talk, and, as with all band breaks, after what seemed like three minutes, the fifteen-minute break was over. The guys climbed back up on stage and Christie hung on to Ronny like he was her favorite stuffed toy.

The place was beginning to fill up fast now, and Gabe noticed a man sitting at a table right up front who looked out of place. Whereas most of the arriving crowd was in their twenties, this guy looked older, mostly by his choice of attire, since his wide-brimmed hat, sunglasses, and floppy coat hid his face. If he was trying to be discrete, his attempt was almost comical.

Gabe always found the second set better than the first. The band settled into the house's groove, and the audience had a chance to get a couple of drinks down. By the time Christie joined them, the place was beginning to rock. She punched out the first tune like a cross between Billy Holiday and Janis Joplin, and the growing crowd responded with applause of honest approval. Christie stood grinning like she'd just taken some angel dust.

A prime rule that a lot of bands never learn is to never let the audience cool down. Gabe launched immediately into the next tune. He had a guitar solo during the third verse, and when he looked up after finishing, he saw Melinda leaning over, talking to the mystery man in the hat and sunglasses. The man said something into her ear. She leaned in further and said something to him. He replied, and then she leaned back and slapped him across the face. This sent his hat flying and there, clear as day, was a brown frog clinging to the man's half-bald head.

It was the zombie!

Gabe missed a beat, but Derrick and Randy eased back and Gabe found his place. The zombie scrambled to retrieve his hat, and made a beeline for the exit without so much as a glance back. Gabe looked over at Ronny, but he seemed to be asleep on Christie's chair. Gabe wasn't sure what to do. He was virtually trapped up there on the stage if the zombie should return with reinforcements.

He needed advice.

When the song ended, Gabe quickly took off his guitar and told Christie to talk to the crowd until he got back. He left her looking stunned while he jumped to the floor and ran to the band table. Ronny stood up on the chair when he saw Gabe coming. Gabe heard Christie introducing the band as he swung the chair around, Ronny and all, so that the back would block the view. He knelt down in front of Ronny and leaned in close.

"Didn't you see the zombie?"

Ronny hesitated only a second. "No."

Gabe craned his neck up and looked around. Everybody in the band plus many in the audience were watching him. The background sound was loud enough that Gabe was sure nobody could hear Ronny. He just hoped they didn't see his mouth moving like an animated commercial.

"Keep your head down low," Gabe said. "He was right over there, right in front."

"I'm sorry Gabe, I didn't see him."

"A fine watch-raccoon *you* turn out to be. What should we do?"

"Proceed with the plan."

"What if they're on to us?"

Think-pause. "We'll just have to chance it."

"Ronny, you're hesitating again . . ."

"Gabe, sometimes I just have to think."

Gabe stuck his head up and looked around. Christie had run out of things to say, and practically everybody in the place was now watching him.

"I've got to get back. We'll talk more after the set. In the meantime, you watch out for any more zombies, got it?"

"I understand, Gabe."

Gabe took a deep breath before sprinting back up the stage steps. As he was putting his guitar back on, Randy asked him what that was all about. "I'll explain later," Gabe replied. "Okay, here we go with *Mack the Knife*—one, two, a-one-two-three . . ."

Gabe was proud of this tune. No combo band that he knew of had covered this well-known song in decades, certainly not with just a guitar and a two-piece rhythm section. Randy and Derrick began the deceptively simple 2/4 intro and Christie joined in, laid-back, but solid. This is the ultimate test for a vocalist since the two-note bass part begins so nondescriptly that the first verse is sung virtually a-cappella. On the second verse, Gabe began building the slowly mounting horn parts. It had taken all of Gabe's imagination and technical abilities to pull off enough phrases to make the instrumentation recognizable as "Mackie".

But it was Christie who carried the night. This was a tune with which everybody is familiar, and Bobby Darin is a mighty high target. Christie sang with Darin's confidence and humor, building the energy verse-by-verse until she nailed the last "look-out-old-Mackie-is-back" line so solidly that Gabe was sure Mr. Darin would have approved, and, judging by the wild applause, the Schooner's guests agreed.

They had the crowd's attention now, and Gabe guided the band from one number to the next with barely a pause. Four songs later they finished their set, and whistles and calls for an encore punched through the sustained applause. The band was all smiles as they hastily tore down their equipment to make room for the headline band, whose lead guitarist greeted them with a simple, sarcastic,

"Thanks!" His meaning was clear: the first band was supposed to warm the audience up, not steal the night and burn them out. Gabe was guessing they'd be returning next time as the headline band.

They loaded the band equipment into their cars, and when Gabe came back inside, his heart sank when he found Christie sitting at the band table talking to Brent. Where the hell was Ronny? He was supposed to be keeping a watch.

Yikes! Ronny was lying right there on Christie's lap!

Gabe felt rising panic. He considered just making a run for it, but decided that he couldn't abandon Ronny. He worked his way around to the side, keeping a good fifty feet away, until he was behind Brent. He then caught Christie's attention by waving to her. She gave him an annoyed look, said something to Brent, and came over, carrying Ronny along. She didn't say anything, but her face explained that she was prepared for the worst.

Gabe didn't let her down. "What the hell are you doing?" he asked, almost hysterically. He looked down at Ronny, but the raccoon returned his gaze without expression.

Christie stared at him a moment, and shook her head. "I'm talking to Brent," she replied, as if she was repeating the obvious.

"I can see that. I mean why?"

Her look implied that she'd had just about enough and was about to walk away.

"Never mind," Gabe continued. "Look I . . . can't deal with him tonight. I don't even want him to see me. You have to get rid of him."

"*I* have to get rid of him?" she repeated.

"Yes. Please, Christie. Just do it, okay?"

She shook her head again as if she couldn't believe what she was hearing.

"Look," Gabe said. "Everything will be clear tomorrow. I know I've been acting strange, but in less than twenty-four hours I'll be able to explain everything."

Christie just looked at him with a wrinkled brow.

"Christie," Gabe pleaded, putting his hand on her shoulder, "I'm asking you to trust me. Just this once. I promise that I'll explain tomorrow night."

Christie took a deep breath and sighed. She looked into Gabe's eyes, and he could see that he'd won her—at least for now.

"Okay, Gabe Wolfekow. But, by damn, you'd better have one hell of an explanation."

Gabe smiled with relief. "Thank you, Christie. I will, I promise."

"So, what do I tell Brent?"

Gabe thought a moment. "Tell him that . . . oh hell, tell him that I'm jealous, and that I want to have it out with him—but not here. Tell him to meet me in one hour outside the Catamaran Hotel on the bay side."

"Have it *out* with him?" Christie looked both angry and worried.

"Please," Gabe pleaded, "just this once."

Christie gave him a hard look, then, without another word, strode off towards the band table.

Gabe moved farther away and watched as Christie talked to Brent. Gabe couldn't see the zombie's expressions from the back, but judging by his violent arm motions, he could guess that Brent was not receiving the news happily. They appeared to argue for a couple of minutes, and then Brent suddenly stood up and stomped away. When Gabe was sure Brent wasn't coming back, be went over to the table where Christie was stroking Ronny thoughtfully.

"How'd it go?" Gabe asked her.

She stared at the floor as if she hadn't heard him. Without looking up, she finally said, "You'd better have one damn fantastic explanation, Mr. Wolfekow."

He grinned. "I promised. In fact, Ronny and I have to go to take care of it."

She looked up at him. "You're going to the Catamaran already?" She looked confused.

"No, that was just to get rid of him."

"You're going to just leave me here?"

"Derrick said he'll give you a ride."

She sighed. "You sure know how to make a girl feel appreciated."

Gabe shrugged. He didn't know what to say. Instead, he kissed her forehead, took Ronny from her, and walked away towards the back door.

There was one more thing he needed to take care of before they left, though. Melinda was taking drink orders at a table nearby, and Gabe caught her attention. She came over to him. "Hey. Cute pet," she said, indicating Ronny. "Do you want a drink?" she asked Gabe.

"No. Can you tell me what that man said to you? The one with the funny birthmark on his head—the one you slapped?"

She looked at him with one raised eyebrow. "I never touched him. He sneezed." She smiled. "That's the official account in case he wants to sue me."

She looked over at Christie who was waiting for Derrick, then back at Gabe. He guessed that she was sizing up the situation—whether she should trust him. She made up her mind. "The guy asked about Christie—"

"About *Christie?*"

"Yeah. He asked if I knew who she was. I figured he was some kind of creep, so I asked him if he was maybe looking for some fun later—you know, to draw him out."

Gabe grinned. "I suppose he said 'yes'?"

In answer, Melinda made a fist and swung it in an arc. "He asked how much I charged," she added. "Listen, I gotta' go, the place is beginning to hop."

"Sure. Thanks."

Gabe watched her walk away before heading out the back door. He made a mental note never to get fresh with her.

Chapter 9

Friday evening, later

"This doesn't add up," Gabe said once inside the car. "Why would the bald zombie be asking about Christie, when the Brent zombie talks to her all the time?"

Ronny was finding a comfortable position on the passenger seat, which he was sharing with Gabe's guitar. "I'm not sure, Gabe. Do you think it's important?"

"How would *I* know? You tell *me*. Also, why would Baldy proposition Melinda? Do zombies' have sexual urges? Is that how they spread their body snatching?"

"I doubt it. Perhaps, like the submarine nuclear bomb, they're studying human capabilities."

"*Sexual* capabilities?"

"Poor choice of word—perhaps human preponderancies. Or, better, human weaknesses."

"Well, if they're looking to explore human sexual experiences, they picked an awfully bad host in old Frog-head. He'll be lucky to buy sex at any price, and even then, I find it hard to believe they'd observe the female orgasm."

Gabe suddenly had an image of the baldy zombie seducing Christie with some advanced hypnotizing device. He shuddered. He'd be happy when this was all over. But of course, this was just the beginning. Once they convinced the authorities that an alien invasion of Demon-zombies was under way . . . well, the fun was only starting.

"Do you still have the containment thingy?" Gabe asked.

Ronny used his little raccoon fingers to open the glove compartment, and pulled out a white plastic shopping bag.

"You kept it in the glove compartment? You said this was the only one. What if somebody had stolen it?"

Ronny thought a moment. "I guess humans do that, don't they?"

Gabe sighed. He'd never have guessed that working with a super-advanced alien would be similar to babysitting.

He still couldn't get over that Ronny had shown up that afternoon carrying the sophisticated device in a used drug store shopping bag, as though it was dirty gym shorts. "The bags are everywhere," Ronny had explained, "and nobody pays attention to them." Gabe guessed that he was right. It just seemed so . . . unromantic.

The device itself looked rather mundane. It could have been a hand ball that had lost some air so that it developed a flat spot. Ronny had explained that this would prevent it from rolling around. It was even slightly soft, like it was made of rubber. Ronny had quickly warned him not to squeeze it too much, or he'd likely break the inner workings. Gabe had asked where the activating switch was, and Ronny had replied that on/off switches were a sure sign of primitive technology. Gabe had been initially offended at that, but remembered that his calculator didn't have a power switch; it just came to life as soon as he hit any key, then went back to sleep after he stopped using it for a while.

The ride to the terrorists' house took fifteen minutes, and they reviewed the plan, if, as Ronny had accused, it could even be called a plan. Ronny confirmed that Isaam and Abdul-Baari had just left to go off to party, leaving devout Nabeeh to mind the house. When Gabe asked him how he knew that, Ronny just looked at him. Gabe understood: off limits. Despite Nabeeh's religious loyalties, Ronny was quite confident that in approximately forty-five minutes the young student would leave the garage, walk into the house, down the hall, go in the bathroom, lock the door, and not come out for about five minutes.

"How do you know that?" Gabe had asked Ronny.

"Although the Koran bans premarital sex, it does not prohibit masturbation."

"You mean, this guy whacks off like clockwork every Friday night?"

"I suspect that the same devotion to structure and ritual that draws him to religion also delays his visit to the bathroom for an hour after his colleagues leave."

Gabe had looked critically at the raccoon. "You know, you could single-handedly start a Jihad war against your people."

"It has nothing to do with Islam, just human psychology."

Gabe had scoffed. "Mr. human psychology, who expected these guys to believe that I was their secret leader."

"It could have worked," Ronny had said.

"Right. Up my ass, it could have worked."

Ronny had thought about that for a couple of seconds. "Apparently some metaphors are not readily accessible on the public communications media," he'd finally concluded.

Gabe turned his car onto Mission Canyon Road and parked a good distance from Crabnuckle's and the terrorists' houses. Now came the part he'd been dreading. He was supposed to place a communications device in his ear so that Ronny, who would be keeping watch, could talk to him. The problem was that this was not a Sony MP3 earpiece, but a tiny alien device manufactured by beings he'd never even seen—and it was going to crawl right inside his head.

In the dim light of the widely separated streetlights, Gabe saw Ronny hold out his hand with his forefinger extended. There, on the tip of his little finger lay what looked like a tiny worm. Gabe held out his palm, and Ronny dropped the device onto it. Gabe then lightly placed the forefinger of his other hand against it, and it wiggled up and clung to it. Gabe had an overpowering urge to open the door and fling it.

He took a deep breath. *For all mankind*, he told himself as he put the tip of his finger to his ear. He shivered as he felt the thing squirm and crawl into his ear canal. He felt panic, and almost cried out.

"Can you hear me?" he heard a calm, clear, and totally unfamiliar voice say.

It caught Gabe by surprise, and he forgot his feelings of horror. Without thinking about it, he'd been expecting to hear Ronny's gravely little voice in his ear. But, as he realized now, Ronny's familiar Louis Armstrong voice was the product of a raccoon's mouth and vocal cords. What he was hearing was the same Ronny, just through a different channel.

"Uh, yeah. I can hear you just fine—is that you, Ronny?"

"Yes," said the voice.

Gabe was looking at Ronny. He just sat there motionless as the voice talked in his ear.

"This is me," Ronny said, and this time the raccoon's mouth moved as well. "You probably find it disconcerting to hear me without associated mouth motion."

"Yeah," Gabe replied. "It's disconcerting, but not even close to having a tiny talking worm living in my ear."

"I have confidence you'll get used to it. Gabe . . ."

"What?"

"If I stop moving my mouth, and you repeat what I say, you could be my dummy, like Charlie McCarthy."

Gabe gave him a pained look. "I'm not sure what's worse, a humorless person, or someone with a bad sense of it."

Ronny thought for just a second. "I'll assume that was an unconnected observation. Shall we get on with the task at hand?"

Gabe nodded. The first problem was the surveillance cameras. Even if Nabeeh wasn't watching, they couldn't afford to be seen in later viewings. There were two cameras: one in front, and an identical one in back. Ronny assured him that the cameras didn't work very well at night. These guys didn't have a CIA budget, after all. Plus, in order to maximize coverage, they both swept back and forth, leaving each periphery unmonitored for eight to ten seconds each sweep.

Gabe got out, opened Ronny's door, and the raccoon climbed down onto the road. Just then, a car came around the turn, blinding Gabe.

Shit! Where was Ronny? He could be squashed! Gabe held his hand up to shield the headlights, and tried to look down to see where Ronny was. The raccoon was right there in front of him . . . and was holding one of his paws up, as if cautioning the driver to take it easy. The driver did indeed slow down, and gave them both an odd look as she passed and then sped up again.

"That wasn't very raccoon-like behavior," Gabe warned, looking down at the animal.

"I was afraid the car might hit you."

"You were afraid for *me?*"

"You're a bigger target."

Gabe nodded. He was right. "Okay. I'll wait for your word."

Ronny immediately hopped up onto the sidewalk and trotted off on all fours towards the houses. The plan was that Ronny would get close enough to observe the camera covering the front. If they happened to notice him, well, who would be surprised to see a raccoon nosing around at night—as long as he didn't wave, or make indecent gestures.

Gabe stepped off the road, onto the sidewalk. He could no longer see Ronny in the darkness. "How's it going?" he asked softly.

Ronny had explained that he'd be able to hear Gabe through the same earworm.

"I'm two houses away from Crabnuckle," came Ronny's reply. "I can see the camera. I'll start looking for an observation post."

Gabe heard a car engine start a little ways behind him. The driver put the car into gear and started up the street. He glanced around, but the headlights blinded him, and he turned immediately away. The car slowed, and stopped next to him. The driver's window was down, and the Brent zombie sat looking at him. "I thought you were supposed to meet me at the Catamaran, asshole," Brent-zombie said.

Oh shit! Gabe thought. *Double shit! They're on to us!* Brent-zombie must have followed him from the Schooner. "Ronny, I've got the Brent zombie here. What should I do?"

Think-pause. "Get rid of him."

"Oh great! That's certainly the most useful advice I've gotten today."

"I don't think this is the time for sarcasm."

Gabe had been talking into the air while Brent-zombie sat watching him, and now his stalker snapped, "Put away the cell phone, jerk, and look at me."

"Fine," Gabe said into the air. "No sarcasm. Now give me an idea how to get rid of the zombie."

"Zombie, my ass," Brent-zombie snarled, opening the car door.

"I suggest you run," Ronny said into Gabe's ear.

"I'm a step ahead of you," Gabe replied, turning and sprinting away down the sidewalk.

He looked back and saw Brent starting off after him. Gabe wasn't in the best of shape. Brent-zombie would catch him sooner rather than later.

His grandmother had impressed instructions on him as a small boy in case he was ever pursued by a strange man. Gabe saw no reason to abandon wise advice. He picked a house that had lights on, ran up to the door, and rang the bell. He heard Brent-zombie's footsteps slapping along the sidewalk. *Come on!* he prayed, knocking with his knuckles, *answer the door!* Brent-zombie reached Gabe just as the door swung open, revealing a skinny, bare-chested elderly man in pajama bottoms.

Before the old man could say anything, Gabe blurted out, indicating to Brent-zombie, "This guy's chasing me!"

The old man looked from Brent-zombie to Gabe. "So, what do you want *me* to do, tell him to stop?" The old man nodded his chin at Brent-zombie. "You, stop chasing him."

Brent-zombie just stood there, obviously flustered at the situation.

"Thanks," Gabe said, "Uh, can I come in?"

"I don't think so," replied the elderly man. "I don't know you."

Brent-zombie finally found his wits. He grabbed Gabe by the shirt. "This is between you and me, weasel. Leave this guy out of it."

"That sounds good to me," the old man said.

Gabe was desperate. "Call the police!"

The old man shrugged and walked away into the house.

Brent-zombie pursed his lips in frustration. "You won't get away with this, asshole," he finally growled, giving Gabe a shove that sent him stumbling into the shrubs. Brent-zombie then stalked away.

"Not the police!" came Ronny's voice in Gabe's ear.

Oops. The police would totally upset their plans with the terrorists. "Uh, sir!" Gabe yelled into the house. "No need for the police. He's left."

The old man reappeared, buttoning a shirt. "I wasn't going to. I was just getting cold."

Gabe nodded. They looked at each other for a couple of seconds. "I'll be going then," Gabe finally announced. "Sorry for the inconvenience."

"What inconvenience? There'd be inconvenience if you'd gotten blood on my walkway, but as it is—no inconvenience. Hey, you want a cup of tea?"

Gabe smiled. "No thanks, maybe another time?"

The old man shrugged. "Always another time. Just like my kids," he grumbled, closing the door.

Gabe took a deep breath. "Ronny, you still there?"

"I'm in position. Gabe you'll have to hurry now. Nabeeh may leave for his sexual activity at any second."

Gabe nodded, and then remembered that Ronny couldn't see him. "Roger. I'm on my way."

The plan was perfect. Ronny would meet Gabe at the outside door to the garage. Once Nabeeh left to do his business, Gabe would hold Ronny in place while he picked the lock with another alien miracle worm device. Gabe would then plant the containment device and lock the door again on the way out. All while Nabeeh was joyously wrestling with his monkey.

Gabe walked out to the street and peered back towards his car. Brent-zombie had just reached his own car, still parked next to Gabe's. He climbed in, but before swinging the door shut, he gave it a good push, smashing the edge of it into the passenger's side of Gabe's car.

The sacrifices of war, Gabe thought.

Brent-zombie drove off and Gabe took off as well at a jog down the sidewalk.

"Ronny, would I have better night vision than the camera?" he asked into the air.

"Considering that your vision is 20/19, I would think so."

"How do you know . . . never mind."

Two houses before Crabnuckle's, Gabe decided he'd gotten close enough. "Okay, I'm ready."

There was silence for a couple of seconds, and then the new, clear voice of Ronny voice intoned, "Three-two-one—go!"

Gabe sprinted up the sidewalk. The camera should be swinging away from him now. As he ran, he searched ahead for the next place to duck out of view. Soon Ronny's voice began again, "One-two-three—stop!"

By the time he heard "stop!" Gabe was crouched down on the walkway of the house just this side of Crabnuckle's. Shrubbery and trees hid him from the camera that was now pointing his way.

"Three-two-one—go!"

Gabe jumped up and made it to Crabnuckle's driveway well before Ronny's next count-up began. He didn't want to push his luck and get stuck with no cover.

"Gabe."

"Yeah. I can hear you."

"Nabeeh has gone to the bathroom."

"Shit!"

"I don't think so. Probably to masturbate."

Gabe groaned. "How can you joke *now*?"

"I thought that humor relieves tension."

Gabe let it go. "Where are you?"

"In the tree in the front yard. The camera is right in front of me."

Gabe thought of something. "You're not moving your mouth when you talk, are you?"

"Of course not, Gabe. I'm not stupid."

"No. Sorry. Okay, listen—change of plan. We're out of time. I'm going through the front door. Give me the next camera window."

"Holy smokes! Be careful, Gabe . . . three-two-one—go!"

Gabe jumped up and sped along the sidewalk, Ronny's sophomoric expletive phrase rattling around in his head. He could see the camera swinging away from him. He was in front of the terrorist house when it started its rotation back. He almost tripped over a sign planted along the walkway warning against trespassing. He glanced up, and there was Ronny, lying on a limb as relaxed as the Cheshire Cat. Gabe made it to the front door and flattened himself against it. He could hear the diligent little whirr of the camera motor just above his head. When Ronny gave him the next mark, he reached out to the side and took a key from under a vase.

Ronny had watched the terrorists use this key through their own camera system. Gabe turned to face the door, and then, still holding himself flat, unlocked it and put the key in his pocket. He eased the door open, slipped inside, and quietly closed it again.

Gabe wasn't sure why he'd been expecting it to be dark inside the house, but he was surprised to find the living room brightly lit by two table lamps. He felt naked and exposed. He'd broken into someone's house, and even if it was terrorists, he felt criminal. He listened, but all was quiet. Whatever Nabeeh was up to down the hall, the junior terrorist wasn't making a ruckus about it. Gabe opened the inner garage door immediately to his left and went through.

The garage was also brightly lit, and there, sitting in the middle of the floor as the star attraction was the bomb. It looked like something kids might cobble together with scraps from a construction site. The terrorists had built it, in fact, from miscellaneous pieces purchased at various hardware stores. A heavy metal drain pipe ran down the middle. Odd braces and boxes clustered together at each end. The whole thing was about six feet long, and lay on a large, wooden pallet.

Ronny had prepared him for what he would find. It was a gun-type atom bomb, the simplest ever devised. The operation was fundamentally the same as Little Boy, the first nuclear bomb dropped on Hiroshima at the end of WWII. The following morning the three terrorists would place a cup of enriched uranium 235 about the size and shape of a small, thick mixing bowl at one end, and another ball of the same stuff, sized to fit into the bowl, at the other end behind a small explosive charge. At two in the afternoon, the terrorists planned to set off the charge, sending the ball hurtling down the pipe to slam into the waiting bowl—a uranium baseball and a perfectly matched catcher's mitt. Together they'd comprise enough fissionable material to exceed the critical mass, and this would start a geometrically expanding chain reaction. In other words, a nuclear explosion.

The only element of sophistication was the production of the enriched uranium, and they'd stolen that. This type of bomb was almost indecently inefficient. Less than 2% of the uranium would actually experience fission before the resulting explosion spread apart the uranium fuel, instantly halting the nuclear chain reaction. More sophisticated bombs—like Fat Boy, dropped on Nagasaki three days after Little Boy, or the later plutonium bombs—managed to use more of the fuel and were significantly more powerful. Even at less than 2% efficiency, though, this bomb would kill thousands in the first second of the blast, and tens of thousands more over the next days and weeks as the mass of radioactive material—the vaporized atoms of the house, and dirt, and tree out front—were flung into the air to drift away downwind.

Gabe pulled Ronny's flattened handball device from his pocket. The appearance was no more impressive than the mod-art bomb assemblage in front of him. But inside was alien magic that could reach out and snatch a mini-sun in the first micro-second of birth, and then hold it tightly in its grasp for centuries to come.

"*Focus!*" he whispered to himself.

He was distracted by the grand scope of it all. Ronny had carefully explained where to hide it. Gabe spun around. Under a built-in bench were wooden cabinets. The smaller door on the left was used to store rags. That's where he was to stash the ball. He reached down and tugged at the knob. It didn't open. He pulled harder. The door didn't budge. Gabe noticed that there was a built-in lock. They'd locked the door? Were they afraid someone would steal their rags? Maybe they were using it now for another purpose. Gabe didn't have time to try to figure it out. Nabeeh would shoot his wad and walk back through the door any second. Gabe had to find another hiding place for the ball. He tried the larger doors. They were locked as well.

"Gabe," came Ronny's voice. "Nabeeh's coming."

At that same instant Gabe heard the bathroom door open and footsteps inside the house. He didn't even have time to find a hiding place for himself. He only managed to crouch down behind the bomb before a shriek suddenly arose outside. It sounded like a baby being jabbed with a hot poker. Gabe heard the front door open, and then Nabeeh said something. The door between the house and the garage flew open, and a young man reached inside, grabbed a rifle leaning against the wall, and ran back into the house. The gun looked serious—a semiautomatic, a type The Terminator might use. Gabe realized that the gun was apparently only a copy when he heard the solid "thump" of pellets fired from a CO2 cartridge. Each shot was followed by an undecipherable curse from Nabeeh.

Gabe searched for an explanation. He concluded that Ronny must be somehow buying him a few precious seconds to find a hiding place for the nuclear containment device.

He saw a trash can sitting in the corner. It was half full of fast-food bags and burger wrappers. He pulled out a handful, jammed the ball down inside, and then shoved the paper trash back on top. He ran to the front of the garage where there was a row of windows in the main garage door. The terrorists had papered over the glass, but Gabe could peek through a corner where the makeshift covering had curled up.

The sight that greeted him made him call out in surprise. Ronny was in the same tree, but had moved to a higher limb. He was holding the no-trespassing sign in front of him like a shield. The sign was riddled with indentations, and Gabe saw it jerk simultaneous with each dull thud of the pellet gun.

Gabe's first thought was to run out and just grab the gun from Nabeeh, but that would completely counter what Ronny was trying to achieve by putting himself in harm's way in the first place. He didn't see any way around confronting the jerked-off student, though. He went to the outside garage door, opposite the door into the house. He turned the knob and it opened to the cool night air. Gabe slipped out and quietly closed the door behind him.

He remembered the cameras. Shit! He was trapped between the terrorists' and Crabnuckle's houses. No time to think it through. He got down on his hands and knees and tried to force his way into the dense shrubbery separating the two properties. He found it impossible. Over the years, the shrubbery had grown thick and tight.

He reminded himself that Ronny could take a killing pellet any second. With a mighty shove, Gabe threw himself forward. He heard shrubbery trunks snapping and his clothes tearing, and felt the claws of the prickly branches digging into his skin. He reached through the remaining shrubbery and grabbed a PVC pipe that was part of Crabnuckle's sprinkler system. He pulled and although it flexed and cracked, he was able to drag himself forward. He was on the other side.

On hands and knees, Gabe scurried around the back of Crabnuckle's dark house. He bumped into a patio chair and it rattled aside. He hoped Mrs. Crabnuckle was a deep sleeper. When he rounded the far corner, he stood up. He could still hear the pellet gun firing. He opened Crabnuckle's side gate, stepped quickly out onto the sidewalk, and immediately began trotting back towards Nabeeh and Ronny.

"Hey!" he called out. "What the hell are you *doing?*"

Nabeeh paused as he was sighting along the barrel, and looked over at Gabe. "Who are you?" he asked with the accent Gabe would have expected of an educated middle-eastern student.

"I'm the owner of that pet raccoon, that's who!" Gabe exclaimed, trying to sound outraged, rather than overwhelmingly anxious. "And if you've harmed it, you're in big trouble!"

Nabeeh let the tip of the rifle fall. "You shouldn't have let it loose to cause trouble."

"What trouble?"

Nabeeh thought a moment, and then pointed. "Look! It's ruined the sign."

Gabe could hardly see the lettering from all the pellet holes. "I think you ruined your own sign trying to murder my pet."

"I didn't know it was a pet! I thought it was just a dirty pest!"

Gabe had him on the defensive. "Well, maybe you'll think twice next time you decide to slaughter an innocent animal."

He reached up, and Ronny handed down the exhausted shield. Gabe dropped it on the ground, and Ronny climbed into Gabe's waiting arms.

Nabeeh was looking at him oddly. "What happened to *you?*"

Gabe looked down at his chest and arms. His shirt was ripped in multiple places, and red lines showed where the shrubs had scratched him. "My pet raccoon gets playful sometimes."

It was the best he could come up with on the spur of the moment.

Nabeeh eyed him skeptically. "Perhaps you should keep it on a leash."

Gabe was losing his advantage. "We're not talking about *me*, we're talking about you and your lethal gun." Gabe had an idea. "Hey! Do you have a license for that rifle?"

It worked. Nabeeh suddenly looked frightened. He obviously wasn't supposed to draw the attention of any authorities. "It's just a pellet gun. A licenses isn't required."

"I don't know. That doesn't look like any BB-gun I've ever seen," Gabe challenged, playing dumb.

"It's not a BB-gun. It's a pellet gun."

"Exactly."

"Look, mister. I'm sorry. No harm done, okay?"

Gabe sighed mentally. He tried to look stern. "Well then, as long as you've learned your lesson."

He nodded goodbye and walked back towards his car. Once past Crabnuckle's house, he looked back and saw that Nabeeh was pulling the sign back out from the ground. He must have tried to reposition it, and decided otherwise. One had to question the effectiveness of a no-trespassing sign that looked like the aftermath of a drive-by shooting.

"Thank you, Gabe," Ronny's voice said into his ear.

"No problem, little buddy. We're partners, right?"

Ronny didn't say anything as Gabe waited through an exceptionally long think-pause. "Right. Partners."

They came to Gabe's car, and he opened the passenger side and let Ronny step down onto the seat. Gabe went around and got in the driver's side. As he was pulling away from the curb, Ronny said, "That was quite a good pile of lies."

Chapter 10

Saturday, early morning

"But Gabe, in the trash can?" Ronny persisted, still in his new, clear inner voice as he watched from a kitchen chair while Gabe made the morning coffee. Punky sat on another chair, his snout resting on his paws, his eyes following Gabe who was apparently speaking to himself. Ronny had explained that using the earworm saved his throat.

Gabe wasn't sure if it was his imagination, but it seemed to him that Ronny was becoming more aware of the raccoon's senses. After all, it had been only a few days before that Ronny first noticed hunger after days of unintended fasting. For his part, Gabe had gotten used to the miniature communication device sitting in his ear, and often forgot that it was even there. He decided that once the Demon-zombie invasion was repelled, he and Ronny could make their fortune marketing the latest, and final, miniaturized cell phone.

"I didn't have time to find a better place," Gabe defended. "You may remember that you were fending off high-speed bullets at the time."

"I am dispensable. *You* are dispensable, Gabe. Nothing is more important than the success of placing the containment device."

"I *know* how important it is. I *know* you're probably right, but the reality is that I just couldn't stand by and let you get killed. It's a human thing, Ronny."

Ronny think-paused on that one, and Gabe let him.

"I think I understand, Gabe," he finally said. "But we do have to keep sight of the big picture."

"Well, hopefully we've managed to juggle both."

"Assuming they don't throw out the trash."

"Look, pointy-face, I've thought about this. The ketchup was long-dried on those french-fry cartons. I don't think they've *ever* emptied that can. Why would they bother today? I can't think of a better incinerator than a nuclear explosion."

"The next trash pickup on that street won't be until next Wednesday." Ronny's voice sounded conciliatory. "Perhaps we'll be okay."

This was new too. Maybe it was just the clearer definition afforded by the earworm, but Ronny seemed to be including more inflections.

Gabe remembered something he'd thought about in the middle of the night. "Hey, once the bomb goes off this afternoon and your miracle device catches an armful of Einstein's energy, I assume the idea will be to then draw as much attention to it as possible—maybe call the Union Tribune and local TV news. I mean, if we just contact the government, they may try to put a clamp on it."

Ronny nodded. "Yes, that seems prudent."

Gabe glanced over at him. "You sound as though you haven't even thought it through."

Ronny thought a moment, and Gabe gave him a sharp look. "There's not much to think about," Ronny finally said.

"What do you mean? Shouldn't we have a press release ready or something?"

"There's time."

Gabe studied Ronny. Sometimes he wasn't sure they were on the same page. "So, what happens when the Demon-zombies hear about it? They'll know then for sure that you're here."

"I guess we'll deal with it when the time comes."

Gabe shook his head. "You guys are supposed to be so smart and advanced, I assumed you'd have the whole thing worked out already. I figured that you'd have already thought through the next thirty moves in the chess game."

"Gabe, I do not constitute the entire intelligence of my people."

"Um, I see. You're saying that there are others who are in charge of things once we establish your credibility with the nuclear containment?"

"Correct."

It occurred to Gabe that he often never got much information from Ronny directly. He would advance scenarios, and then Ronny would either agree or disagree. For example, they'd established that Brent and Frog-head were zombies only after Gabe asked about them specifically.

Quite a coincidence.

This line of thought bothered Gabe. It tickled something inside that he couldn't put his finger on, yet seemed crucial. The Wizard of Oz came to mind.

He went over and pulled out the tiny communiqué from Ronny that he'd stuck under the coffee jar. He scanned down to the last response:

> 5. *We cannot answer that; a Demon-zombie would perhaps want to get information about your pet.*

Gabe tried to remember his exact question. Ronny could tell him word-for-word, but he wanted to keep him out of it for the time being. It had been something like, "Why are the Demon-zombies after me?" He remembered that he'd actually said, "stalking," but it was the same thing. Ronny's colleagues supposedly couldn't lie. If so, then every word in the response was true. "We cannot answer that." Did that mean they didn't know, or that they decided they could not *allow* themselves to answer it? What about the, "would perhaps," part? Gabe had assumed that this meant they were simply conjecturing about what this particular Demon-zombie was after, but as he looked at it now, he saw that it could also mean that they were conjecturing about a *hypothetical* Demon-zombie.

Suddenly a flash of insight hit Gabe between the eyes. Ronny was a trained liar. How did he know that Ronny had asked the questions exactly as originally asked? Ronny could get almost any response he wanted by wording the question carefully.

Gabe put the basket into the coffee machine and flipped the power switch, then pulled a chair next to Ronny and sat down in front of him, elbows on knees. "Ronny, buddy."

Ronny must have sensed something important was up, for he sat up. "Yes, Gabe?"

"You're a trained liar, right?"

"Correct."

"What does that mean?"

"I'm not sure I understand what you're asking."

"I'll try to be specific. When would you lie?"

Think-pause.

"No hesitation, remember?" Gabe gently reminded him.

"I'm sorry, Gabe. I had to think about that myself. I realize that I've become so used to lying that it's almost second-nature."

Gabe grinned sardonically. "It's probably the only way to be successful at it."

"But to answer your question," Ronny went on, "I would lie when I concluded that it was necessary to achieve a goal."

"And, what are your goals?"

"Gabe, I've already explained them."

"Yes you have, but how do I know they themselves weren't lies?"

Think-pause. "I'm thinking, Gabe . . . I don't know the answer to that."

Gabe studied the raccoon a minute. "You promised not to lie anymore, remember?"

"Yes, Gabe. I did promise that there'd be no more lies."

"Ronny, what was the exact wording you used to convey my last question to your colleagues?"

"You know that we do not speak with your words. I had to translate your question."

"I understand. Translate what you asked them back to English—as accurately as you can."

Think-pause. "Gabe, can I suggest that we put this off for just a while? Let's wait and see how things go this afternoon."

Gabe sat back in the chair. "I see. The shenanigans are continuing, aren't they?"

Think-pause. "I don't understand."

Gabe leaned forward again. He was almost nose-to-nose with Ronny. "Tell me what you asked your colleagues for the last question."

"There were two parts: 'Gabe wants to know the complete truth,' and, 'Assuming Mr. Schultz was a Demon-zombie, why might he be stalking Gabe?' "

Gabe sat back. "Thank you, Ronny. Why did you add the first part? That wasn't part of my question."

"Like I said, there's no direct translation. I had to interpret."

Gabe looked at Ronny for a few seconds, and then shook his head. "I don't buy it. That wasn't a matter of interpretation. It was a whole different concept you introduced. In fact, you added that specifically because you knew what the response would be, didn't you? You knew it would be something like, 'We cannot answer that.' "

Think-pause. "Yes."

Gabe closed his eyes and sighed. After some seconds he opened them again. "Mr. Schultz is Frog-head?"

"Yes."

"Is he a Demon-zombie?"

"Yes."

"Then, why did you phrase the question with 'assuming' he was?"

"I maintain that he is, but my colleagues, being unable to conceive anything but absolute truths, must hold the idea only as an assumption until definitive proof is obtained."

Gabe leaned in close again. "But the bottom line is that you reworded my question to produce the answer you wanted, right?"

"Yes, Gabe."

Gabe nodded slowly. "We're going to do it again, but this time, I want your colleagues to repeat my question."

Think-pause. "I don't think so."

"What do you mean?"

"I don't think they'll allow it."

"What 'allow'? I demand it!"

"Gabe, I don't think you understand. You are no longer in a position to make demands."

Gabe sat back as the words registered. His face felt warm. "I've been used, haven't I?"

"That seems an extreme description, Gabe."

"But it's true. You've gotten your nuclear containment device planted, and now I'm not needed anymore."

Think-pause. "That is somewhat correct."

Gabe found that he was breathing hard. He felt the world spinning, like when he overdid the hash.

"Gabe," Ronny went on, "I want you to know that I feel badly about this. This is unexpected."

Gabe barely heard the words. "Unexpected? You didn't think I'd start probing?"

"No, I mean that I didn't expect I would feel so badly about how this is turning out."

Gabe took one, deep breath. "We're not done yet. I want you to take one question to your colleagues, and I want them to repeat my question."

"I've told you, Gabe. I'm quite sure they won't go for it."

"They may think that they don't need me anymore, but perhaps they haven't thought through enough chess moves. I could still wreck their plans by blowing the whistle to the terrorists."

Think-pause. "Gabe, that's ridiculous. You could be condemning your species to annihilation."

Gabe raised one eyebrow and shrugged. "It's a high-stakes game. Successful poker requires subtle lying. I think I have the leg-up over your species."

"This is neither chess nor poker."

Gabe smiled. "Don't forget that I'm human. *Everything's* a game."

Think-pause. "Very well. What's your question?"

" 'Has Ronny and his colleagues come to Earth to save humans from invading Demon-zombies?' They have to repeat that back verbatim."

"Very well."

The doorbell rang. Gabe nodded at Ronny, and the raccoon jumped down and headed off towards the bedroom and the open French doors. Gabe went to the front door, and swung it wide. Christie was standing there.

"Good morning, Gabe," she said, twisting her nylon jacket in her hands.

Gabe thought that she was the best thing he was going to see that day. "Hey, Christie," he said, stepping aside to let her in.

"Am I interrupting anything?" she asked.

"Kiddo, my whole life could use some interrupting."

She studied him searchingly.

He shook his head and smiled. "Don't look so serious. What could be so bad?"

"Maybe you can tell me."

Gabe's smile evaporated. "Christie, what's up?"

"Gabe, why are the FBI after you?"

Gabe's eyes went wide. "What are you talking about?"

Christie continued to study him. "A middle-aged man claiming to be with the FBI showed up at the Schooner last night asking about you, just after you left. At first we refused to talk with him, but then he showed us his ID and asked whether we thought you'd been acting strange lately. Gabe, what's this all about?"

Gabe sighed. "Was his name Weston?"

"Yes! That was it...." She pulled a business card from her pocket and looked at it. "Paul Weston." She handed it to him. "Gabe, are you in some sort of trouble?"

Gabe glanced at it. "Oh, there's plenty of trouble, but not with the FBI . . . at least, not yet."

"So, what's going on? Is it drugs?"

Her face was earnest, and Gabe was so touched, he suddenly wanted to tell her everything.

"No, not drugs. It's very complicated, and quite frankly, hard to believe."

Christie was watching him intensely, listening to his every word. He made up his mind. "Christie, you're going to think I've lost my marbles, but I'm going to explain everything—*ouch*!"

Gabe felt a sharp pain in his left ear, the one in which he'd placed Ronny's earworm.

Christie was looking at him questioningly.

"I've got something in my ear," he said in explanation. The pain had eased as quickly as it had come. "Maybe we should sit down."

He led her to the sofa and they sat down together. Gabe reached out to take her hands, and she offered them willingly. "I want you to understand first of all that I haven't lost my mind—at least I'm convinced I haven't. Do you remember a few days ago when you first came here and thought I was talking to Ronny? Well, I was actually—*OUCH!*"

The pain was sharper than before.

Christie's brow was furrowed with concern.

"Those bastards," Gabe said under his breath.

"What bastards?" Christie asked. She looked as though she doubted his authority to declare his own sanity.

Gabe sat and looked at her. He could feel the invisible wall of incomprehension between them. She was struggling to understand, but he wasn't providing her anything tangible to work with.

"Christie," he finally said. "I've gotten myself into some trouble, but you need to believe me that it's not with the law, nor the mob, nor drugs, nor anything you know of, in fact."

She squeezed his hands in response. She was listening, continuing to try to understand.

"I'll tell you as soon as I can," he went on. "In the meantime—"

He was interrupted by the doorbell. He sighed and went to answer it. When he opened the door, he found Brent standing there. Gabe could see that he was angry, and this was confirmed when he shoved Gabe and said, "You're a real prick, aren't you? Is Christie here?"

Gabe sensed that if he let Brent inside, things could get broken, including him. He pushed his way past Brent, and tried to pull the door shut, but Brent kept his foot firmly planted preventing it from closing.

"That's forced entry," Gabe said, as levelly as he could. "You're committing a crime."

Gabe didn't know if this was even true, but Brent apparently didn't either, for he pulled his foot back and let Gabe close the door.

On a hunch, Gabe continued the crime track. "I've already contacted the police about you," he said. He remembered Weston's card that Christie had just given him. Gabe pulled it from his pocket, and handed it to Brent. He took it and looked at it, and Gabe could see that his bluff was working. "In fact, he's on his way right now."

A good bluff can't be timid, Gabe thought.

He was rewarded with a flash of panic across Brent's face, leaving behind despair. "Why can't you just leave us alone?" Brent implored.

"What makes you think there's even a 'we'?" Gabe challenged. His heart thumped away in his chest and he could hardly believe his own brashness.

Brent's face scrunched with inner pain. "You *prick*," was all he could manage.

Gabe almost felt sorry for the guy. He knew what it felt like losing Christie.

There was no time to dwell on sympathies, though. Gabe nodded at a car he saw coming down the street some distance away. "That could be Weston, now."

Brent glanced around, then gave Gabe one last hateful glare before he strode off towards his car. Gabe watched him leave, and as the broken man walked away along the sidewalk, Gabe realized that he wasn't thinking of Brent as a Demon-zombie, but just as his adversary in romance.

Gabe noticed that one of the parked cars that Brent passed had an occupant. Gabe could clearly see that it was Frog-head. There was no end, it seemed. He turned his back on that problem and came back inside the house.

Christie was standing near the front window. "You heard?" he asked.

"Most," she said. She looked troubled.

"I thought it was best just to get rid of him. I lied."

"I know, I heard. It's okay. He would've just caused trouble."

"I didn't expect that police ploy to work so well."

Christie gave a sardonic grin. "You as good as punched him in the gut with that. I didn't tell you before, but Brent spent a couple of months in jail once for hitting his girlfriend du jour."

"Caveman love. Maybe that's where the expression 'to hit on somebody' came from. "

"Gabe," she continued, "you promised last night that you'd explain what's up with you and Brent."

"I know I did, and I *will* keep my promise." Gabe flinched but there was no pinch in his ear. "But I can't just yet. Christie, I have to ask you to just trust me. I promise I'll explain as soon as I can."

She looked deeply into his eyes, as if searching for something she could indeed trust. Whether or not she found it, Gabe was relieved when she finally nodded. "Don't let me down, Mr. Wolfekow," she warned.

He shook his head. "I promise."

Punky barked once and tore off towards Gabe's bedroom. A minute later Ronny came strolling out with Punky following, tail wagging.

"It is as I predicted," Ronny said. "They refuse to answer your questions."

Gabe glanced at Christie to see what her reaction was to hearing the raccoon talk. She was returning his gaze, as though wondering why he was staring at *her*. Gabe realized that Ronny's mouth hadn't moved. The damn earworm.

"Christie, I need a moment alone with Ronny," he said, picking up the raccoon and heading off towards the bedroom.

"You need to be alone with a raccoon?" she asked behind him.

He paused and turned to her. "It's one of those things I'll explain later."

She was still staring at him, puzzled, when he turned and closed the bedroom door behind him.

"What about your people's devotion to complete honesty?" Gabe asked in a rushed whisper, setting Ronny down in his usual chair.

"It's not dishonest to refuse to answer. They are being totally honest when they indicate that they choose in their best interest not to respond."

"Agreed. But refusing to answer is an answer in itself. They didn't want to contradict some lie you've fabricated."

"I suggest you don't pursue this."

The sense of being manipulated was tearing at Gabe. He paced the bedroom. "And who's best interest is that suggestion for?"

"Yours, Gabe."

He stopped and looked at the raccoon who sat gazing steadily at him. "Are you threatening me?"

"I am not. I was speaking for my people."

Gabe understood. "It's the earworm, isn't it?"

Ever since the sharp pain, he'd had the urge to grab a pair of scissors and dig out the foreign abomination.

"Yes. That's part of it."

"The earworm is only *part* of it?" Gabe could feel panic bubbling. "What the hell else have you planted on me?"

"I cannot say more. I'm sorry."

"You *bastard*!" Gabe yelled.

"Please understand," Ronny said, the voice in Gabe's ear calm with authority. "This is not my doing."

Something inside Gabe broke loose. "I can't believe anything you've told me! It's all lies!"

He stormed out of the bedroom, slamming the door behind him. Christie sat on the sofa like a poised statue, gripped with fear. Punky was on her lap, growling.

"Who were you yelling at?" Christie asked tremulously as he stormed past her towards the front door.

"Ronny," he replied, knowing that his answer wasn't really an answer. "I'll be back in a minute," he added, slamming the front door as he left.

Gabe strode out to the sidewalk and directly to Frog-head's parked car. The engine started up as he approached, but Gabe held up his hand, and stood so that he was blocking the car's exit. "Who the hell are you!" he called. "And why are you watching me?"

Frog-head looked flustered, like he'd never considered this scenario. "Look, I don't know what you're talking about, mister," he replied.

"Don't be an asshole," Gabe snapped as he walked around to the open driver's window. "You've been following me for days. You can either tell me who you are, or I'll drag you from the car and extract it myself."

"Look buddy," the man said, lifting his hands in defense. "I haven't done anything illegal. You touch me, and I'll call the police." He fished his wallet from his pocket and took out a card, which he handed to Gabe. It read:

Stan Schultz
Private Investigator
"Your eyes: seeing, but unseen."
No case too large or too small.

Gabe handed it back. He leaned in close, so that he was looking directly into Schultz's eyes. "Are you an alien?" he asked.

Schultz pulled back, as though Gabe might suddenly go berserk. "What the hell kind of question is that? I'm American! My grandfather moved here before World War II . . . hey, I don't have to take this." He turned the steering wheel, as though he was going to pull away, Gabe or no Gabe.

Gabe took a step back and held up his hands. "Okay, okay. Just tell me who hired you."

"I don't have to tell you that," Schultz replied, keeping his hand on the steering wheel, ready to pull out any second.

Gabe had to come up with something convincing. He had an idea. It had worked with Brent . . . why not? He fished Weston's card from his pocket again and handed it to Schultz. "I've already contacted the FBI," he said. "You might as well come clean."

Schultz looked at the card and handed it back. "Is that so? Then how come Weston was asking *me* about *you?*"

"What!"

Gabe felt out of breath, like his abdominal muscles had become paralyzed.

Schultz shook his head in disgust. "This is the lousiest case I ever took. I should of just said no. If Crabnuckle wasn't an in-law—"

"Mrs. *Crabnuckle* hired you?" Gabe exclaimed.

Schultz contemplated his mistake. "Aw, to hell with it," he finally said. "I probably ain't gonna' get paid anyway. Yeah, ol' Crabnuckle wanted me to get proof that you'd kidnapped her pooch—Pinksty."

"Punky," Gabe corrected distractedly.

"Whatever. I'll tell you, it's a sorry day when an investigator has to follow a mutt kidnapper around. How low can you sink?"

"Punky's not a mutt, and I didn't kidnap him, he chose to live with me."

The new reality was beginning to sink. Ronny had indeed lied about the two supposed Demon-zombies. What *hadn't* he lied about?

"Whatever," Schultz said. "Look, Wolfekow, it's over, okay? I've got nothing to tell Crabnuckle except that you're a nutcase who talks to his pet raccoon. Can I go now?"

Gabe stepped aside and Schultz drove off. He called after the retreating car. "If you want to be unseen like it says on your card, *use some makeup on that birthmark!*"

He felt bad about that. To hell with it. The guy was prying into his life, for Christ's sake.

Gabe stormed up the walkway and into the house. He slammed the front door shut like a crack of thunder. Christie sat on the sofa, wide-eyed. Even Punky sat frozen, awed. Ronny sat on a chair across from Christie. "How the hell did he get in here?" Gabe barked.

"He crawled through the side window," Christie answered cautiously.

"Gabe, you're angry," Ronny's voice said into his ear.

"You're damn right I'm angry."

Christie watched him closely, not sure how to respond.

"I suggest you calm down before you get hurt. Please, Gabe."

"Who's going to hurt me? You?"

"No Gabe, not me."

"Right. Your colleagues, the all-knowing space aliens. Well bring them on. I've had enough."

"Gabe, you don't know what the stakes are here."

He went to the kitchen and grabbed a bowl from the cupboard. "And you're going to tell me, right?" he called, pouring a few cups of water into the bowl. "And I'm supposed to believe you, like I was supposed to believe that Brent and that PI are Demon-zombies." He came back to the living room carrying the bowl.

Christie looked terrified. "Gabe," she said carefully, "I'm going to leave now."

Shit. How was he going to explain?

Later. "Just one minute. I'm almost done here."

He opened the door to the coat closet next to the front door and set the bowl inside.

"Gabe don't do this," Ronny's voice warned.

This was immediately followed by an intense stab of pain in Gabe's ear. He yelled out and bent over with his hand to his head. The pain eased as quickly as it had come.

He looked at Ronny who sat watching him. "You're a son-of-a-bitch," Gabe spat.

"Gabe, that wasn't me. Please believe me."

"That's one thing I can't do," Gabe declared, picking up Ronny and carrying him to the closet. He fully expected that Ronny would squirm and try to scratch him, but the raccoon passively allowed Gabe to carry him. As Gabe set him down in the closet, another stab of pain hit, but it was gone so quickly, he didn't even have time to react. He closed the door and Ronny's furry, impassive face disappeared.

In taking action, Gabe found that his anger subsided a bit. He was thinking clearly again, and different puzzle-pieces began to slide into place. When he and Punky had been caught by Crabnuckle a few days ago, she said, "*We'll* get you," not "*I'll* get you." She'd obviously already contacted Schultz. And then, the message from Ronny's people: *a Demon-zombie would perhaps want to get information about your pet*. Ronny had probably worded the question something like: "If we were referring to Schultz as a Demon-zombie; why would he be after Gabe?" Gabe had let Ronny lead him to think that the "pet" was him, when, in fact, it was Punky. His colleagues had indeed responded truthfully . . . to the question posed.

The pain stabbed Gabe in his ear. A few seconds later it happened again, this time harder.

"Gabe," came Ronny's inner voice. "You must let me out. I don't know how long I can hold them off."

"What are you talking about?" Gabe called through the door.

"Gabe, ten minutes ago you asked Christie to trust you."

"So what?"

"Look at her."

Gabe did. She was trembling with fright as she watched him, wide-eyed. What in the world could she possibly think, other than that he was stark, raving mad, as he stomped around, apparently talking to some invisible person? Yet she stayed because he'd asked her to, because she trusted him.

"I'm looking at her," Gabe replied.

Christie's eyes went even wider when he said this. She probably thought some evil part of his schizophrenic brain was telling him to stab her with a kitchen knife.

"You're looking at blind faith. I need that from you, Gabe. I want to help you."

"Why should I? You've only lied to me."

Silence reigned for an endless minute. Christie sat frozen, as if already dead. Every ten or twenty seconds a fleeting pain stabbed his inner ear.

Ronny's voice finally spoke. "A man walks into a bar . . ."

Chapter 11

Saturday, mid-morning

Gabe could hardly believe his ears. Ronny had apparently gone mad.

". . . he looks around and notices that the place if full of rats—rats sitting at tables drinking, rats playing darts, rats dancing to music. He notices that one rat sitting at the bar is wearing a baseball cap. The man sits down next to this rat and orders a drink, and the rat with the baseball cap leans over and remarks, 'I don't know if you noticed, but the place is crawling with rats.' The man looks at this rat and says, 'You look an awful lot like a rat yourself,' to which the rat replies, 'I know, the damn cap makes my nose seem longer.' "

Gabe stood suspended in the surrealism of the moment. It was as if someone fleeing from a burning building had suddenly stopped to tuck in his shirt.

A stab of pain broke the spell. He needed help. He dug Weston's card out of his pocket and went to the phone in the kitchen. He cradled the handset against his ear as he dialed Weston's number. The instant he punched the last button, an intense pain exploded in his head. This was the worst one yet. He cried out, and had to put his hand against the wall to steady himself. Reflexively he slammed the handset back into its cradle and immediately the pain disappeared. This time, though, it left a slight buzzing behind. He wondered if they could be causing permanent damage.

Gabe strode to the closet with tears of pain trickling down his cheeks. He pounded on the door. "Stop it! For God's sake, have mercy!"

"Gabe," came Ronny's voice in his head. "I'm telling you, it's not me."

"What do they want from me?"

"They want you to sit down with Christie and wait until two o'clock."

"And then what?"

There was silence, broken only by the nervous tapping of Punky's tail on the sofa. Ronny's voice finally came through again. "Did you hear the one about the accident litigation lawyer who was disbarred for advising his client that his injury was just a scratch, that he should walk it off?"

Another joke. What the hell was the matter with Ronny? Was he just being cruel? Just teasing him?

No, Gabe didn't believe that. In this he did trust Ronny. He trusted that Ronny would not try to hurt him. *He trusted Ronny.* It was true. Despite the evidence, Gabe was convinced that Ronny wasn't hurting him. It was indeed that blind trust that Ronny had invoked.

If the pain wasn't Ronny's doing, then it must be his colleagues. But why the jokes? Gabe remembered what Ronny had said when they were sitting on the floor discussing humor: "Humor is sometimes truth wearing a silly hat." Was that what these jokes were about? Ronny had explained that his colleagues found humor incomprehensible since they lacked the faculties for lying. Maybe Ronny was trying to communicate something that would be hidden from Gabe's tormentors, a message encrypted in humor.

Gabe tried to remember the first joke. He wished he'd listened more carefully. It was about a rat in a roomful of rats, trying to convince a man that he wasn't a rat. Well, how much more obvious could *that* be? It was hard to believe that even Ronny's humorless colleagues would have missed it.

What about the second joke? Again, the meaning that Ronny was trying to convey was clear as day: in order to do the right thing, a lawyer was giving up his membership in a group that was universally despised.

Ronny was trying to tell Gabe that he wanted to turn coat and help him.

But, how could he believe Ronny when the alien agent had already acknowledged himself to be a liar? *I lie, and Christie trusts me*, Gabe thought. This was the ultimate test for a human: deciding who to trust in a world of people programmed to lie. Some people never lower their shield at all and lead secure but lonely lives. It wasn't really something you calculated. There was no formula to apply. You went with your feelings.

Gabe opened the closet door. Ronny was sitting there looking up at him. He tried to close just one eye, but this was apparently not possible for a raccoon to do and it ended up looking like a twisted blink. Gabe understood, though. Ronny had given him a wink.

"Come on out, you hairy little beast," Gabe said, returning a wink.

Punky jumped down and ran over to say "Hi!" as though Ronny had been gone a month.

"Thank you, Gabe," Ronny said into Gabe's ear as he climbed up onto a chair. "I hope you understand that everything is safe and that you can talk about anything you like." As he said this, Ronny twisted out another sorry wink.

Could Ronny's colleagues be so easily fooled? Ronny was essentially saying, *Watch what you say because they're listening*. The wink put the italics around the words, turned them around into sarcasm. He could only hope that the real message was indeed going over the aliens' heads—assuming they had heads.

Ronny's colleagues had completely bugged the terrorists' house for sound and vision. Gabe had no reason to think they hadn't done the same to his house. He'd have to assume they could both hear and see everything he did.

"So, you think we need to go see Mrs. Crabnuckle?" Ronny said, accompanied by yet a third wink. Again the meaning was clear: *we need an excuse to get out of here*.

Gabe realized that a wink was not an easy thing to define. Its meaning changed subtly with the context.

The ball was back in his court. They needed a pretext for going back to Crabnuckle's. Ronny's colleagues had not liked the idea that Gabe was going to call the FBI, who would interfere with the nuclear containment plan. Okay, he'd use that.

"Schultz showed me a note that Crabnuckle had given him," Gabe finally lied. "It said that she was going to call the police about both me and the suspicious men next door. It looks like she's almost on to the terrorists."

He'd almost said that Schultz had *told* him this, but remembered just in time that the aliens could hear everything he heard through the earworm.

"Right," Ronny agreed. "We'd better get over there right away. There's no time to lose."

It sounded like pitifully bad script reading. Hopefully Ronny's colleagues weren't movie fans. They didn't seem to be catching on, though, for he'd been pain free since he'd let Ronny out of the closet.

"We'd better take Punky," Ronny added, "he might be useful in negotiating with Crabnuckle."

Gabe wasn't sure what that was about. Maybe he was just trying to make it more convincing.

He looked over at Christie. She still sat on the sofa, watching Gabe carry on a one-sided conversation. Her fear seemed to have dissipated, and she was now simply watching him with cautious curiosity. "We're going to Crabnuckle's now," he told her.

She grinned grimly. "So I heard. Gabe, what the hell is going on?"

"She can't know, Gabe," Ronny's voice came immediately into his ear. He sounded urgent.

Gabe walked over and sat down next to her. He took her hands and looked her in the eye. "I know that it sounds like I'm stark mad, but I have a good reason for it all—I just can't tell you right now." Gabe added the last part quickly, circumventing a stab of pain. "I asked you to trust me before. I need you to continue just a little longer. Can you do that for me?"

She looked at him seriously for a few seconds, and then grinned. "This is going to be one whopper of a story. I want to stick around just to hear it."

"Great," Gabe said, standing up. "Move em' out!"

He hustled them all into the car, and Ronny made a point to scamper into the front seat, leaving Christie to sit in the back with Punky. "Quite the spoiled brat," she observed.

Once they were under way, Ronny stood up on his hind legs and, facing around to both Gabe and Christie, held his forefinger up to his mouth—be quiet.

"Where did he learn *that!*" Christie exclaimed.

Shit! "That's a good trick, isn't it?" Gabe enthused. "He can do all kinds of stupid stuff." As he said this, Gabe turned to Christie and held *his* finger to his lips.

Christie was taken aback by this. It clearly unnerved her that both Gabe and a raccoon were telling her to keep her yap shut.

"We should tell her some jokes to keep her occupied," came Ronny's voice.

As they drove to Crabnuckle's, Gabe related the one about the man in heaven who happens to find God standing next to him at the urinals. Taking advantage of the rare opportunity, the man asks God why he made women so soft. "So that you would like them, my son," comes God's reply. "Okay," says the man, "why did you make them so beautiful?" Again comes the reply, "So that you would like them, my son." "Okay," the man finally asks, "then why did you make them so stupid?" God answers, "So that they'd like *you*, my son."

Gabe then told the one about the sadist man who meets the masochist women, and they decide they should get married, and on the honeymoon the woman runs ahead all excited to the hotel room and takes off her clothes and lies on the bed, and when the man comes in she tells him, groaning, to beat her, and he answers, "No."

Gabe told more, even worse. Some jokes he related that Ronny made up, and by the time they arrived, Christie looked like she was now sure he was nuts.

"Park directly in front of Crabnuckle's house," Ronny said.

Gabe had been trying to figure out what Ronny was up to. He'd initially thought that the Crabnuckle ruse was just and excuse to get out of the house, but now it seemed that Ronny really did want to come here.

As soon as Gabe pulled up on the parking brake up, Ronny jumped over the seat and took Christie's purse from her. "Hey!" she said, "There's no more candy!"

Ronny was searching through the contents. To Gabe she explained, "Before you came in the house, he was rooting around in my purse. I gave him an old jelly-bean that had been in there forever."

All Gabe could do was shrug.

Ronny finally pulled out something small and metallic, and hopped back over the seat.

"Hey! He took my tweezers!" Christie yelled.

Instantly, intense pain exploded in Gabe's ear. This was far worse than anything before. It was so intense, he couldn't even cry out. Ronny had climbed up next to him, and Gabe was dimly aware that the little raccoon hands had pushed his head to the side and was doing something. Suddenly, with a final lightning jab of pure agony, the pain was gone, leaving behind a dull ache and echoes of the almost unbearable torture.

Ronny was holding the tweezers out in front of him, and Gabe could see, caught between the pincers, a tiny, blood-soaked, squirming worm—the earworm.

"In another few seconds, it would have dug its way into your brain," the familiar gravelly voice of the old Ronny said.

Gabe heard a thump. Christie had fainted in the back seat.

Chapter 12

Saturday, late morning

It was as if a small nuclear bomb had gone off right inside the car. Gabe was incapacitated, recovering from the ordeal of having a mechanical worm try to bore its way into his brain. Christie was passed out in the back seat, apparently overcome by the sight of the bloody operation and a talking raccoon. Ronny, inexplicably, was cowering on the front seat. He had pushed in the cigarette lighter, and then carefully placed the earworm on the glowing coils before, himself, collapsing. He was now trembling as though a grizzly bear was about to pounce on him. Only Punky seemed normal, standing on Christie's chest, tilting his head back and forth trying to figure out what was the matter with her.

"What's wrong?" Gabe finally asked Ronny.

"I'm lonely," the raccoon replied without uncurling form his fetal position. "I didn't realize it would be like this."

"They've cut you off, haven't they?"

Ronny nodded his head up and down. "I knew they would, but I still wasn't prepared."

Gabe finally lifted himself up. "You've still got me, my friend," he said, laying his hand on Ronny's head. He felt the trembling subside.

"I'm very sorry about Christie," Ronny said. "I thought I could save her."

Gabe glanced back at her. She looked like she was sleeping peacefully. "She just fainted."

Ronny lifted his head. "No, Gabe. I'm so sorry. I'm afraid she's dead."

"*What!*" Gabe looked at her again. "Christie! Wake up!"

She didn't stir. Punky must have intuited what Gabe was after, for he leaned down and licked her face. She lay there, still as death. Gabe felt the world falling away, and braced himself to accept the worst thing in his life. Punky continued to lather her face with his saliva, licking her mouth and nose, then caressing her cheek with his tongue. Her head twitched. She shook it. Her eyes popped open, and she sat bolt upright, sending Punky falling away.

"Thank God!" Gabe exclaimed.

Christie was staring at him. He put his hand to his head and his fingers came away bloody. "It's okay. Ronny got it out in time."

Ronny hopped up and lifted himself with his paws so that he could see around the back of the seat. "Why did you do that?" he asked her.

Christie didn't answer. Her eyes were nearly bursting from their sockets as she looked from Ronny to Gabe.

"She fainted," Gabe said.

"Why?" Ronny asked.

Gabe shrugged. "She's a girl."

"You scared me," Ronny said to her.

"Gabe?" she asked tremulously, watching Ronny as though expecting him to whip out a sword and challenge her to a duel.

He smiled. "It's time to explain, like I promised."

She nodded. She was ready.

"Ronny's an alien . . . the raccoon's not, just the part that's talking . . . the part that's thinking too . . . actually, I'm not sure what part's what. I'm not off to a very good start, am I?"

She shook her head slowly.

"Maybe I should back up some. You see, there are these other aliens, the Demon-zombies, who are starting an invasion of Earth—"

"Actually," Ronny cut in, "there are no Demon-zombies."

"Huh? None?"

"I made that up."

"Why?"

"To get you to help me plant the detonator. I was still learning human subtleties. The whole Demon-zombie ruse seems embarrassingly clumsy now."

"You said, 'detonator.' You mean the nuclear containment thingy?"

"I lied about that as well. It's not a containment device, but just the opposite. It will cause the bomb to detonate at two o'clock."

"It will *cause* . . . but, that's when the terrorists are going to set it off anyway!"

"I lied about that too. They don't intend on setting it off here. Their plan is to fly it over Las Vegas in a couple of days and set it off a thousand feet in the air where it will do the greatest damage."

It was now Gabe's turn to stare wide-eyed. That explained why it was sitting in the garage on a pallet. "For God's sake, why would you want to set off a nuclear bomb in San Diego?"

"First, please understand that I no longer wish this to happen. But to explain why my ex-colleagues wish it requires some background. We're part of a very small expeditionary mission. We punched through what I'll call hyperspace—you have no word for this—some distance from your sun. From our launching point, 320 light years away—"

"You said you came from sixteen light-years away," Gabe said.

"I lied. As I was saying, from our distant starting point, we couldn't know that Earth had spawned intelligent life. Remember, we only had light speed information, and that was 320 years old. All we knew was that there was a favorable planet for the next base in our expansion. Open-ended punches through hyperspace are inherently inaccurate, and we were lucky to come through only ten billion miles from the sun—"

"That's not even in the solar system!"

"Correct. Twice as far as Pluto, in fact. It took many years to reach Earth from our arrival point. The original plan was to then spend many more decades building a hyperspace marker. With this, our companions at the base, 320 light years distance, could precisely punch through the materials needed to build a far-station—the other end of a two-way link through hyperspace. When we realized that an industrial species had arisen on Earth, we changed our plans. With your technology, we could create a crude, temporary marker and use it to receive the permanent marker, saving many years of time. Can you guess what technology of yours we could use to establish a temporary hyperspace marker?"

"Cell phones?" Gabe replied.

"Good joke, but this is technology that you've had for over half a century."

"Lasers?"

"You're on the right track, but a laser is nothing more than organized light. The energy density can be sufficient, but the total magnitude, at least for your lasers, isn't nearly enough to be detectable across hyperspace."

"Energy density is important?"

"Correct. Actually, it's a combination of density and quantity. Energy creates perturbations in hyperspace, similar to what mass does to normal space-time."

"I thought energy and matter were different forms of the same thing."

"Mr. Einstein was correct, but hyperspace interacts more closely with the energy form. In fact, matter is nearly undetectable in hyperspace, which is why we can push it through at all."

Gabe pondered what technology would have enough energy to be visible across hyperspace.

"I'll give you a hint," Ronny continued. "Think more Mr. Einstein."

"Atom bombs," Christie said almost tonelessly.

"The submarine!" Gabe exclaimed.

"Precisely," Ronny said. "We managed to arrange that detonation. More importantly, we believe we were successful in sending a message."

"*You* set off that bomb?"

"Well, not me. Another hybrid agent similar to myself."

"What message?"

"Our colleagues 320 light years away did not know, of course, about the situation that we'd found here. This message basically said 'We're here and we can communicate with nuclear bombs.' Ever since we left, they have been watching very carefully in this direction for some message. Close attention on their part is necessary. Even using a nuclear explosion, the perturbations of hyperspace are quite faint, and your nuclear bombs are but tiny sparkles in hyperspace next to the disturbances produced by your sun."

Gabe felt like he was floating in a dream, sitting in his car on this sunny morning, talking to a raccoon about hyperspace mechanics. "What are they planning to communicate with the terrorists' bomb?"

"Nothing but a location. There was a bit more to the message we already sent. We told them that we would be setting off a second bomb. The obvious implication is that they'd use it as a temporary location marker to punch through the permanent one. Once that arrives, we will have achieved a nearly limitless one-way link."

"But, why two o'clock this afternoon?"

"They have to know a very exact time. They need to launch the hyperspace puncher virtually simultaneously with the extremely faint and fleeting nuclear hyperspace perturbation. We calculated that the timing of the explosion has about a plus/minus .3 second window. The actual target time is 2:03 and 17.4 seconds."

Gabe felt numb, like when he only half-woke in the morning as the reconnection of his muscle motor control functions lagged behind consciousness. His mind was awake, but he was paralyzed for a brief second or two.

Christie was the first to speak. "Won't the permanent marker be destroyed when it appears in the center of a nuclear fireball?"

Gabe was impressed. There was more to her than he knew.

"The punch won't be aimed directly at the point of explosion. It could come through ten, or even one-hundred miles away."

Silence hung in the car as Gabe and Christie struggled with the information.

"Why are you coming to Earth?" Christie finally asked.

"Part of our general expansion. To you it's the most significant event in your history. To us, it's just the next small step in many."

"Towards the final stage-three intelligence," Gabe said, remembering their previous conversation.

"Correct."

Ronny had tried to distract Gabe with stories about Demon-zombies, when all along it was his own race who were about to invade Earth.

"Why did you think Christie was dead?" Gabe asked.

Ronny paused a moment. "You're going to be angry with me, Gabe."

"I'm beyond angry. I feel half dead myself."

"Christie has been booby-trapped."

"*What!*" Gabe exclaimed, snapping out of his paralysis.

"Agents have been introduced into Christie that are prepared to kill her upon command from my colleagues."

Gabe thought he too was about to faint. "Why?"

"In case we needed to control you. Essentially to blackmail you. Gabe, I have to confess that this was my idea. It was conceived early on when I first discerned your attachment to her. This was before I felt myself turning."

"The ants," Christie murmured. She was staring off into space, as though in a trance.

"Correct," Ronny said. "I placed them in your tea that night in Gabe's kitchen."

Gabe remembered. "You tricked me into going to the front door. You said that you thought somebody was there!"

"That's right, Gabe. I'm really very sorry about this. I wish I could go back in time and change it."

"Why *her*? Why didn't you just feed them to *me*?"

"That was the same question my colleagues asked me at the time. The truth is that I was already growing fond of you, Gabe, and as an excuse, I told them that I didn't want to risk making you suspicious."

"But, you put the worm in my ear."

"I couldn't get around that one. That had been the plan from the beginning, and it really was necessary in order to plant the detonator. It wasn't built to be a weapon. My colleagues figured that one out on their own."

From some dream place, Christie spoke. "We have to get that detonator thing back."

"That's right," Ronny confirmed. "There's a complication, though."

Gabe sighed. "And what's that?"

"Christie is alive right now because of the detonator's placement."

After a moment Gabe said, "Your sense of the dramatic is developing just fine, fur-face, but can we cut to the chase? Christie and I are holding our breaths here."

"Right. Unlike the detonator, which is autonomous and will detonate the bomb on its own at two o'clock, the poison agents ingested by Christie must be activated by my colleagues via a signal. Because of the poison agent's small size, this signal is specialized—powerful, directional, and very high frequency. On a whim, and unbeknownst by my colleagues, I reconfigured the detonator's de-activation signal to be the same signal. I informed them of this once we arrived here at Crabnuckle's house."

Gabe saw the pieces falling into place. "We had to get Christie out of the house and here, near the detonator, before they decided to activate her poison agents. *That's* why the whole charade about Mrs. Crabnuckle calling the police. If they knew why we were really coming here, they would have activated the agents immediately. They don't dare try now for fear that they'd also deactivate the bomb."

Gabe looked at Christie. She was pale, like she was staring at her own ghost.

"And," Ronny added, "that's why I had to wait until we got here before extracting the earworm—"

"Because," Gabe finished the sentence, "if they realized you had turned, they would have understood that we were coming here on a ruse and might have activated the agents."

"Precisely. It was an interesting balance of deception."

"Interesting?" Gabe questioned.

"In truth, I was most vexed. I believe anxiety is the word that expresses my state. I was expecting that they'd see through me at any moment, but they didn't until they heard from Christie that I had tweezers."

Christie finally spoke. "That's why we can't remove the detonator."

Gabe could see that the color had come back to her cheeks.

"That is unfortunately true," Ronny agreed. "If we remove the detonator, my colleagues will have no reason not to activate Christie's agents."

Christie shook her head as though waking up. "If we remove the detonator, or if I leave the vicinity of the bomb, they'll activate these . . . agents, and I die. If we don't, then the bomb goes off and I die anyway." She looked at Ronny. "Obviously we have to remove the detonator."

"No!" Gabe exclaimed.

She looked at Gabe, as if seeing him for the first time. She shook her head again. "We can't let the bomb go off."

"No, wait! How do we know Ronny's not lying right now?"

"Gabe," Ronny said, raising his right paw in the air, "I swear I'm not lying."

"You said that before when I caught you the first time."

"That's true from your perspective. You might perhaps interpret that I didn't keep my word, but I took my promise seriously. You see, you may remember that I promised that I would tell no *more* lies. I took that to mean that I would not fabricate any *new* ones. I had to follow through with the ones I'd already presented. Remember, I hadn't turned yet. My loyalties were still with my colleagues. Gabe, I swear that I speak the truth and nothing but the truth now."

Gabe thought about this. "I specifically asked you after you promised to tell no more lies if Frog-head was a Demon-zombie, and you said yes."

"Again, that was true in the context of an already-established lie."

Somehow that sounded twisted to Gabe. How could you have a truth about a lie? Maybe you could. It was making his head spin.

"Look, Gabe," Ronny continued, "it really all comes down to faith. You either have faith in me, or you don't. But, you have to decide which it is."

I do, Gabe decided. *I believe the mangy vermin.* "Okay, you've got it, but I will not let Christie be killed by removing the detonator device."

"I think I may have a way out," Ronny said. "But, we'll need the cooperation of Mrs. Crabnuckle."

ж ж ж

Gabe knocked on Crabnuckle's front door a second time. Normally she was sneaking around and popping up to surprise him. Now when he really needed her, she wasn't home. He'd had to walk from the car to her front door in full view of the terrorists' camera. He could only hope that Nabeeh wouldn't recognize him from the previous night. He was holding Punky now, and he hoped this would be a bit of a distraction if the terrorists were observing him.

Crabnuckle's door suddenly opened, and she was standing there in curlers. "Well, well," she said. "If it isn't Gabe Wolfekow. I was expecting you." She looked down at Punky and her face lit up. "You finally decided to bring back my little Pinksty! I can't imagine what use he could have been, but I'm just glad he wasn't hurt."

She reached out, and Gabe handed Punky to her. What else could he do?

But what was this about expecting him?

Punky growled and nipped at her as she took him. "My, my," she reproved, "he's gotten all uppity working with secret agents."

As she said this, she tried to snap his nose with her finger like she used to do, but Punky was having none of that now. He grabbed her finger in his mouth and gave her a good bite. "Ouch!" she exclaimed.

What the devil is she talking about? Gabe thought. *What's all this about working with secret agents?* "Mrs. Crabnuckle, can I come in and talk to you?"

She stepped aside. "Of course. We have to get to the bottom of this."

Gabe took a deep breath and stepped inside.

Ever since Ronny popped his head up next to his bed, it seemed that he'd been stumbling along, just trying to stay on his feet. "Mrs. Crabnuckle, we have a problem—"

"You bet your sweet heinie we do, and let me tell you, I'm not one bit happy that it took you so long to get around to talking to me. Why, I knew those Arabs were trouble the day they moved in."

Gabe stared at her. What in God's good name was she was talking about? He had come to the door planning to simply ask for help and hoping she wouldn't throw him out on his ear.

He decided to play along and see what she knew. "I'm sorry for the delay,"—*delay of what?*—"but things have been busy. Maybe you can fill me in on the latest."

"Some agency *you* belong to if you don't know. For all the taxes I pay, I expect the CIA to be more on the ball."

CIA?

"First it's the FBI poking around," she went on, "and now the CIA has to come to old Crabnuckle for help."

"The FBI was here?"

"Of course! You boys had better get your heads together or this country's in big trouble. A man named . . . Winston—no, that's not it—"

"Weston?"

"Yes! Weston. He was finally looking into those terrorists next door."

"He *said* they were terrorists?"

"Well, no. But it was obvious he knew."

"How did *you* know?"

"Oh, I figured it out right after they moved in there six months ago. I called the police on them. They were banging around in their garage at all hours of the night—sometimes until ten o'clock. Anyway, the policeman didn't do a thing, just talked to them for a few minutes. To tell you the truth, I don't think he took me serious—thought I was just some batty old woman too nosey for her own good."

Gabe struggled to keep a serious face.

"I saw them," she added. "That policeman and them had a good laugh on my account."

"I'm sorry, Mrs. Crabnuckle, but I don't understand. How did that convince you that they were terrorists?"

"I'm getting to that. Keep your pants on. After that, they were just as nice as could be."

Gabe waited for the rest, but Mrs. Crabnuckle seemed to think she'd made her point. "And *that's* why they're terrorists?" he said. "Because they've been *nice* to you?"

"Of course, you ninny. Any normal person would have held a grudge, but these boys were just sweet as pie. Obviously they were up to no good. They're trying to hide something, sure as I'm standing here."

Gabe just looked at her. She wasn't crazy. In her little world it made complete sense.

". . . plus one of them curls up in a ball in the back yard and points at my house. He does it real early in the morning so's I won't see it, but I see it. You don't get anything past old Crabnuckle."

That would be Nabeeh. "He's probably doing his morning prayers, Mrs. Crabnuckle. They're supposed to face Mecca. I think your house is just in the way."

"That's what they want you to believe. I know what's really up."

"And . . . what's that?"

"He's pointing me out to their spy satellite."

Gabe blinked. "The terrorists have a spy satellite?"

"Of course they do . . . wait, I can tell from your grin that you already know that. You have to play dumb. I understand, and don't worry. I won't blow your cover. You should talk to Weston, though. He's blabbing about you all over the place."

"He is, huh?" Gabe tried to look professionally concerned.

"Oh yeah. I have a confession, Wolfekow. When he started asking about those terrorists, I thought you were part of their gang, and I said so to him. That's when he told me that you weren't a terrorist. 'He's on our side, Mrs. Crabnuckle.' That's what he said. So, if you're not with the FBI, you must be CIA."

Gabe just stood looking at her, wondering what an undercover CIA agent would say now.

"Oh, don't worry," she continued. "I won't push it. You're secret's safe with me."

Mrs. Crabnuckle's delusions were opening doors for him. "You're very perceptive, Mrs. Crabnuckle. I'm sorry we didn't recruit you long ago. This is going to make things a lot easier for us now that you already know about the terrorists."

"You going in and arrest them? To tell you the truth, I'll be sorry to see them go. They're quiet, polite boys, and you never know what kind of renters you'll get in their place. They might have dogs."

Gabe looked down at Punky. The irony floated in the air between them, unacknowledged.

"Actually," Gabe said, "we want to do some surveillance first. In fact, I have a couple . . . er, I have a colleague that will be joining me. If it's all right by you, we'd like to use your house as a base for a few hours."

"It's all right by me, but you've got to clean up your own messes. I'm not no servant here. You gonna' clean the toilet before you go?"

"Er, yes, sure. We'll take care of that."

"You've got to clean the rim of the bowl, you know. You men pee all over everything. Sometimes I think you just like to see it splash."

"Sure, sure. We'll clean up completely."

Oh, what the hell. *A good bluff can't be timid.* "We have a special crew. You know, they specialize in cleaning up blood."

This didn't faze her. "Well, you'll be paying for any blood stains that don't come out."

"Of course." Actually, if they weren't successful, all of her pesky stains—blood and all—would be vaporized at two o'clock. But he wasn't going to go into that.

Gabe went to the front door and waved to Christie, waiting in the car. In a wash of panic, he realized that he didn't remember her last name. He knew it a year ago, but he'd forgotten since then. She came carrying Ronny, and when she was inside, Gabe said, "Agent Christie, this is Mrs. Crabnuckle. She already knows that we're CIA agents." Gabe gave her a studied look as he said this.

Christie didn't miss a beat. She shifted Ronny to her left arm, and extended her right hand. "Good to meet you, Mrs. Crabnuckle. The agency appreciates your help."

Mrs. Crabnuckle looked sourly at Ronny. "What kind of name is that, 'Agent Christie'? And what the devil are you doing with that vicious raccoon?"

"Mrs. Crabnuckle met Ronny before," Gabe hastily explained to Christie. Then to their host, "Agent Christie is a code name—like double-oh-seven."

"What the devil do you carry that vermin raccoon around for?" Crabnuckle repeated.

A good bluff can't be timid. "Ronny is specially trained for reconnaissance. He's been genetically altered. He has the intelligence of a six-year-old."

Ronny looked at Gabe. He tried to lift one skeptical eyebrow, but it came off looking like the reverse of his clumsy winks.

Mrs. Crabnuckle was watching Ronny as though she expected him to leap from Christie's arms at any second and clamp his jaws around her ankle. "What kind of name is 'Ronny' for a raccoon?"

What the hell. "It's short for Ronald Reagan."

Crabnuckle nodded with approval. "I'm glad that fine man is being remembered."

Ronny just stared at Gabe, but he knew what he was thinking. "Don't let it go to your head," Gabe said.

"Huh?" Mrs. Crabnuckle said.

"He can understand rudimentary English. You have to speak slowly and use simple words, though."

Crabnuckle nodded. She was eating it up like candy.

She cautiously put her face close to Ronny's. "Don't—poop—in—the—house," she warned as though she were indeed talking to a child.

Ronny nodded, and Crabnuckle jumped back, startled.

"We should get on with our business," Gabe suggested. "We'll need to use the shop."

He knew from his previous Punky-sitting that Mr. Crabnuckle had built a workshop out back, which Mrs. Crabnuckle had left intact since his death some years before.

"Help yourself," Mrs. Crabnuckle said. "I don't expect the terrorists will be going anywhere soon."

Gabe checked his watch. It was 11:15. *Actually,* he told himself, *unless Ronny's successful, they'll be leaving rather abruptly in less than three hours.*

Chapter 13

Saturday, lunchtime

"Mr. Crabnuckle apparently had no interest in electronics at all," Ronny's voice came from somewhere within the depths of boxes and miscellaneous junk piled against the workshop's back wall. His head appeared at the opposite end from where he'd entered. "There's not even a transistor to be found, let alone a transformer. This is the only wire I could find," Ronny announced, holding up an old cloth-covered cord with cobwebs still clinging to it.

Gabe and Christie sat at the workbench watching as Ronny scoured the shop. "From the tools," Gabe said, "it looks like he was a carpenter. Without special training in electronics, there's not much he could have done with it."

Ronny dove under the bench for the second time. From underneath he said, "I'd have expected it to be a basic part of your education. Most of the people on Earth live in a world they don't understand."

"We live in a society of specialization," Gabe explained. "Everybody can't understand *everything*. An electronics technician can't be expected to understand what a doctor knows about medicine."

Gabe found himself on the defensive. He had two years of physics, but his understanding of the nuts and bolts of electronics consisted of soldering his guitar cords when they broke.

"He could if he didn't stop learning as soon as he was done with school," came Ronny's voice. "People get an education just to get a good job. The founding fathers of America thought that an education was meant to enlighten the spirit and lift the soul."

"Yeah, and a lot of them had slaves to do the work so they could sit around contemplating whether 'all men are created equal' meant *all* white males, or just those who owned property."

Ronny came out from under the bench and reached up so that Christie could lift him onto her lap. Gabe had noticed that ever since he'd been excommunicated by his colleagues, Ronny seemed to be nearly always in contact with either him or Christie. He was happiest when they were rubbing his back or scratching his chin—a super-intelligent space alien who needed constant cuddling.

Gabe heard footsteps, and Mrs. Crabnuckle appeared at the door carrying a tray of lemonade. "Who were you talking to?" she asked setting the tray on the bench.

"Uh, Christie, I guess," Gabe replied.

"Well, young woman, you sound like you're coming down with a nasty cold. You'd better take care of that."

Suddenly Ronny leaped from Christie's lap onto the workbench. He grabbed a foot-long piece of molding and swung it at Gabe's head as though it were a Samurai sword. Gabe ducked and heard the swoosh of the wood go by. "What's gotten into you!" he yelled.

Gabe realized there was another sound as well: the insistent buzzing of a bee. Gabe kept his head down as Ronny took a second swing, this time connecting with a *thunk*.

"Step on it!" Ronny called out.

Christie jumped from her stool and stomped. "It crunched!" she reported.

Gabe lifted his head, checking to make sure Ronny wasn't about to swing again. "What was *that* all about?"

"I'm afraid my colleagues are not going to forgive and forget. That was a device of their manufacture—an assassin, in fact."

"They *made* that bee?"

"It only looks like a bee, although it was designed specifically with that goal. Its sting consists of actual melittin bee venom, plus a smaller dose of a fatal nerve agent, which decomposes within an hour of doing its job. These were originally built to protect my colleagues' base location. An autopsy of an inadvertent intruder would conclude an extreme allergic reaction to the bee sting. These assassins were built when my colleagues were still concerned about keeping their presence hidden. This issue is, of course, becoming less important to them with each passing hour."

Gabe looked down at the spot on the floor where Christie had squashed the tiny device. "You saved my life," he said. "You're my hero."

"I doubt it was after you," Ronny predicted, "although you're probably second on the list. They're after me. They understand that I'm now their greatest threat."

Gabe remembered Mrs. Crabnuckle. She was standing at the door, hands clasped in front of her, eyes staring wide. "Mrs. Crabnuckle?" he asked. "You okay?"

She nodded, never taking her eyes from Ronny. "That's no six year-old mind," she said.

Gabe shrugged. "Emotionally, he's just a child."

She seemed to break out of her trance. "I'm sorry I voted for that stem cell research," she said, turning and walking away.

"Where'd the bee come from?" Gabe asked.

"Their base. There were no bees stationed here. The last thing we wanted was a dead person found near the nuclear bomb, apparent bee sting or not. No, it must have begun its journey even before they knew that I'd turned. They were obviously becoming suspicious when I kept thwarting their attempts to punish you."

"The earworm," Gabe said. "The pain that started hitting me every thirty seconds or so after I locked you in the closet."

"Correct. It wasn't easy convincing them that I knew best how to handle you. I was lying to them, of course—I'd already decided my course. I had, for example, already checked Christie's purse to make sure she had tweezers."

Gabe put his hand to his ear. Just talking about it was enough to make him cringe. "Too bad you weren't successful in convincing them. It *hurt!*"

"Oh, but I *was* successful. Each of those momentary stabs of pain ended after protracted and complex arguments with them. If they'd had their way, the worm would have entered your brain before you even put me in the closet."

That was a sobering thought, indeed.

Gabe puzzled over the fact that each occurrence of pain had "ended after protracted and complex arguments." How much arguing could you do in ten seconds? Gabe imagined only getting in a few "Did not!"/"Did too!"'s . . . unless your thoughts zipped along at a rate many times that of a human's.

"There are certain to be more bees on the way," Ronny warned, "so I suggest we keep the doors and windows shut, and have a stick handy to swat them. I needn't remind you that one sting, and you'll be dead within sixty seconds."

ж ж ж

Ten minutes later Ronny gave up. "The materials I need just aren't here," he said, climbing back up onto Gabe's lap.

"What kind of materials are you looking for?" Gabe asked.

"Nothing elaborate: a medium-sized microprocessor, a microwave modulator, and an RF transmitter."

Gabe rolled his eyes. "I could have told you that those sorts of things wouldn't be here. Ronny, we're running out of time."

Ronny's plan was to build a decoy. He'd explained that the principle of the alien detonator device was actually fairly simple. This simplicity was in turn possible due to the simplistic operation of the gun-type atom bomb itself. Earlier that morning, the terrorists had added the two uranium components—the baseball and the catchers' mitt. All that was left was to set off the explosive charge behind the baseball. The explosives in turn used a firing pin for detonation. Since the firing pin was activated with an electric current, the alien detonator would simply emit a short-lived, but powerful and focused, EMP pulse that would induce enough current to ignite the explosive (Gabe had explained to Christie that EMP stood for electromagnetic pulse).

The only elegance at all lay in focusing the EMP pulse on the firing pin's two lead wires; otherwise the large amount of metal of the bomb casing would absorb and ground the transmitted energy. During the first few micro-seconds of operation, the detonator device would use micro-wave, radar-like, fingers to probe its surroundings looking for the electrical signature of the firing pin wires. Ronny planned to have his decoy gizmo emulate those wires and fool the detonator device into throwing its energy at it instead of the firing pin. The decoy would be melted in the process, but the alien detonator device only stored enough energy for one burst.

Ronny was confident of that. At least, he was pretty sure this was so. "Greater than fifty-fifty likelihood," he had confessed when pressed.

Gabe had asked why they didn't just plant their own bomb and blow up the detonator device three minutes before it goes off. Ronny had explained that although it seems that a bomb explosion happens instantaneously, the blast travels outward at around five times the speed of sound. This indeed seems instantaneous to a person, but there are many micro-seconds for the alien detonator to react and do its job. Although not ideal, Ronny's colleagues would set off the nuclear bomb before the 2:03 target time if they had to. "In fact," Ronny had noted, "they'd likely set it off even now if they felt threatened enough."

Ronny's plan was only so much mental masturbation at this point, though. They didn't have a single piece of the required electronic components. "Maybe we could run to Radio Shack?" Gabe offered.

Ronny paused before answering. Whereas Ronny's pauses usually indicated contemplation, this one seemed simply sarcastic. "This is so that we can perhaps indulge in a hobby as we while away the time waiting for the nuclear bomb to go off?"

"I was just trying to help," Gabe said. He had another idea. "Maybe you could use a laptop for the microprocessor."

Again the sarcastic pause. "Gabe, laptops run Windows."

"So?"

"So, the detonator device will set off the nuclear bomb and the laptop will be separated into individual atoms before the operating system could even decide whether to hand over execution to my routine."

Gabe gave up. It was vaguely disquieting that Ronny could formulate a technically sophisticated plan to thwart the alien detonator, yet be so off the mark on its execution. Ronny had actually had the idea that the average American dabbled in microprocessor coding and micro-wave electronics in their bedrooms.

He could feel himself fighting waves of anxiety. They could climb into his car and drive away from the blast zone, but they couldn't take Christie with them. He told himself he would never run away and leave Christie to her death. But what was going to happen when the last minutes started ticking away? Would he really stay with her to his death? He realized that it was this pending decision that was really depressing him.

"So that's it, then?" Gabe challenged.

Christie looked pale and ill, but she'd said nothing as he and Ronny argued over the impossibility of Ronny's plan. *No*, Gabe decided, *he'd stay with her, no matter what*. He felt relieved that he'd resolved his decision, even if it meant his own demise.

"Maybe not," Ronny said, jumping down from Gabe's lap. "Perhaps brute force takes the stage when elegance crumbles in defeat. Go call your band. Christie and I will move on to Plan B. I'll explain when you get back."

Gabe headed for the house. He smiled at Ronny's metaphor, the first he'd used. They had needed some distraction in order to gain entry into the terrorists' garage and plant Ronny's erstwhile decoy, and they'd settled on Gabe's band. They were hoping that the aliens wouldn't know what to make of the activity.

Gabe closed the door behind him and took only two steps when he heard the bee. He'd completely forgotten the danger, and it only came to him because this bee's buzz was slightly odd, slightly metallic sounding.

He'd left his stick lying on the workbench.

He sprinted for the house, and the buzz followed, seemingly inches behind his head. He burst through the back door, and the bee ticked against the door's window as Gabe slammed it shut behind him. *Shit, that was close!*

Mrs. Crabnuckle was sitting in the living room, knitting. Punky sat on a chair next to her, not looking too happy about his situation. He jumped down and tore across the room to Gabe, barking madly. "I know, boy," Gabe soothed, picking the dog up and turning his head to avoid the probing tongue. "We're *all* in a pickle right now."

"Let me know if you need anything," Mrs. Crabnuckle called, her knitting needles clicking away. "That raccoon hasn't pooped yet, has he?"

"No, he's being good. Can I use your phone?"

She pointed at a small table next to the front door.

It took about ten seconds for Derrick to agree. He was ready to play anywhere, anytime, for any reason. Randy wasn't so easy. Gabe had to convince him to leave work early. Gabe pleaded that it was a real emergency, and, to Randy's credit, he finally agreed without asking how a sudden life-and-death emergency could be solved with a jump-blues band.

When Gabe hung up the phone, Mrs. Crabnuckle said, "We're going to have a band playing in my back yard?"

"It's a distraction," Gabe explained.

Her needles clicked industriously for a few seconds. "You sure you know what you're doing?" she finally asked.

He smiled. "No, I'm not sure, but I am hopeful."

She nodded, satisfied. Her fingers twisted and dipped as the sweater took form, stitch by stitch. She didn't know that an atom bomb sat armed, barely fifty feet from her. He had the idea that her knitting would proceed the same if she did.

Gabe explained to Mrs. Crabnuckle that she had to stay in the house and keep the windows and doors closed, and if any bees got in, she should kill them, kill them with a vengeance. She held Punky, and Gabe went to the back door where he paused a moment. He didn't see the alien assassin bee out there, but it was surely waiting for him. He searched the kitchen drawers until he found a spatula. He gave it a trial swing. He could feel his heart thumping away. *Don't think, just run.* And with that, he swung the door open, stepped out, and slammed it shut behind him.

He immediately heard the metallic buzz. A copper-colored bee came swooping in, directly for his face. Gabe leaned back and swung the spatula. He thought he missed, but he must have just nicked it, for the bee fell to the ground like a stone. It was already on its feet and walking towards him when Gabe looked down. Gabe decided that they must be fragile, for one wing was completely gone. Its progress across the cement towards his shoes was valiant, but painfully slow. Gabe almost felt sorry for it as he stepped on it. It crunched. Instead of bee-juice, the walk was smeared with entrails of amazingly tiny complexity. It was as if

Gabe was looking at an exact micro-miniaturized model of the space shuttle squashed on the ground.

Back in the shop, Gabe found Christie watching as Ronny drew on a tablet. An old, plastic drinking cup sat next to them. The pen was nearly as big as Ronny's arm, and he had to hold it with both hands. Gabe found an old pencil and snapped off about an inch. He then sharpened the point with a carpet knife and handed this to Ronny, who, although still using two hands, was able to handle it much better.

Gabe looked over their shoulders. Ronny was drawing what looked like a vase containing a giant golf tee instead of a flower.

"Making Valentine's cards to kill time?" Gabe asked.

Christie gave him a shove, shoulder to shoulder. She pointed at the vase. "That's a plastic cup filled with gunpowder. This," she said, pointing to the golf tee, "is our surrogate firing pin. Ronny thinks a wire bread tie will do nicely."

"It looks like a homemade bomb."

"It is, silly."

"I don't get it, Ronny. I thought you said we couldn't just blow up the detonator, that it would detect the explosion and set off the atom bomb anyway."

"That is indeed correct," Ronny replied. "But that scenario applied to a bomb that we set off. This one will be set off by the detonator device itself."

Gabe saw it in a flash. "The detonator will find our firing pin and focus the EMP energy on it. It'll think that the resulting explosion is the atom bomb going off." Gabe laughed. "It'll be blown up, happy in its misconception that it did its job."

Ronny laid the pencil stub down and sat back on his haunches. "That's the theory."

"That doesn't sound very optimistic."

Ronny took a deep breath, apparently emulating a sigh. "The detonator device will need to be fooled into thinking our simulated firing pin is the only one. We'll need to place it close—within a couple of feet. We'll be counting on the detonator finding our closer position first, and hope that it won't look further. Finally, the resulting small explosion needs to be close enough to render the detonator device inoperable, but not so close that it will be suspicious."

Ronny put his little paw to his forehead and shook his head, an imitation of a human's gesture of near hopelessness.

"I'm familiar with this processor," Ronny went on, "and he's not too intelligent. I'm afraid we're counting on him being a bit gullible as well."

Him? Gabe wondered. Did Ronny know this detonator thing personally?

No time for that now. Gabe looked at his watch. It was nearly noon. Only two hours left. "Where am I supposed to get gunpowder?" he asked. "I don't remember seeing the armament aisle at the grocery store."

In answer, Christie stepped over to a cupboard and opened a door above her head. Inside, Gabe saw several boxes of shotgun shells. Piled next to them were many small, clay Frisbees. "Mr. Crabnuckle apparently enjoyed skeet shooting," she explained.

Gabe took down the boxes, and he and Christie began the tedious task of extracting the powder from the shells. They opened the folded end, spilled the BB shot, pulled out the cotton wad with tweezers, and then gently tapped the precious powder into a bowl. Gabe was surprised at how little each shell contained. They'd have to open all the boxes of shells to fill even half the cup. It could take an hour or more.

He could feel the tension tightening his chest. They were running out of time. If they weren't successful, this very spot where he sat, opening shell after shell, was going to be obliterated in a fireball blast that would make all the gunpowder in San Diego seem like a firecracker.

He heard a car pull up out front, and then a horn toot a couple of times. That was probably Derrick.

Shit! Gabe remembered the bees. He grabbed his spatula and ran out. From his left, a bee came in low. He heard another coming in high from his right, behind him. He swatted the spatula at the assassin going for his bare legs and caught it square. It hurtled away in an arc as Gabe ducked and spun around to deal with the second one. He couldn't see it, but he still heard it right behind his head. It had circled behind him. He could almost feel the stinging prick of lethal venom on his neck and he wanted to scream. Hardwired with millions of years of experience stealing honey, he instinctively ducked his head forward and shook it vigorously, simultaneously leaping ahead and again twisting around. The bee hovered there in front of him. It was slowly beginning to move towards him when Gabe smacked it square. He held up his spatula in victory. "I dub thee Bee Killer," he pronounced.

Gabe had the impression that these robot bees weren't as maneuverable as the real thing. It could have been just luck that the second one had managed to get behind him.

He found the last one he'd smacked and squashed it mercilessly under his heel, but he couldn't locate the first one. He hated leaving it, but he had to see if Derrick was already lying dead out front.

Gabe found Derrick alive and well, whistling an old Elton John tune while he unloaded his drums. "You'll only need the bare basics," Gabe told him, "maybe just the bass, snare, and one tom. I wouldn't even bother with the symbols."

"Really tight spot, eh?" Derrick said.

"No, but we're only going to play a couple of tunes."

"This some sort of audition? If so, I'd rather use the full set."

"No, not an audition." Gabe glanced around as if one of the terrorists might be standing there listening. "To tell you the truth, we're just a diversion. I know it sounds crazy, but I don't have time to explain. I really appreciate this, bro."

Derrick slapped him on the back. "Hey! You never know when you'll need to do something crazy for me."

Gabe smiled. It was good to have good friends.

They both picked up a load of drums and headed around back. Gabe kept his eyes peeled for alien assassin bees, but he'd either gotten them all, or they were biding their time. Ronny, the traitor, was their prime target.

He surveyed Mrs. Crabnuckle's back patio. Shrubbery surrounded it on all sides. He picked a spot for the band where it was the thinnest, affording the best visibility into the terrorists' back yard. He then checked on Christie. Ronny had crawled up next to her and was helping her remove the gunpowder from the shells. He didn't have the strength to peel open the pinched ends, but he was pulling out the cotton wads. He didn't need the tweezers, as he could fit his hand right inside the casing.

Gabe was turning to leave when he heard the dreaded buzzing sound. A bee flew across the room straight for Ronny. With one smooth swipe, Gabe knocked him down with Bee Killer. Once you had a little practice, he decided as he squashed the fallen soldier with his toe, it was pretty easy to deal with them. The sneaky ones would be the problem.

He walked across the room and found the hole in the wall where this one had come through. He jammed in a splinter of wood. He rushed back outside, now concerned for Derrick. This was going to drive him crazy.

His friend was busy setting up his drums, and Gabe heard another car out front, hopefully Randy. Gabe ran back into the shop and returned with two foot-long pieces of molding. "Listen," he told Derrick, handing him one, "keep this with you at all times. If you see any bees, whack them. It's really important that they don't sting you—I mean *really* important."

Derrick took a practice swing. "Sure. Are they killer bees or something?"

"Yeah, in fact they're a new strain. They're deadly. One sting will do it."

Derrick looked to see if he was joking. Gabe shook his head solemnly. "Right," Derrick said, "kill the bees."

Gabe headed off for the front yard and found that it was indeed Randy, but he wasn't nearly so cooperative as Derrick. He refused to unload his equipment until he knew what was up. Gabe tried to convince him to go along until there was time to explain later, but the bass player was being stubborn. Randy could be that way.

Gabe finally gave up in exasperation. "Okay, you win," he said, waving his arm towards the house next door. "A pack of terrorists live right there, and they have an atom bomb that's set to go off in"—Gabe checked his watch—"one hour and thirty-two minutes. We're trying to plant a counter-bomb to stop them."

Randy stared at Gabe a few seconds. "Fine," he finally groused, "don't tell me. But you owe me, buddy. Big time."

Together, they carried the large bass amp around to the back. Gabe tried to explain about the bees, but Randy just gave him a look that said, "Give it up, already."

Great, Gabe thought, *now I'll have to watch out for him the whole time as well.*

He showed Randy where to set up. As to why they were playing to the bushes, Gabe answered, "Just do it—and watch out for the bees, for God's sake."

Back to the shop. Christie continued pulling apart the shotgun shells, building a pile of empty cases next to her on the table. Ronny sat in a far corner loading the powder into the plastic cup a teaspoon at a time, pressing down each addition with his bee-swatter stick.

"Is that dangerous?" Gabe asked.

"Very," Ronny replied.

"Is that why you're in the corner?"

"No sense getting Christie hurt if I make a mistake."

Gabe was touched by Ronny's consideration, since his alien friend knew as well as he that if he prematurely set off their bomb, Christie would be vaporized soon afterwards anyway. Gabe kept his thoughts to himself, though.

Before he left, he searched the walls for more holes. He had the idea that, being made of metal, or at least some manufactured substance that went crunch when stepped on, the assassin bees couldn't squeeze through holes as small as one that a real bee could. To be safe, though, he plugged up any he could stick a pencil through. When he was done, he looked around to see if there was anything obvious he'd missed. There was.

"Ronny."

Ronny paused in his delicate tamping and looked at him.

Gabe pointed to the floor. Three feet from Ronny was the missing bee Gabe had disabled earlier outside. The wings were mangled, and one leg seemed to be twisted out of shape. The little sucker was limping along like the last soldier in the platoon who knows he's a goner anyway, so by damn he'll go down fighting. Ronny reached over with his stick and deftly obliterated the assassin with one whack.

"Did you know him?" Gabe asked.

"No," Ronny replied, returning his attention to the cup-bomb.

Gabe had meant it as a joke.

Randy! The bees might be strafing his band member right now just for revenge. Gabe needed a couple of clones.

He stepped outside and listened for buzzing. Randy was tuning his guitar, apparently unmolested. Time was flying by. Gabe ran to his car and grabbed the old, little solid state amp and cheap Mexican guitar from the trunk that he always carried around. He lugged them back to the patio and set up on the other side of Derrick. They had no PA. Christie would have to sing through the second channel of Randy's amp, the ultimate in amateur cheese. Randy protested when Gabe plugged the mic into his amp. "Are you worried that some talent scouts are hiding in the shrubs?" Gabe responded.

Gabe looked at his watch and saw that it was 12:50. Panic overwhelmed him in a wave. This would never work. It was totally crazy. There were far too many things that could go wrong. What if their bomb didn't work? What if the alien detonator device perceived the ruse? What if the terrorists just ignored their distraction? Even if they didn't, what if he wasn't able to plant the cup-bomb? And, even if all that worked flawlessly, even *if* they disabled the detonator device, Christie still had the lethal agents inside her. The aliens would probably instantly activate them once they realized the atom bomb didn't go off. Ronny had assured him that he had a plan, and Gabe had been putting that whole problem aside, but now it loomed before him, impossible to ignore.

Way too many what-if's.

Derrick and Randy were ready. Gabe finished tuning (*why?*, he asked himself), and he was ready. All they needed was their cup-bomb. He put down his guitar and heard a buzz. The sound suddenly stopped. *Uh-oh!* The sons-of-bitches had found a new tactic. Gabe glanced around. Where the hell was it?

To his horror, he saw it sitting on Randy's shoulder.

Chapter 14

Saturday, afternoon

"Randy!" Gabe cried.

His band mate looked at him, startled by his tone.

"Randy, don't move. Just don't move."

The bee sat, motionless, almost daring Gabe to come closer. Perhaps it realized that Gabe would have difficulty swinging at it while on Randy.

Randy must have seen where Gabe was staring, for he looked down at his shoulder. With one swift motion, he slapped the assassin. "The little bastards!" he muttered, and continued practicing a new song he was learning, letting the little mechanical marvel fall to the ground.

Gabe leaped over and stomped on it, even though it already appeared pretty mangled. Randy looked at Gabe as though he was sadistic.

Derrick leaned over from his position on his throne stool. "Hey, was that one of those killer bees?"

"Yeah," Gabe said, "Randy's our fearless protector."

Randy looked down, curious now. He swung his bass guitar around his hip so he could bend over to look closer. *"That's* not a bee!" He looked at Gabe with shock. "What the hell *is* that thing?"

Derrick answered for him. "A killer bee. Dude, you could have been dead right now."

Randy stood up, but kept glancing down at the squashed remnant.

This wouldn't do. Eventually one of them would let their guard down and get stung, particularly when they were playing and couldn't hear the buzzing. They needed a guard.

Punky!

Gabe set his guitar down and ran to the house. When Punky saw him, he jumped down from his chair and tore through the house to greet him.

"I have to ask you to risk your life, Punkster," Gabe said letting him lick his face this time.

Punky barked.

"I knew you'd understand. But you have to be careful. Promise?"

Punky barked again.

"Okay, then."

Gabe explained to Mrs. Crabnuckle what he needed from the two of them, then took Punky outside and showed him the squashed carcasses of the various fallen alien assassins. Punky sniffed and then barked at each one. Gabe wasn't sure if Punky would even associate these little machines with the bees he hated so much, but it was worth a try.

Mrs. Crabnuckle came out wielding a fly swatter. Gabe dubbed it Alien Terminator. She carried a patio chair off to one side under an umbrella and sat down, then decided it was too far away and moved it directly behind the band. She looked like a groupie waiting for her heartthrob to be done. Punky wandered around here and there, checking out all the myriad smells of the back yard.

Gabe checked his watch: 1:05. One hour. They had to *move!* He sprinted to the shop. Ronny was still tamping powder into the cup. He had bent the bread-tie makeshift firing pin in half and embedded it in the packed powder, leaving the two ends free. He had then stripped, twisted, and attached each of the two conductors of one end of the lamp cord to these. The other end of the lamp cord hung free. Ronny had explained that, together, these should look electrically close to the actual firing pin of the atom bomb. The lamp cord would also serve as an antenna to pick up the detonator device's EMP energy.

"Time's up, guys," Gabe called. "We've got to *go!*"

Christie lay down the tweezers and looked at Gabe. She'd probably been finding some solace in the bomb-manufacturing activity. She was at least doing *something* to save herself. Now, it was out of her hands, and her final hour was looming. Gabe could see the fear hiding in her eyes. "You ready, girl?" he asked her. "We're going to need your best attention-grabbing performance."

She gave him a smile, somewhat melancholy, Gabe thought. "Ronny," he said, "let's go!"

"I just need to seal the top," Ronny replied, handing the cup carefully to Gabe. "Set this on the bench and plug in the hot-glue gun. Our deterrent-bomb will be ready in about five minutes."

Gabe could feel his heart doing double-beats. His panic was barely under control. He really just wanted to stand and scream. "I'll be back in exactly five minutes. It *has* to be ready."

Christie was waiting at the shop door. They stepped outside. Instinctively glancing around for bees, Gabe held Bee Killer ready. There was only the chirping of birds and Punky sniffing here and there among the bushes. Christie greeted Derrick and Randy, and Gabe handed her the microphone. There'd been no sign of their stinker neighbors. *Lord! This had better work*, Gabe thought.

He needed one more piece to complete the plan. He sprinted off to his car and rooted around the piles of junk in the back seat until he found a McDonald's paper bag filled with discarded sandwich wrappers. He rooted around some more until he uncovered a paper soda cup as well. He pulled off the plastic top and saw that the unfinished soda inside had dried into a crusty layer at the bottom. Sensibilities were now a luxury he couldn't afford. Gabe sprinted into the house and tried to rinse out the dried soda crust. The effect was similar to pouring water on a dry lake bed: what had been dried mud was now mud-mud. No time to do more. He poked around inside the refrigerator and found some grape juice. It would have to do. He poured it into the cup.

He hurried back outside and found Punky barking and jumping at one of the shop windows. Mrs. Crabnuckle was peering at it as well, and as Gabe watched, she gave Alien Terminator a quick flick and then spun it around and jabbed at something on the sill with the handle. Gabe saw an assassin fall to the ground where Punky stood barking at it, ready in case it miraculously sprang back to life.

Gabe picked up Punky and kicked some dirt over the fallen alien. "Good boy!" he said, rubbing Punky's head. "Go find more!" Gabe launched him onto the patio—an insect-detecting torpedo, the target selector set to "Bee."

Gabe picked up his guitar, and reached behind the amp to flip the power switch. "We'll start with *Hit the Road, Jack*," Gabe announced.

He started to count it down, but Randy held out his hands and asked, "Exactly to whom are we playing?"

Derrick sat facing the shrubbery, content to play to thin air if asked.

"Let's just say ourselves for now," Gabe replied. "Pretend it's a practice. If we're lucky, maybe the neighbors will appreciate it."

"Or call the cops," Randy muttered, but positioned his bass guitar, ready to play.

Gabe counted down a second time and they kicked off the Ray Charles tune. It sounded terrible. Playing outside was always a problem; the bass notes dissolved into the empty expanse, and Gabe's guitar sounded like he was playing through a transistor radio. Add the fact that Christie's vocals were jostling with Randy's bass lines, and under other circumstances Gabe would have been depressed. As it was, he was immensely relieved to simply be moving along towards their goal.

The relief melted as the song progressed and there was no sign of the terrorists. At least one of them had to be home. Maybe they were afraid to be seen. Maybe they too just thought the band sucked. The last verse was winding down when Gabe saw, for just a second, a face at the garage door window.

The song ended and Mrs. Crabnuckle clapped appreciatively behind them. Gabe yanked off his guitar and ran to the shop with the paper bag and cup of grape juice, remembering at the last minute to grab Bee Killer. He threw open the door, and walked in. Ronny was sitting on the bench, holding out the plastic cup trailing the lamp cord. "It's ready," he said.

Suddenly Gabe heard Punky barking.

He'd left the door open! He turned just in time to see an assassin making a bee-line for Ronny. Gabe swung Bee Killer as it buzzed by, but missed. As the assassin reached Ronny, he used the cup-bomb to deflect the slow motion bullet, but it maintained control and landed on Ronny's back.

No time to think! Gabe swung Bee Killer and clubbed Ronny hard on the back. He saw the bee fall onto the bench. Gabe swung again and smashed it. Punky was still barking up a storm outside. Gabe turned in time to see another one almost in his face. He instinctively swatted at it, and felt it tap the back side of his hand, then heard its revving buzz as it struggled to regain control. He stepped back and saw it floating in the air, spinning slowly in circles. He must have damaged one of its wings. With one swipe, Gabe batted it to the ground and stomped on it.

Gabe hurried to the bench and leaned over the motionless body of Ronny. "Are you okay, little buddy?"

Ronny opened his eye. "Did you get it?" he asked.

"Yes. Are you okay?"

"Yes. Just a lot of pain, that's all."

"I'm sorry! Geez, Maybe I broke your back!"

"No," Ronny replied, getting slowly to his feet. "You did exactly the right thing. Luckily these devices were designed to emulate an actual bee sting. Their stingers are not as efficient as they would be otherwise. He didn't have time to work his way through my fur."

Gabe rubbed Ronny's back where he'd clubbed him.

"Gabe, that hurts," Ronny said. "But I appreciate the thought," he added.

Gabe took the sandwich wrappers from the McDonald's bag and gently placed the cup-bomb inside, coiling the cord loosely around it. He then shoved the wrappers back in on top. Anybody seeing him drinking his soda wouldn't think twice about the matching sandwich bag in his other hand.

This is it, he thought, careful to close the shop door behind him. He set the bag and soda down and picked up his guitar. "Okay," he said to his band, *"Got my Mojo Working.* This is our last chance, so make it good . . . and make it loud. Christie, give it all you've got."

"Like my life depends on it?" she asked, struggling to hold a smile.

"Last chance for what?" Randy asked.

"Never mind. Just play like a maniac. And, whatever you do, don't stop until I tell you. You hear me? *Don't stop!*"

Derrick tapped out the count with his sticks and they hurled into the song. Christie's life did depend on this, and she sang with passion to prove it. Although apparently playing to the bushes, with their only audience member sitting behind them with a fly-swatter, Randy nevertheless played handsomely, holding the rhythm rock-solid and allowing Derrick to work the back-beat.

Come on, Gabe thought, *are you guys deaf?* Whatever their cultural background, the terrorists *couldn't* ignore the tearing emotion of Christie's performance.

Gabe was right. The face that had appeared at the garage door came back. After a minute, the door opened and Nabeeh stepped out. He was obviously curious, but it seemed to Gabe, also enchanted. Who wouldn't be? How could any human male resist the plaintive heartbreak of Christie's soul? Nabeeh stuck his head back inside and said something, and then one of the others, probably Abdul-Baari, stepped out as well.

Here goes nothing, Gabe told himself. He took off his guitar and, casually picking up the soda cup and paper bag, nodded to the band to keep playing. The loss of the guitar seriously crippled the song, but Christie carried on, holding the center of the tune steady. Gabe strode purposefully through the bushes into the terrorists' yard. For effect, he took a big swig of grape juice and then restrained himself from spraying it back out across their grass. His mouth was full of the taste of mold from the dried coke at the bottom. He forced himself to swallow the nauseating liquid.

Halfway across the terrorists' yard, he turned and faced the band as though giving a critical listen. After a moment he turned and continued on towards the two men standing just outside the garage. They appeared concerned about his approach, but allowed him to come up to them. Their attention was split between him and Christie.

"SHE'S GREAT, HUH?" Gabe yelled above the loud music, forcing himself to take a tiny sip of his fake coke.

Abdul-Baari gave a noncommittal shrug, obviously wary of Gabe, but Nabeeh nodded enthusiastically. *You* would, *you weenie-whacker*, Gabe thought. He stood with them for a minute, thankful that the music was too loud to allow conversation. He held out the cup, offering Abdul-Baari a drink, but he held up his hand, declining.

The time had come for his pivotal move, perhaps the most important of his life. He could hardly breathe against the thumping of his heart against his ribs. "I NEED TO USE YOUR BATHROOM!" he yelled, and immediately, before they could react, opened the garage door and stepped inside.

Coming from the sun-drenched yard into the dark garage, Gabe was momentarily blind. He heard a chair scrape on the floor, and perceived movement across the room. As his eyes slowly adjusted, Gabe saw that Isaam was standing there holding an automatic rifle aimed at his chest. This was no pellet gun. Some rational corner of Gabe's mind noted that this was the first time in his life that somebody had pointed a loaded gun at him. The slightest twitch of that finger and his chest would explode in a mass of blood.

Gabe willed himself to shrug. Every movement required his entire willpower as he stared down the barrel of the gun. "I was looking for a bathroom," Gabe explained.

Abdul-Baari rushed in, saw that Isaam had Gabe covered, and then with a nod, stepped back outside.

Isaam said nothing. The black hole of the gun barrel floated before him like the tip of God's accusing finger.

Gabe willed the McDonald's bag in his hand to appear natural. He took a drink of grape juice, and suppressed a wince. "Look," he said, nodding at the atom bomb lying there between them, "I won't tell anybody."

Isaam's eyes narrowed.

"I've made whisky myself," Gabe went on.

The terrorist's eyes morphed into a question. "What do you mean?"

The accent was thick and, to Gabe, seemed ominous.

"I know a still when I see one. A still . . . to make whisky."

Isaam kept the gun trained on Gabe's heart. He seemed to be trying to decide what to do with him. This was a man who was willing to sacrifice his own life for his cause. He'd hardly hesitate to kill an American musician if he thought it necessary. Gabe realized that the loud music worked against him now, for it would cover the gun shots.

Gabe spread his arms wide in the universal show of surrender, the soda in hand, and the precious bag in the other. *Whatever happens, you have to place Ronny's cup-bomb*, he told himself.

Slowly, slowly, he leaned over and set both the bag and soda on the floor, next to the garbage can, then straightened, arms held high.

Isaam seemed to make up his mind. Gabe saw a resolve come to the man's eyes, and the aim became more purposeful. *Should I try to make a dive for the door?* Gabe's mind raced. He felt paralyzed.

Just then, he heard the mechanical buzz of an assassin bee above the music. It seemed to drift in from a dream—a familiar one where Gabe knew that doom was descending, but he was powerless to do anything. Death by either bullet or venom. He apparently had his pick.

From the corner of his eye he saw it—a tiny flurry of beating wings disappearing behind his head. He closed his eyes, waiting to feel its mechanical legs touch his neck. The buzzing continued. He opened his eyes and saw it fly by, past his other ear, and head across the room, straight for Isaam. *Was it confused?* Gabe didn't understand, but it was clearly headed for the terrorist.

Gabe held his breath. Isaam deserved what he was about to get. He was a man who was planning to kill thousands upon thousands of innocent citizens. Granted, they were Las Vegas tourists, but innocent nevertheless. Just a few more seconds and it would be done.

"Watch out for that bee!" Gabe yelled. He couldn't help himself; he couldn't stand by and watch the man murdered. "It has deadly venom."

Isaam's eyes narrowed once more. He obviously thought Gabe was trying to distract him.

"I'm serious," Gabe said, "it'll kill you."

As the assassin flew by the tip of the barrel, Isaam waved the gun slightly in an ineffective attempt to shoo it away, then trained it back on Gabe's chest. Gabe watched as the bee landed on Isaam's arm. The terrorist took his eyes off of Gabe and glanced down, as though wondering whether to try to knock it off. An instant later he yelped in pain and slapped it with his other hand. The bee fell to the garage floor, its job done. Isaam raised the gun back up at Gabe, but a perplexed look wrinkled his brow. The confusion changed to alarm, and Isaam crumpled to the ground, joining his killer.

Gabe stood frozen. Isaam had disappeared behind the atom bomb. He waited for the terrorist to get back up and finish the job, but there was only the sound of the band and Christie starting the first verse over for the third time.

Shit! What should he do? Call an ambulance? Call the police?

Forget it! What's done is done, and besides, the bastard got what he deserved.

Gabe took a deep breath, and then stepped outside. "A BEE STUNG YOUR FRIEND ON HIS ARM!" he yelled to Abdul-Baari and Nabeeh. "I THINK HE MIGHT BE ALLERGIC!"

A good bluff can't be timid.

Gabe took off, sprinting back across the terrorists' yard before they had a chance to ask questions.

He hated to leave now, not knowing how Abdul-Baari and Nabeeh would react to the death of their co-conspirator, but he had no choice. He and Ronny had to deal with the aliens before they realized their plans for the atom bomb had been foiled. If not, Christie would follow Isaam as the next victim at their hands (if they *had* hands).

Gabe jumped through the low shrubs and swung his hand in a rolling circle, indicating that they should keep playing. Christie gave him a distressed look. She'd sung the entire song through three times and was starting the fourth. Gabe shrugged. On impulse, he leaned over the microphone as she sang and kissed her on the forehead. She looked up at him and smiled. He winked and sprinted off for the shop.

He noticed Punky barking madly off at the back corner while Mrs. Crabnuckle took careful aim and swung Alien Terminator. No time to check on them; he'd just have to trust them to take care of themselves.

Inside the shop he found Ronny waiting patiently on the bench. Gabe grabbed him under one arm and ran back out and around the house towards his car.

"ISAAM'S DEAD!" Gabe yelled over the music.

Ronny said something which Gabe couldn't understand. He leaned closer. "I said, did you kill him?" Ronny asked.

"NO! A BEE!"

Ronny nodded, as though he understood completely.

Gabe hadn't questioned it until now, but why *did* the bee go for Isaam instead of him? A million questions and—he checked his watch—*only forty minutes left!*

They'd done all they could do to thwart the detonation of the terrorists' atom bomb. Now, unless he and Ronny could somehow stop them, the aliens would be free to activate Christie's poison agents at 2:03 when the atom bomb failed to go off.

Chapter 15

Saturday, 1:25 PM

"Where are we going?" Gabe asked, practically yelling as he pulled the car away from Crabnuckle's house.

He had asked Ronny when they were building the cup bomb where the alien base was, and the turncoat had been evasive, saying only that it was a short drive. They were in the middle of developed San Diego. Where could you hide an alien space ship?

"Go to your house," Ronny instructed from the passenger seat.

"Why my house? We don't have much time!"

"That's where my colleagues are."

"At *my* house? Since when?"

"From the beginning."

Gabe looked over at the raccoon. "Ronny, if you're joking, I'm going to break one of your little legs."

"Gabe, I am not joking . . . although I assume *you* were about breaking my leg."

"Of course. How could they possibly have been at my house all along?"

Ronny didn't answer for a few seconds. "There's something I haven't been very specific about," he finally admitted. "Let me ask you, what do you imagine my colleagues and I are like—our physical form?"

It had been a while since Gabe had thought about that. "I don't really know. Maybe like those kid actors playing the aliens with huge heads in *Close Encounters*. In bad dreams you have tentacles and big teeth."

"You're way off on both counts. Gabe, you're making a basic assumption that we're animals."

"You're a *computer*?"

"I no more resemble one of your computers than your brain resembles the nerve bundles of a worm."

"Huh! So, you're super-advanced AI?"

"What is artificial? The Concise Oxford Dictionary defines it as 'made as a copy of something natural'. In the sense that our far-distant prototype ancestors were originally conceived by living beings, then we are artificial. But only in the way that your house is an artificial cave."

Gabe realized that he had come to think of Ronny as the raccoon and his colleagues as . . . something else. Maybe big-brained alien things sitting in a softly lit control room twisting knobs and flipping switches.

"Where are you now?" Gabe asked. "I mean, where is your program—your software—when you're part of Ronny ... I mean, the raccoon?" Gabe's mind was spinning like a top.

Ronny took a deep, sigh-emulating breath. "Gabe, you are familiar with two types of intelligence: your own brain, and rudimentary forms of software which run on computer platforms. Try to understand that I am not lines of software code. Nor am I a re-configurable hardwired machine like your brain. The best I can describe is that I am several billion logic algorithms interacting in patterns that self-correlate over time. In other words, I learn as I go. I reside in a processing machine about the size of your shirt button. It sits on this raccoon's neck. Rather than transistors, this machine uses individual molecules for storage and logic processes. My intelligent 'essence' can be transferred to another machine, but it's a complex process and takes some time."

"You're a computer chip."

"I could take that as an insult, but I know that you're trying to understand. Comparing me to a laptop is like comparing you to a bacterium."

They drove in silence for a minute. "Are the beings who made you waiting at this home base 320 light years away?" Gabe asked. "Is *that* your home planet?"

"Gabe, there are no 'beings,' at least not the biological organism kind. Although my ancestors were originally conceived by living beings, that was millions of years ago. They are but a very dim memory. More a myth than a history. There is no one planet that we consider home. I doubt you think of Africa as your home because your species originally evolved there."

"What happened to your creators, those mythical biological organisms?"

"Gabe, I suspect that you you're probably imagining something out of a poorly done science fiction movie. My ancestors did not one day rise up and take over the planet of their creators, perhaps turning them into slaves. That's silly. The reality is simply that animal species are transitory things. Their very nature is to change and evolve. Also, there are fundamental biological limits to the complexities associated with advancing intelligence. Humans view themselves, quite naturally, as the supreme, inevitable result of evolution. In fact, you, and dolphins, and any other large-brained animal, are examples of extreme evolutionary niche specialization. Your brains are the peacocks of the thinking department. Like any specialization, it's a precarious evolutionary position. I know this is difficult to see from your perspective, but I'm talking time spans of many hundreds of thousands of years."

Gabe felt depressed. It wasn't fun to think of yourself as a short evolutionary way-stop in the big scheme of things. Maybe it was just the fatigue from all the anxiety of the last hours and days.

Oh hell, it *was* a depressing thought.

"Don't forget that animals were the creators of my kind," Ronny went on, as though reading Gabe's thoughts. "Without you, we would never exist. Think of yourself as the fetus that grows into us."

"Like the end of *2001: A Space Odyssey*."

"I think Mr. Clarke and Mr. Kubrick were using a metaphor, but in a sense, yes. The fundamental difference being that the movie envisioned that mankind could evolve to a higher form. There is, in fact, no higher form for biological beings. You may be interested to know that there are probably no animals in this galaxy very much more intelligent than humans."

That was only more depressing.

Ronny continued. "It is inevitable. Intelligent biological organisms eventually either develop our form, or they fade away into extinction, leaving only archeological evidence behind."

Gabe had trouble focusing his thoughts. Random ideas and questions popped and dissipated like the grand finale of a fireworks display. An obvious one gestured wildly for attention. "Why didn't you tell me this earlier?"

"I was afraid that it would alienate you."

Gabe glanced at his watch. Time was flying by. "Look, it's fine to talk philosophically about how living beings are the revered mythical creators of your kind, but the hard reality now is that your 'kind' wants to exterminate us."

"That is not true. That is not the goal. My colleagues would prefer to work with you as we expand. It's more accurate to say that my colleagues will not hesitate to kill humans if necessary to achieve their goal. Note that no humans were killed prior to Isaam, but that was simply because my colleagues wanted to avoid drawing attention. Your fellow humans take a killing *very* seriously."

Gabe realized he was way over the speed limit. It would just slow them down if he was stopped by a cop.

"Has it ever happened?" he asked. "Has your kind ever worked cooperatively with a living species?"

Ronny took a few seconds to reply. "Yes, but not for long. I'd be lying to say that your race should welcome my colleagues."

"No shit, Dick Tracy. Not when they won't hesitate to kill us."

"Like the Europeans did to the American natives?" Ronny countered.

"Um, right. Good point."

"I was joking, Gabe."

"I wasn't. Hey, why did the bee kill Isaam and not me?"

"Simple logic. The prime goal is to detonate the nuclear bomb at 2:03. My colleagues undoubtedly concluded that this would be most jeopardized if Isaam were allowed to live."

"Because his gun shots might have brought the police?"

"Partly that, but mostly because they feel they have control over you through Christie. If Isaam were to learn of the detonator device—because, for example, you reveal its location in the trash can in a moment of panic to save your life—they'd have limited means to stop him from removing it."

Gabe glanced at Ronny. "They killed Isaam because I might have talked to him?"

"Correct. They would have tried to kill you as well if there'd been another bee in the area."

Gabe swerved to miss a car in an intersection. He realized that he'd ran a stop sign.

Things were beginning to make sense, though. "You didn't even know that you were hungry," he mused out loud.

"Excuse me?"

"When I first fed you, you had to learn what hunger was. If you were a living organism, you would've known hunger, even if you were some super-advanced fish or insect."

"You're probably right."

"And your idea that I should pose as the terrorists' cell leader. That was just dumb. Considering how smart you are otherwise, that seemed incongruous. It was naïve, but only from the perspective of a social animal."

"I see." Ronny was silent a moment, then said, "I still think it could have worked."

Gabe snorted, and then laughed. "I think you just proved my point. Hey, those jokes you told when I had you locked in the closet, did you make those up?"

"I did. I considered some candidate jokes that I had previously read, but I decided that you'd be more likely to pick up the intended message if you hadn't heard the joke before. My colleagues inquired as to why I was telling them, and I lied and told them that I was calming and strengthening the rapport with you, that it was a human thing they didn't understand."

Gabe still winced at the memory of the earworm. "I can see another puzzle piece that now fits into place. You said that there were a lot of arguments with your colleagues between each of those stabs of pain from the earworm. I couldn't see how there was enough time for that, but to you thirty seconds is probably like an hour to me."

"Something like that, yes."

Gabe slammed the breaks as an elderly man stepped into a crosswalk. "Sorry!" he called out his window, but the old fart just threw him the finger.

There were ramifications to their last point. "So, when we're talking—like now—it must seem like forever, waiting for me to answer you, word—by—slow—word."

"I've gotten used to it. I think about other things while I'm waiting."

"Hold on a second, you used to take several seconds to answer me, many minutes by your time."

"I was getting my lies straight. Understand, lying does not come natural for me. It's a complex process, weighing the many possible consequences and keeping it all straight. It's similar to a complex game of chess. You don't understand the difficulty since evolution has pre-wired you for the job."

Gabe finally turned the car onto his own street. His heart had migrated up next to his Adam's apple. His apprehension about the atom bomb and Christie's peril was now aggravated by the knowledge that the aliens weren't even living beings.

"I still don't understand why your people will kill Christie when they find out we've prevented the atom bomb from going off. What do they have to gain from that?"

"There is no direct gain. They will simply be completing the implementation of an established threat, a demonstration of the resolution of their intentions."

Gabe could feel his cheeks getting hot. "That sounds like the thinking of a machine."

Ronny lifted his little shoulders in a shrug. "From your perspective, I'm sure it does."

Gabe's house came into view, and he was mildly surprised to find that it looked the same. He'd been expecting to see a flying saucer hovering overhead, or maybe all the windows pulsing with an eerie, alien glow.

"Why did you want me to bring Punky along to Crabnuckle's?"

"I was afraid he'd get too curious about my colleagues as they prepared to come forth after the bomb went off."

"What about Mrs. Jones!" Gabe exclaimed. They'd left the cat behind.

"I thought about her, but she's not a persistent pest like Punky, plus my colleagues appreciate that she keeps the rats away. We're not fond of rats."

"Because of the terrorist pellet-guns?"

"They chew us."

"Why don't you just send assassin bees after them?"

"The rotting carcasses might draw attention."

"Right."

Gabe pulled over along the street, rather than in his driveway. He didn't really imagine that this would fool them, but pulling into a driveway seems somehow blatant, a deliberate trespass, like stepping provocatively across a line scratched in the dirt.

Besides, he was very nervous and not thinking very clearly.

He looked at his watch. "Oh Christ! We've only got twelve minutes before they think the atom bomb will go off. What do I need to know? How will they try to stop us?"

"The bees, mainly," Ronny replied calmly. "They didn't plan for this, a deliberate assault. They never imagined that I'd turn traitor on them and give them away. Early on I heard references about an electric field defense, but I don't think they ever went anywhere with it."

Gabe picked up Bee Killer. He reached under the seat and took out his tire iron with his other hand.

"What's that for?" Ronny asked. "You're not going to use that on my colleagues, are you?"

Gabe shrugged and nodded.

"That's like trying to kill a moth with a shotgun. Your cooking utensil will work fine. I don't think you understand. Think very small."

Gabe reluctantly laid the iron on the seat and opened the door. He listened. There was nothing but the distant sound of traffic—no bees. He got out, went around, and took Ronny from the passenger seat. Bee Killer in one hand, Ronny in the other, he walked to his front door.

"Open it," Ronny said.

"Shouldn't we peek in a window and check it out?"

"I don't think so. We don't have much time."

"Right." Gabe thought he could see his heart beating under his T-shirt.

He opened the door a crack, and when no bees flew out, he threw it open. Everything was just as they'd left it. He stepped cautiously inside. "Where are they?"

"Your attic."

"They've been right above me all this time?"

That would explain the static on his radio, and all those weird silver ants. His kitchen was their basement. This would also account for his high electric bills. The little bastards were stealing his power. In fact, when the utility meter-man came, Ronny had obviously high-tailed it back to the attic. That's why Gabe saw him up on the roof. They probably thought that a utility man might do some snooping around, and would have wanted to be prepared . . . to sting him.

Gabe walked through the living room and down the hall towards his bedroom. In the ceiling at the end of the hall were the pull-down stairs to the attic. The cord with the little plastic ball at the end hung above him. All he had to do was give it a tug, and the alien base would open above him. "What do I do next?" he asked.

The Ronny paused a moment in his arms before answering. Gabe knew that for his accelerated time sense, this was an extraordinary amount of deliberation. "Destroy them," Ronny finally said.

"How?"

"With your cooking utensil. Bees should be our only threat. They haven't had time to manufacture anything else. Before we go up, though, you should put on some clothes."

Gabe glanced down at his shorts and T-shirt, feeling for a fleeting moment that he was living one of those dreams where he discovers he's in class with no pants on. "I'm *wearing* clothes!"

"I mean long pants and a jacket. There may be a lot of bees up there."

"Oh yeah. Good idea."

Gabe went to his bedroom and put Ronny on the bed. He tossed clothes from his dresser drawers. "Other than weddings, I haven't worn long pants since grade school. I don't know if still own any!"

He was on the verge of total panic. Each passing second felt like another rock piled on his chest, making it more and more difficult to breath. Soon, all too soon, their time would be up, and Christie would be killed.

"I'll have to wear my blue suit," he concluded, giving up hope of finding anything in the drawers.

Gabe turned to find that Ronny had climbed down from the bed and was rooting through a box in the closet. He held up the sleeve of a jacket. "Perhaps this," he said.

It was the Polartec pants and jacket his grandmother had given him when he'd gone skiing with his senior class. He hadn't worn it in years and had completely forgotten about it. It was perfect. Not only did it have elastic around the wrists and ankles, but it also had a hood with a draw string. "How did you know it was there?"

"Earlier reconnoitering," Ronny explained, pulling the jacket and then the pants from the box and handing them up to him.

Gabe pulled the pants on over his shoes and shorts, and then put on the jacket, zipped it up, and pulled the hood over his head, tugging on the drawstring so that only his eyes and nose stuck out. On a warm, sunny afternoon in San Diego, Gabe looked like he was out to sweat away a few pounds. "What about you?" Gabe asked.

"My fur will protect me to some extent. In any case, neither of us can afford to let any bees sit on us very long. They'll work their stinger through your fabric or my fur."

Gabe looked at the clock next to his bed. "Oh God! We only have eight minutes left."

"That should be plenty of time."

Gabe nodded inside his hood. The cloth rustled and scratched against his ears. "Let's do it."

He picked up Ronny, who'd found a small spoon to use as a bee swatter, and walked back out into the hall. He hesitated only a second before reaching up and pulling firmly on the cord. The stairs unfolded and extended down to meet Gabe, revealing the darkness of the attic above. Gabe flinched, expecting a swarm of attacking assassin bees, but the darkness offered only the silence of old attic air.

Gabe looked at Ronny. The raccoon gave him his wounded version of a wink. With a nod, Gabe climbed up into the blackness.

He could feel the hairs standing at attention all over his body, tickling against the Polartec material.

He reached for the light cord that hung immediately above the stairway, and, from the depths of the darkness, came the buzz of a bee. Gabe swung his hand to find the light cord, and felt a tap as he connected with the invisible mechanical insect. He heard the buzz modulate, and then steady as the assassin regained its equilibrium. Gabe swung his hand around some more. *Where was the damn cord?* He felt the bee land on the back of his hand. Gabe yelled and gave his hand a violent shake, almost losing his balance and falling back down the stairs. He heard the bee's buzz whine and whir as it fell away and tried to maneuver back. But, in shaking away the bee, he'd knocked the light cord. He tried to grab it, but it was swinging around now, an invisible moving target. He heard the buzz of a second bee. He forced his panic into submission and held his arm far to one side and swung it slowly in an arc through the darkness. He felt the cord fall against his forearm. No, it must have been one of the bees, for the cord then fell against his hand. He grabbed the cord and gave it a yank. Light flooded the attic.

Gabe saw that there was indeed a bee crawling along his arm towards the exposed skin of his hand. He heard the second bee circling somewhere behind him. He gave his arm a shake, but the bee hung on. It was barely an inch from his hand and moving closer by the second. He couldn't use his other hand, which was holding Ronny. He was about to try banging his wrist against the floor of the attic when Ronny reached over and gave the bee a precise little tap with his spoon. It stopped moving and Gabe easily shook it off.

Gabe realized that the buzzing of the other bee had stopped. Where was it? His skin crawled in anticipation of a fatal sting. He looked down. It was on Ronny's back! Ronny must have felt it, for he was groping behind him, but his arm wasn't quite flexible enough. Gabe could see the bee wiggling, burrowing itself down into the fur. He had laid Bee Killer down when he'd reached for the light string, and the bee would be in position to sting at any moment. Gabe reached over, picked the assassin out of Ronny's fur, and flung it away. Wings whirred as it gained control and made a wide circle back towards them. Gabe had Bee Killer ready now, though, and he batted it away with one swipe.

For the first time Gabe had a chance to look around. He wasn't sure what he was expecting, but it wasn't this. All around him, covering every surface, including old, broken chairs, appliances, and cardboard boxes, were intricate constructions of the minutest detail. It was as though he'd grown a hundred-fold and was gazing around at a large city from a giddying height. Except that this city had neither wall nor window, just tinker toy structures supporting God-knows-what. Instead of streets, the tiny metropolis had slender, but apparently rigid strands connecting different areas of apparent functional specialization. Rather than a regular grid pattern, this city seemed to have been designed by someone devoid of a sane sense of uniform structure. Gabe could get lost in the complexity without moving an inch from the stairs.

One object stood out by its substantive form. Hanging from the ceiling, about five feet above the floor, was what appeared to be a small satellite. All the rest of the alien construction was tiny and fragile, but this looked solid and durable. A central core was surrounded by a dozen or more radial, vertical fins so that the whole thing looked like a three inch Christmas tree ornament. Every surface was polished and reflected like mirrors. Orbiting around the finned satellite some three or four feet away were perhaps a dozen assassin bees, circling and circling, never straying from their perfectly calculated paths.

Other than the bee-electrons orbiting their finned atom nucleus, there was no movement. The alien city was deserted.

It took a total of about four seconds for Gabe to take all of this in.

"It is as I predicted, Gabe. They have all gone for cover."

Gabe looked down at Ronny. What the hell was he talking about? As he'd "predicted"?

Gabe was about to question him when he saw that Ronny was twisting his eyes into his pseudo-wink. He then lifted his little shoulders in a shrug. Ronny was obviously trying to tell him that this was a lie in formation.

Why? Gabe had no idea, but he had enough sense not to undermine the ruse. "Yes, you were right. What now?" Again, Gabe had the feeling he was reading script lines, badly.

"Since I know where they're hidden, we'll go there." He gave Gabe another twisted wink.

Gabe didn't know what to do. Did Ronny want to go up, or down? Ronny solved his dilemma. "The quickest would be if you put me down on the hallway floor," he suggested.

Gabe climbed back down and did just that. Ronny scampered off towards the front door and waited for Gabe to come and open it. Outside, Ronny began circling the house with Gabe following behind. Charlemagne, the neighbor dog, sat in the yard watching them. It seemed incongruous that the neighbor's dog should be idling in the sun while they hunted for alien invaders. They rounded the first corner, and Gabe caught a smell of something putrid. They were halfway to the next corner when a swarm of bees emerged from a small hole located near the end of the wall.

"Run for it!" Ronny called, and scampered back, choosing the shortest path, which took him between Gabe's legs.

Chapter 16

Saturday, 1:56 PM

Gabe hesitated only long enough to see that the bees were headed straight for them before he turned and followed Ronny. Gabe slammed the front door behind them, and Ronny pointed at his shoulder. Gabe slapped at it with Bee Killer. Ronny indicated "higher." Gabe slapped nearer his neck, and an assassin fell to the ground.

He turned around in a circle for Ronny to look, but he was now clean.

"You tricked them," Gabe said.

"That's right. If they thought I already knew where they were hidden, they'd have no reason to keep their location hidden and would attack when we came near."

"They're pretty dumb, aren't they?"

"Only when it comes to lying."

"But you knew they were somewhere in the ground near the house."

"That was just an educated guess. I have to admit, this development took me by surprise. It makes perfect sense in retrospect. They're expecting an atom bomb to go off soon, and they want as much protection as they can get. Even with the hill between us and the bomb, they wouldn't take any chances. Although dirt and house foundation provides only minimal shielding from EMP, they'd still want to get as low as possible. My guess is that they've lined that hole deep down with tin foil."

"Their city—in my attic—I didn't imagine that they'd be so . . ."

"Small?"

"Yes."

"That's your human-centric perspective speaking, Gabe. You are the size you are because you compete with other animals of similar size, and also because it takes a head the size of a soccer ball to house a complex organic brain. There are many advantages to a smaller size. For example, it requires far less resources. More importantly, space travel practically demands it. The Space Shuttle and Saturn rocket that sent men to the moon were most impressive, but almost ludicrous in the extravagance of materials and fuel. All because you insist on sending organic brains."

"True. But, it seems so fragile, so vulnerable. I could have laid their city to waste with just Bee Killer."

"Again, your human perspective speaking. Dangers come in many forms and sizes. There was a time when the size of a man was important in battle, but modern war technology has made a soldier's size almost completely irrelevant. Isaam was killed by an assassin that weighed a few grams. In the face of a nuclear bomb, if anything, a small size has its advantages."

The atom bomb! "Shit! What do we do now?"

Ronny didn't speak for a couple of seconds as he apparently mulled a multitude of options. "This is unfortunate," is all he finally said.

"What?"

"They kept this move hidden from me. They obviously didn't trust me."

"You sound hurt. What did you expect? You turned traitor on them."

"They were obviously planning to retreat to a temporary safe bunker well before they knew I'd turned. Actually, it would be more accurate to say they don't know how to trust at all. From their non-organic perspective, they'd view the ability to lie as an unmanageable cancer. Lacking the capacity to lie, they don't understand how to trust another who can."

Gabe could feel his anxiety mounting. "But, what do we *do* now?"

"I don't know, Gabe."

"We have to stop them from activating Christie's booby trap. Does that mean we have to destroy them in their hole?"

Ronny thought a moment. "Yes."

"How?"

"There are many ways. The key is how to do it in the next few minutes."

"Ronny, that's obvious. You're not helping."

"I know. I'm sorry, Gabe. I thought about pouring some caustic liquid down the hole, but I imagine that the animal that originally dug it probably included some sort of rain trap. Also, we have to be sure that we get them all."

Gabe's mind raced, exploring and abandoning ten different ideas in succession. "You said they're sensitive to EMP. Could we use that somehow?"

"I don't see how. We don't have the means. Plus, remember, they've probably shielded themselves against electro-magnetic radiation."

"Well . . . what about just straight electricity?"

Ronny thought a moment. "Yes, perhaps. But, it would have to be a sufficiently high voltage."

"Straight wall AC wouldn't do it?"

"110 Volts? I don't think so. It would just give them an opportunity to sting us."

Gabe glanced at his watch. *Five minutes!* Panic caught in his throat, seeming to strangle him. High voltage. They needed high voltage. *Think!*

"The microwave oven! I remember reading that they transform 110 AC up to a few thousand Volts."

"No. We need both high voltage and sufficient current. The microwave oven transformer wouldn't push enough current through the ground."

Voltage and current. Something that was powerful. Gabe remembered a bad shock he'd gotten a few years before. He'd been repairing his guitar tube amplifier and accidentally brushed a high-voltage point. It knocked him on his ass. *That was it!* High-powered tube amplifiers developed six-hundred volts or more on the tube plates. That was DC voltage, but the large input transformer put out the equivalent amount as AC. "I think I've got it!"

Gabe ran to his bedroom. He'd brought the vintage Fender Showman amp head in after the Schooner gig. He never left it in his car. He picked it up and tossed it on the bed. It weighed 40 pounds, and half of that was the input transformer. He could see it through the opening in the back, a fat, hulking mass of metal and wire windings. The primary side was connected to the AC wall cord. All he had to do was get to the secondary wires. They were buried inside the cabinet, though. Leo Fender had designed the amp for easy servicing, and Gabe knew from experience that it took about five minutes to get the chassis out from the cabinet. In five minutes Christie would be dead.

This amplifier was Gabe's pride and joy. It had been built when the Beatles were learning their chops. It was the only thing he owned besides the house that had intrinsic value. It was an irreplaceable token of musical heritage. Gabe picked up the vintage amplifier, held it high over his head, and smashed it to the floor.

Gabe felt a shower of glass shards against his legs as the tubes shattered. The black Tolex covering ripped at one corner where the interlacing wood finger-joint had parted slightly. Otherwise, the cabinet was intact. Leo Fender had also built his equipment to last. Gabe picked up the glass-speckled wreck and threw it against the floor again, this time making the weakened joint the point of impact. The cabinet finally fell apart, but left the chassis still bolted to the top piece of wood. The secondary wires from the transformer remained hidden inside.

Gabe picked up this remnant and smashed it to the floor. Nothing. The four top bolts held. He got down in his knees and began pounding the chassis on the hardwood floor like a hammer. Chunks of hardwood floor flew in all directions. One bolt gave way. The wooden piece was now loose, but there wasn't room to get his fingers inside. He hammered some more, and another bolt broke. He was now able to use the board as a lever and pry it away from the chassis. Gabe finally saw the secondary wires that could deliver his killing voltage.

He got up and carried the ruined chassis to the kitchen, dragging the AC cord behind him. Ronny had opened kitchen cabinet drawers and used them as steps to climb up onto the counter. He was at the sink pouring salt into a pitcher he'd filled with water. Gabe understood. The dissolved salt would form an electrolyte to enhance conduction of the electricity through the ground.

He dropped the remnants of his prize amp on the table, ran back to his bedroom, and grabbed two wire clothes hangers from his closet. Back to the kitchen. He looked at his watch. *Two and a half minutes!* He picked up the chassis and headed for the front door. "Come *on*, we're almost out of time!"

"Gabe!" Ronny called, "I can't carry the water."

Shit! Gabe sometimes forgot that Ronny was just a little animal.

Gabe moved the chassis and coat hangers to his right hand, ran back, picked up the pitcher of salt-water with his left hand, and then hobbled as fast as he could with the load to the front door. Ronny would have to follow as best he could.

He had closed the front door when they came in, and now he leaned over and extended his fingertips from his grip on the broken amp chassis to turn the knob. The metal chassis and broken glass tubes cut into his wrist. He pulled the door open and waddled outside.

He couldn't carry it all. He knew he'd drop the water before he got to the far corner, so he put it down on the front walk, and then, carrying the chassis and hangers in both hands, jogged off around the house.

When he rounded the first corner, Gabe caught another whiff of the rotting flesh, and he also saw that Charlemagne had moved. The mutt was now sitting next to the house, between Gabe and the next corner where the aliens had taken refuge. The dog looked at him impassively, appearing to hardly take notice of him. Gabe recalled that Charlemagne had reacted the same way when they'd come out before. He'd been preoccupied then, and it hadn't registered. This was uncharacteristic of the playful animal. Gabe stopped fifteen feet from the dog. His instincts were calling to him. Something was wrong.

Gabe heard Ronny come around the corner behind him. The dog turned its head slightly at a sound down the street. For one brief moment Gabe saw it—the wound on the back of the

Charlemagne's neck. The incision hadn't been closed properly, likely due to haste in placing the implant. Gabe sensed that, although appearing relaxed, the dog—the *alien*—was poised for action, just waiting for some trigger point.

"Let's go, Gabe," Ronny said just behind him. "We're almost out of time."

Ronny didn't see the danger, but Gabe hesitated, afraid that blatantly pointing it out would propel the commandeered animal into action.

Ronny began walking around him. Gabe put his foot out and stopped him.

"Did you hear the one about the ventriloquist who was arrested during a show in Mobile Alabama for child molestation?" Gabe asked quickly. It was the best he could come up with on a moment's notice.

Ronny stopped and looked up at him.

"The sheriff in the audience saw his hand in the dummy's pants."

Ronny glanced at Charlemagne and immediately backed up behind Gabe. Thank God for his friend's kilo-thoughts-per-second synthetic brain.

Charlemagne lifted his head and whined. Gabe had heard Punky do something similar when he wanted attention. The whine modulated up and down as Charlemagne twisted his mouth into bizarre contortions, and ended in a low growl.

"It's over," Ronny said.

At first Gabe thought that Ronny was talking to him. The dog began whining again, only this time Gabe could discern that the whines and growls formed barely understandable words. The effect was chillingly eerie, stranger than when he'd first heard Ronny talk since this was not very different than what he heard from dogs his whole life. It was as if all the hounds, collies, and dachshunds had been trying to talk to him, but he just hadn't heard.

"The liar and his pet," the dog whimpered and growled.

Gabe wondered why Charlemagne would call him "the" liar. He realized that the alien was calling *Ronny* the liar, and *Gabe* the pet.

"You'll never be welcomed back to the nest either," Ronny said from behind Gabe. "Join us and live."

Charlemagne howled in an earsplitting imitation of a human laugh. *"But I have not been trained as a liar. I am not defiled."*

A thin, tenuous string rose like a vertical snake from the corner of the house—a whole platoon of assassin bees, the ones that had swarmed after them before.

"Nevertheless," Ronny warned, "we will terminate you unless you let us pass."

The dog howled another laugh. *"I have not become ensnared in the emotions of these animals. We began to suspect you, you know, when you refused to feed your pet the poison agents."*

Ronny started to walk around Gabe. "Come on, he's trying to stall us."

Charlemagne sprang to his feet and whined, *"Be warned! I have caused your human pet to ingest the poison agents. They will be activated if you don't stop."*

Ronny paused the barest moment, and then continued past Gabe, saying, "He's lying."

Charlemagne leapt forward with a fierce growl, and Ronny instinctively crouched low to the ground. The dog could break his back with one quick snap of his jaws.

"No!" Gabe yelled, and threw himself between the helpless raccoon and the attacking dog. Gabe caught a glimpse of bared canines and a blur of leaping fur, and then felt shocking pain as the dog's teeth sank into his left forearm. Gabe had been bitten by big dogs before, and only realized now that they'd actually restrained themselves. The alien within Charlemagne held nothing back. Gabe heard the sickening sound of the dog's teeth grinding against his ulna and radius bones. Despite the searing pain, Gabe held the thought that the same treatment would kill Ronny.

They fell to the ground and Charlemagne growled and shook Gabe's arm like it was prey he was finishing off. The alien was tapping into the dog's hunting instincts. From some detached and isolated place Gabe heard himself screaming from the pain.

Charlemagne let go of his arm and lunged for his neck. Gabe fell onto his back and managed to put his hand in the way, and the dog's teeth now sank into that flesh. Suddenly Charlemagne loosened his hold, and his eyes went wide with confusion, like Isaam's had before he toppled over dead. The dog started to turn on Ronny, but collapsed as though shot through the heart. Gabe saw Ronny pull his miniature hand away from the dead dog's flank. The raccoon was holding an assassin bee between his little fingers. A whole flurry of the lethal killers swarmed around them. Ronny had apparently picked one out of his own fur and pressed it against Charlemagne.

A bee swooped in and tried to land on Gabe's exposed nose. He swung his hand to block it, and the assassin became embedded in the blood streaming from his wounds. Gabe could see it wiggling, trying to get its stinger into position. He shook his arm and it fell away.

Suddenly Ronny's face was above him. He was waving his tail back and forth over him, fanning the bees away. Two had managed to land on him, though, and were working their way slowly towards his head, probably not able to penetrate the thicker fur of his main body. *So that's what fur is for*, Gabe thought from the detached place far from his arm and hand and the tearing pain. Gabe reached over with his good hand and flicked his finger at one of the bees on Ronny, as though it was a marble. It spun away. He did the same for the second.

Out of nowhere, another lone assassin zoomed in and landed on Gabe's cheek. Ronny reached out and knocked it away. That's why he'd come over to Gabe, to keep the bees off his vulnerable face.

"You have to get up," Ronny said.

Gabe nodded. He could do this. He could lift himself with the elbow of his wounded arm, then if he put his good hand under him
. . .

He heard the pop in the distance. It sounded like a balloon bursting, except that this one echoed majestically among the hills and canyons. He flinched, expecting to be blasted away in a 500 MPH shock wave, but it came to him immediately that this was not the atom bomb, but their own homemade cup bomb. The precise time had arrived, and the alien detonation device had attempted to carry out its final task. Ronny's cobbled ruse had worked.

The consequence of this, what they had been so desperately trying to circumvent, settled in Gabe's chest, and he couldn't breathe. Christie had trusted him, and he'd let her down.

He leapt to his feet. Grief and anger boiled his blood. He pressed his clenched fists to his forehead, smashing an assassin bee in the process. *At least they'll pay.* He would finish what was started.

He reached down, picked up his ruined amplifier, and stormed along the wall towards the hole at the corner of the house. Bees swarmed in mass behind him, trying to follow. He saw the rotting carcass of a ground squirrel lying a few feet away, the source of the putrid smell. The bastards had killed it and stolen its home.

Gabe took one clothes hanger and bent and twisted it into some semblance of a rod. He tried to shove it into the ground, but it couldn't penetrate the hard-packed dirt. He untangled it and bent one section back and forth until it broke, and was then able to push the resulting straight segment a good foot down before it hit a rock. Bees buzzed in a flurry all around him. He didn't care; he swatted them away like so many mosquitoes. He could feel them desperately trying to attach themselves to his hands as he swished them away. One was trying to find a way through the holes in his Polartec jacket pierced by Charlemagne's teeth. He slapped it viciously, and it crunched under his palm.

"Put the other one around the corner," Ronny said beside him. "The squirrel hole probably goes under the foundation—we need the current to pass through the whole lair."

His little friend held a broken paint-stirring stick, which he used, along with his tail, to swat away the bees.

Gabe took the other clothes hanger around the corner, broke and straightened it, and pushed it into the ground against the wall. It immediately hit a rock. He pulled it out, moved a few inches to the side, and this time was able to shove it a good two feet down. He picked up the amp chassis and slammed it to the ground at the house corner, mid-way between his two ground posts.

"It needs to be insulated from the ground," Ronny reminded him.

Gabe reached over and savagely tore off a piece of wooden ivy-lattice along the wall. He threw this to the ground and placed the chassis on it. A bee suddenly landed right on his eye. Gabe slapped it with a smack and felt the pain as it squashed against his closed eyelid. Sooner or later, he knew, he was bound to smash one of their stingers right into his skin and the game would be over, as it was already over for Christie.

He needed the salt water. Where the hell was it? He remembered he'd set it down at the front door. He sprinted back to the front of the house. It was right where he'd left it. *An extension cord!* The nearest outside outlet was at the front of the house. *And wire to connect to the ground rods.* What else had he forgotten?

The bees caught up with him again, and he slapped and swatted them once more. Gabe ran into the house. He yanked open kitchen drawers and found a light-duty lamp extension cord. It would never reach from the front of the house around to the hole. Gabe howled out in frustration.

You don't have to reach to the front of the house, a calm voice said from the detached place.

No, he didn't. Gabe carried the extension cord into the spare bedroom located in the corner of the house. He plugged the cord into the wall below a window, but then he couldn't get the window open. In a rage, he threw a large book through the glass. *You could have hit Ronny out there,* he thought. Bees wandered in through the broken window. He tossed the free end of the cord through the broken window and went in search of wire. To hell with it. He grabbed a table lamp from the living room and carried it out with him. He ripped off the shade, held the porcelain lamp high over his head and smashed it to the cement of the front walk. It shattered, and porcelain pieces shot off in all directions. The light bulb socket lay exposed on the walk, the cord still attached. Gabe put his foot on the socket and yanked the cord until it broke free.

When Gabe came around the corner of the house carrying the saltwater and lamp cord, he saw Ronny squatting next to the hole along the far wall. As Gabe came closer, he saw that the bees were no longer attacking the raccoon. Instead, they were orbiting him in exact counter-plane circles like the ones in the attic guarding the shiny ornament. Gabe realized that they were no longer attacking him either. He too had a contingent of little satellites.

He poured a small amount of saltwater at the base of each ground rod. As he leaned over to pour the rest down the hole, his bee satellites suddenly spun in close so that they were flying inches from his face. He was caught by surprise and straightened back up. The bees dutifully spun away into their more distant orbits. They obviously didn't want him to pour the water.

"They've opened my channel," Ronny said, perched at the edge of the hole.

Gabe looked at him. The raccoon appeared to be in a trance, staring into the distance.

"They had closed it off when I turned traitor," Ronny went on, seemingly talking to nothing. "They're speaking to me again."

Gabe didn't say anything. He didn't really care. He just wanted to finish this. Vengeance was all that mattered.

"They're offering me clemency."

It came to him that Ronny might be changing his mind. "*No!*" he cried. "They're lying! They just want to save their skins!"

"Of course they want to save themselves. But remember, they don't lie."

Gabe shook his head. He didn't know what to say.

"These were my colleagues," Ronny continued. "I've known them for hundreds of years."

Would Ronny try to stop him? If he did, what was he willing to do? Would he hurt Ronny to finish this job?

"I have to do this," Gabe declared. He was surprised at how calm he sounded.

Ronny finally looked up at him. "I know. Let's get on with it."

The bees immediately attacked Gabe's face in mass. He jumped away and spun in a circle to break up their swarm. He twisted back and splashed the rest of the saltwater into the hole. It gurgled and bubbled as it sank away out of view.

"That was most unwelcome," Ronny informed, as though he were an on-the-spot reporter. "The saltwater alone is damaging to them. Several that were posted near the entrance are gravely injured."

"Good," Gabe replied.

He was on his knees swatting away bees and pulling at the transformer wires. *There were so many!* He'd forgotten that there were multiple secondary windings and taps—some for the power section tubes plates, some for the pre-amp, and still others for the tube heating elements. Which was the high-voltage pair? There was one quick way to find out. He plugged in the power cord and began brushing his fingers against the various wires. He felt his arm jolt as he contacted some high voltage. Not enough. He tried some more. He got another jolt, this one somewhat smaller. The last pair he tried jolted him so fiercely he felt his jaw shake. That was it. He unplugged the extension cord and began twisting the high-voltage transformer wires to the two prongs of the lamp cord AC plug.

"They understand only now what we're going to do," Ronny reported. "They're most distraught. They're offering you riches."

Gabe paused. He didn't care about their bribe, but he remembered that they couldn't lie. "Ask them if they've killed Christie," Gabe said.

Ronny listened for a moment. "They refuse to answer." He looked up at Gabe. "I'm sorry, my friend. That almost certainly means that they've sent the activation signal."

It was what Gabe already assumed, but it nearly brought him to his knees to hear it. He resumed his task with a renewed vengeance. He took the other end of the lamp cord and pulled the two strands apart, carrying one to each ground rod and twisting the bare ends around the exposed coat hangers. He could hardly see with the bees so thick in his face, and he knocked three or four away with each swipe of his hand.

The electrocution was ready. Gabe picked up the amplifier power plug and extension cord.

The bees suddenly moved away from him. "Hold it!" Ronny called. He looked up at Gabe again. "They offer you anything you want, anything within their power to give you."

"Can they bring Christie back to life?" Gabe asked quietly.

Ronny looked at him, but said nothing.

Gabe shoved the power plug into the extension socket.

He half expected a crack of thunder, an explosion, and billows of smoke. Instead, the transformer hummed softly as it efficiently delivered Amperes of current at six-hundred volts. The makeshift connections where he'd twisted wire together snapped and sparked.

"They're screaming," Ronny said woodenly.

"They can scream?" Gabe asked.

Ronny looked up at him. "Their equivalent."

Gabe heard a faint rustling, like the mouse that scampering through the wall next to his bed at night. Suddenly a swell of motion appeared at the entrance to the hole, and a veritable sea of insects flowed out. Gabe fell back with a yell. He saw that they were not insects, but tiny machines with flexible legs, claws, hands, and tentacles. They flowed out of the hole, and crawled around him in seemingly random circles. Some limped crookedly, some barely crawled along with only one functional appendage.

Ronny took no notice, ignoring them completely.

"What *are* they?" Gabe exclaimed.

"My former colleagues," Ronny replied.

"I thought we were going to kill them?"

"We *have* destroyed them." Ronny looked down at the myriad of flailing mini-machines. "Their movements are merely the result of motive co-processors that were not completely disabled. These are simpler, more robust sections of circuitry. My colleagues, their intelligent essences, are gone. I hear only silence."

Gabe stepped on one machine that happened to wander close to his foot. It crunched like the bees. He had thought he would feel satisfaction, but, instead, his grief now overwhelmed him. He fell to his knees crying.

Through his sobs, he heard a tap-tapping. He looked up to find Ronny calmly but forcefully striking each tiny machine in turn with his stick. One by one, the horde of mindless devices was stilled.

Chapter 17

Saturday, 2:10 PM

After five minutes of weeping, Gabe wiped his face with the sleeve of his jacket and stood up. He felt drained. The pain in his arm and hand where Charlemagne had bit him grew as adrenaline dissipated. He should probably clean and bandage the wounds. The whole front of him was bloody. He really just wanted to crawl into bed and pull the covers over his head.

There was one last task, though, which he had to do. He needed to see that Christie's body was taken care of. In fact, he wondered what the scene was like at Crabnuckle's. He hadn't known how much damage their cup-bomb would inflict, but he considered it good fortune that it was even enough to put the alien detonator out of action. He was surprised they'd heard the bang from his house.

As if on cue, Gabe heard sirens wailing in the distance. He wondered why it had taken so long, but it came to him that it had only been minutes since their homemade bomb had gone off and Christie had dropped over dead. It just *seemed* like hours.

Also . . .

"The bees are gone," Gabe remarked with wonder.

Ronny put his whacking stick down, letting the last of the crippled monstrosities continue their mindless wandering. "They've gone back to the attic."

That made sense. The attic would be the closest thing to home for them, now that they had nothing more to protect.

"Let's go clean up the mess," Gabe said walking off towards the front of the house. This was going to be the hardest thing he'd ever done. He wasn't sure if he wanted to get there before the ambulances took her body away, but, regardless, he was going to try.

"Which mess?" Ronny asked from behind him.

"The only mess that means anything right now." He hadn't really answered his friend. "I have to take care of Christie . . . and, I guess, see what happened to the terrorists."

He hadn't thought about them until now. Their leader had mysteriously died, and then a small bomb had gone off, drawing the attention of the police to their nuclear weapon. If they hadn't been caught in the explosion, they were probably half way to Tijuana.

"Gabe!" Ronny called, running up next to him, "I'm afraid we aren't finished here yet."

"We can deal with the bees later, unless you think they'll go after the neighbors."

"I'm not talking about the bees."

Gabe stopped, and Ronny turned around in front of him to face him.

"What do you mean?" Gabe asked.

"There's a second nuclear detonator."

Gabe couldn't quite catch what this meant. "If there was another one, why didn't the terrorists' atom bomb go off?"

"There's another detonator that was placed next to a different nuclear weapon," Ronny elaborated.

Gabe shook his head. He wasn't sure he could deal with this. "Where? Why?"

"It's a backup, in case the terrorists' bomb failed to detonate—for this very situation. They didn't envision themselves destroyed as well, though."

"Where is it?"

"Another submarine, off the coast of British Columbia. It's much less preferred since the marker then comes through over the ocean."

"When?"

"My colleagues, 320 light years distant, will be looking for it approximately eighteen minutes after the first, if that should fail to appear."

Gabe looked at his watch. "Fourteen minutes from now," he said, like one might repeat their doctor's prognosis that they'd be dead from their cancer in sixty days.

"Thirteen," Ronny corrected.

Gabe continued towards the front door. "Then there's obviously nothing I can do about it."

Ronny ran ahead of him again. "But there is. It will not automatically go off on its own. Like the agents planted in Christie, it needs to be activated."

Gabe stopped again. "By whom? Your colleagues are all dead."

"It's a little more complicated than that."

Gabe felt numb, unable to process any more information. He didn't want to hear it. *It's over, done.* He walked around Ronny. "I can't deal with it. I'm going to Christie."

"You're not thinking straight, Gabe!" Ronny called after him. He could hear the raccoon running to catch up. "You're sentencing the crew of the submarine to death, and ensuring my colleagues will take Earth as their next foothold. They'll likely find the human race an unacceptable obstacle."

Gabe nodded as he went through the front door. "Yeah, yeah, the fate of the entire Earth rests on my shoulders."

Ronny jumped up onto the sofa. "I believe you're being sarcastic, Gabe, but you shouldn't be. Your statement is absolutely correct."

Gabe fell into a chair and held his head in his hands. His mind seemed blank. He waited, but no thoughts came. He seemed to be floating in a soundless pool of despair and exhaustion.

"Twelve minutes," was all that Ronny said.

"Why did you wait to tell me?" Gabe asked without lifting his head.

"I suspected you'd be overwhelmed, as you appear to be now."

"You're right . . . on both counts."

Ronny didn't reply. Gabe knew his friend was simply waiting for him to be ready.

"So, who's left to send the activation signal?" Gabe asked, sitting up.

"Two or three of my colleagues would have risked EMP damage to stay and protect the Source."

"We didn't kill them all?"

"All but these few."

Gabe shook his head. "What is this 'Source'?"

"It is the heart and soul of my race. It's essentially an information cache, but it's more than that, really. It contains everything that we are—everything that we know, that we did, that we *should* be doing. It's like a combination of your genes and all your history books, philosophy texts, bibles, and Korans. Any number of us could be destroyed, but as long as the Source remains, we live on."

"The Christmas tree ornament," Gabe deduced, wondrously.

"If you're referring to the multi-planed object hanging from the attic roof, yes."

"Why would you have brought it with you? I would think you'd have kept it safe back at your home planet, wherever *that* is."

"I've already explained that we no longer have one home planet, but to answer your question, this is not the only Source. Ours is a copy of the latest generation that existed on the previous planet 320 light years away. Should Earth become an expansion post, our Source will represent the outermost instantiation of our total being. At some point in the future, new experiences and knowledge gained on Earth would be back-filled to other Sources. Across the galaxy, over the millennia, information about our total being, our gestalt, flows endlessly, updating and expanding all Sources. Any one Source, any thousand Sources, could be lost, and our being persists, as long as even one remains."

The scope was dizzying. Gabe had thought that the little insect machines they'd destroyed in the hole *were* the aliens. He saw now that they were just one piece in the puzzle, gears in the bigger machine, ants in the colony.

"Conversely," Ronny continued, "destroy a Source, and all of my colleagues associated with it are rendered purposeless—harmless curiosities."

Gabe shrugged and stood up. "Okay, let's go smash it."

He headed for the kitchen to get the hammer from a bottom drawer.

"It's not that simple," Ronny said from behind him.

Gabe stopped and turned around. He gave Ronny a tired look.

"My colleagues in the bunker hole were easily destroyed because they weren't expecting to be attacked there."

Gabe didn't think it had been all that easy, but he didn't say anything.

"However," Ronny continued, "you shouldn't assume the same for the Source."

Gabe held out his hands. "Then, what?"

"There are protective mechanisms."

"Like *what?*"

"Mostly focused energy generators."

"That sounds like techno mumbo-jumbo they use in science fiction movies."

"I know, but it's true."

"What? They use 'heat rays'?"

"Infrared has poor penetration and is difficult to focus."

"I was joking."

"Right. Micro-waves and proton guns mostly."

"Could they stop a speeding bullet?"

"Of course, remember that a bullet seems fast to you, but is an easy target to devices whose thoughts are processed at pico-second speeds."

"What chance do *I* have if a bullet can't even get through?"

Ronny sat looking at Gabe for a moment. "Pick me up and take me for a walk," the raccoon said. "I have to shit."

Gabe was stunned. Ronny gave him one of his twisted winks.

Once out on the sidewalk Gabe said, "I assume we needed to get out of the house."

"That's right," Ronny said in his arms. "The monitor sensors will still be functioning. To continue—we need to disable the Source's defense devices I described."

"Burn down the house?"

Ronny was silent.

"I was kidding," Gabe added.

"I see. In any case, I'm not sure that would be effective. The Source is fairly immune to heat. It's possible that it would be smashed by a falling beam, but, more likely, my remaining colleagues would carry it to safety."

"I assume you *have* some plan?"

"I do. You must distract them while I disable the main power supply."

"Why don't I just go up and smash *that* with a big rock?"

"This is technology beyond your comprehension, Gabe. This power supply has been storing energy tapped from your electric lines for well over a month. Now imagine all that energy released in one millisecond."

Gabe moved decimal points around in his head: two hundred kilowatt hours condensed to one millisecond . . . "Uh, that's the equivalent of like a hundred million kilowatts!"

"720 million kilowatts, actually."

"That's like an atom bomb all by itself!"

"It would seem that way if you were nearby when it was released."

"Okay, what's plan B?"

ж ж ж

Gabe could barely stand it. Again they were racing against the clock. He stood at the bottom of the fold-down attic stairs holding Ronny. He looked at his watch: two minutes left. Ronny had explained that his remaining colleagues would send the activation signal to the detonator device on the submarine early if they decided they had no choice. He and Ronny had just one chance. Slip up, and the submarine would vaporize and a hyperspace marker could appear somewhere over the north Atlantic. Endless armies of insect aliens would then follow.

Gabe had added gloves and goggles to his ski outfit. He'd also wrapped a scarf around his mouth, nose, and forehead. The attic was be full of bees, and he would be too busy to fend them off. In his left hand he held a flashlight and a broom. He needed the flashlight because the aliens had somehow disabled the attic light. He'd use the broom to give them a good poke.

Gabe set Ronny on the hall floor and carefully climbed the stairs into a darkness filled with aliens who wanted him very dead.

Inside his sweaty cocoon, anxiety seemed to be producing a tangible pressure.

As soon as his head rose above the attic floor, he heard a storm of buzzing, and could feel the assassin bees striking and clinging to his face scarf. He wiped them away with his glove before one of them got lucky and poked its way through the thick wool. He turned on the flashlight. He had to use both hands through the clumsy padded ski gloves. He swung the beam around the attic. The deserted miniature alien city lay as it had before: silent and ghostly, waiting for the return of inhabitants who had been massacred inside a squirrel's hole. Assassin bees flicked like flying snow through the beam of light.

Gabe swung the flashlight up. The Source hung there, reflecting the light like a miniature disco-ball, so that little squares of white glided around the attic. Gabe had asked Ronny why the precious Source hung out in the open, so exposed and vulnerable. His friend had explained that this allowed wide-range access by his colleagues. But, there was another, more telling reason. If the aliens had anything resembling a religion, it was a devotion to the Source. Essentially, it made them feel good to see it.

Gabe swung the flashlight down and picked up a small piece of scrap wood the size of a wallet. Shining the flashlight back on the Source, he tossed the wood under-armed across the room. It flew invisibly through the darkness, and he jumped when a blinding flash and loud crack exploded near the alien Holy Grail. Gabe noted that there was no sound of remnant wood falling to the floor.

The bees attacked with fury now. If he hadn't known otherwise, Gabe would have thought the non-organic beasts were angry. This was good. It would distract them.

Gabe strode towards the Source, holding the broomstick handle in front of him like a jousting lance. In the darkness below, whole tracks of miniature city crunched under his boots—Gabezilla on a rampage; a Gabeasaurous-Rex loose in San Diego.

Suddenly the tip of the broomstick flared into a blinding point of light as it met the protected zone around the Source. This was it. Gabe had to keep that fierce little star alive. If he pushed the handle through too fast, Ronny wouldn't have enough time to finish his deed. Too slow, and the star would extinguish and the aliens would see what Ronny was up to. As long as this star burned in the darkness, ionizing energy would keep the aliens semi-blinded, hopefully enough that they wouldn't see Ronny disabling the power supply.

The broom handle disappeared inch-by-inch as Gabe fed it steadily forward. He heard a rustle in the darkness behind him. That would be Ronny going for the power supply. The scattering radio noise generated by the white-hot broom handle tip must have confused the assassin bees as well, for here and there tiny, fleeting mini-novas flared near the Source as the winged soldiers strayed too close. He wondered what the few alien survivors thought he was doing. How could they not see that this was just a ruse to distract them from Ronny's sabotage? What was obvious to Gabe, Ronny had explained, could be inexplicable alien animal behavior to the synthetic intelligence of his colleagues. Who among them could guess what incomprehensible emotion drove the human to this apparently senseless action?

Gabe's eyes adjusted to the stark, white light of his disintegrating broom stick. Sharp, menacing shadows groped inward towards him from all directions. He turned his head, and he could see Ronny crouched against the wall over what looked like a frozen mound of sea foam, apparently the power storage unit. Gabe looked forward again just in time to see that the hissing white tip of the broom was only inches from his hand. Before he even knew what happened, his fingers could be gone, fuel for the hungry star that burned before him.

It was time to reposition his hold. He first moved his rear-most hand farther back along the broom handle, but just as he was following with the forward hand, now so close that he could smell the heat burning his glove, a blind assassin bee flew headlong into his goggles. Taken by surprise, Gabe let the broom dip slightly, and the star flickered and sputtered before he jammed the broom handle back in place and the tip flared again to a steady glare.

Had it been enough time for the aliens to see what Ronny was doing? Gabe glanced around. Ronny was still working at the pile of foam. Gabe repositioned his hands a second time. The broom was now only a couple of feet long, though, and easier to hold. *Hurry Ronny!* Gabe prayed. He repositioned his hands yet again, and now he was holding the broom by the straw; he'd be out of wooden handle in a matter of seconds.

A motion other than dancing shadows caught Gabe's eye. He looked over and, to his horror, saw one of the aliens working its way along the bottom of the sloping attic roof towards Ronny. It looked like an over-sized daddy long-legs spider, and it moved along as if drunk, bumping into each beam before groping and climbing laboriously over. It carried among it's appendages a little space gun, complete with tiny, tiered disks along the barrel. A thread, barely visible, trailed behind it, disappearing in the shadows below.

Gabe had barely three inches of handle left. "Ronny, they're on to you," he called above the hissing of the star. Gabe looked again, and the alien had stopped and was aiming the gun.

"Got it!" Ronny called, just as Gabe heard a *bzzrrtt* from the direction of the alien.

There was no more broom handle left. Gabe tossed the bound bristles into the field area and jumped back as the straw fibers disintegrated into a thousand spitting meteors.

The attic was once again dark and silent.

"Ronny?" Gabe said into the blackness.

No answer.

"Ronny! You there?"

Still only silence. Not even the buzz of a bee.

He'd dropped the flashlight when he begun feeding the broom into the mother of all bug-zappers. He took off his right glove and felt around his feet. Alien construction that he hadn't trampled now disintegrated under his probing hands. Some pieces were like needles and jabbed him, piercing his skin. He found the rubber cylinder of the flashlight, and picked it up, but it wouldn't come on. He knocked it against his other palm, and it sprang to life. He pointed the flashlight straight ahead. The Source hung before him, turning slowly on its suspension wire. He swung the beam to the side. The alien with the space gun was gone. Gabe swung it around further, to the power storage foam-pile. Ronny lay there lifeless.

"Ronny!" Gabe yelled and stomped over, smashing and kicking aside the alien city. Before he got to Ronny, he heard a scuttling sound to his left. He whipped the flashlight beam in that direction, and saw the alien daddy long-legs on the floor. It still held the tiny space gun, but it didn't seem to be aiming it at anything in particular.

Gabe probed the floor around him with the beam. He needed a club. He saw the outline of his old baseball bat under the ubiquitous covering of alien city. He kicked away the fairy-delicate snowflake structures and picked up the bat. The alien was still there, swaying back and forth slightly, as though listening to some internal music. Gabe waded over to it. Holding the flashlight beam on it with his left hand, he lifted the bat to strike, but before he could swing it down, the alien sprang into action. It simply disappeared from the circle of his beam. An instant later, Gabe felt it scrambling up his leg, and then up his coat towards his face. Gabe let out a fearful yell and danced around, wiping his left arm along his body in a desperate attempt to get it off him. He stood still, trembling. Where was it? He swept the floor around him with the flashlight and found it. It lay on its back, two ineffectual appendages waving helplessly in the air. Gabe must have broken most of its legs when he'd knocked it off.

Without hesitation, he lifted his foot and stepped on the creature that had traveled 320 light years to get here. The crunch was significantly more substantial than that of the bees.

Gabe now turned his attention back to Ronny. His friend looked dead.

"Ronny, oh Ronny!" Gabe moaned, squatting down and gently laying his hand on the fur of the raccoon's back.

The raccoon's eyes opened.

"Thank God!" Gabe sighed.

Ronny lifted himself onto all fours somewhat unsteadily, as though he'd forgotten how to do it.

"Let's get some air," Gabe said, "it stinks in here." He reached down to pick up his friend, but felt a sharp pain in his hand. "Hey! What's the matter?" Gabe cried.

Ronny had bitten him!

Gabe shined the light on the raccoon. Gabe could see fear in its eyes. There was something else in the face as well, something he hadn't seen until now—it was plain and simply the face of a raccoon, nothing more. The significance was in what was missing: intelligence. The raccoon was just a raccoon.

It was then that Gabe noticed small swirls of smoke rising from the raccoon's neck. In fact, he realized that this was the source of the stink—it smelled like burnt-out resistors in his amplifiers.

For the second time that day Gabe fell to his knees and buried his face in his hands. After a moment he felt tears wetting his cheeks. Letting go, his shoulders shook as he sobbed. Loneliness settled over him like a cold, heavy blanket. He cried until his tears and snot fell dripping to the attic floor.

After some time, he knelt quietly, holding his head wrapped in his hands. He uncurled and stood up. Propping up the flashlight on the floor so that its beam fell on the Source, he picked up his bat and strode to the alien repository hanging there innocently by its thread. He heard something drop to the floor. In the dim reflection, Gabe could see a second alien crouched on the floor. This one had shorter legs, but four long manipulating appendages with tiny hands. It didn't seem to have a weapon. A third alien dropped to the ground on the other side of the Source. They made no move towards him. It seemed to Gabe that they were pleading for mercy, or perhaps, simply wanted to give witness to the end.

Gabe cocked the bat and took a mighty swing, and this time no focused energy stopped him. The alien treasure, the source of everything they had been and could be, shattered into a hundred pieces, which bounced off the walls of Gabe's attic and fell among the ruined city of its progeny.

Chapter 18

Saturday, 2:30 PM

Gabe drove like a madman. He was lucky that the police were already at Crabnuckle's. The raccoon that used to be Ronny cowered in the passenger seat watching Gabe. After the initial bite, the little guy had let Gabe handle him. Gabe suspected that it remembered, if not comprehended, all that had happened to it the last days and weeks. It probably remembered that it had spent a lot of time with him.

He wanted to believe that it remembered that they'd been friends—friends who had trusted each other to the end.

Gabe could only drive to within a block of Crabnuckle's. It looked like the entire San Diego police, fire, and emergency departments had converged here. He left the car double parked, and locking the doors so that some inquisitive fool didn't let the raccoon out, sprinted down the street towards the eye of the storm. He pushed his way past uniformed city employees and curious onlookers. As he got closer, he saw that their cup-bomb had indeed done some damage to the terrorists' garage. One section of the wall bulged outward, and some boards had broken away.

A new flurry of sirens announced the arrival of soldiers carrying serious-looking guns. Gabe guessed that the government was waking up to the fact that it had an atom bomb sitting in its lap. Soon they would surely put a clamp on the whole area to prevent a mad panic as citizenry tried, en mass, to evacuate the city.

He ducked under police tape, and one of the patrolmen watching the perimeter grabbed his arm. "No you don't," the policeman said.

Gabe knew he was near a breaking point. He restrained the urge to just push the cop away and force his way through. Instead he said, "That's my friend. She was killed . . ."

He didn't know how to begin to summarize the situation to this man.

The annoyed look of the cop turned serious. "Who's been killed?"

"Christie—my friend. Look, just let me go. I belong here."

"What's your name?"

He saw an emergency crew wheeling a portable gurney towards a waiting ambulance. "Gabe. Gabe Wolfekow. Look, let me go."

Understanding lit up the man's face and his grip tightened. "All right, Gabe. Just hold on here."

Gabe could tell that the policeman was reaching for his handcuffs. He twisted, trying to break the policeman's hold, but the cop was used to this and deftly turned his wrist behind his back while grabbing his other shoulder. "Take it easy, son. You don't want to get hurt."

"*It's okay, officer!*" someone called.

Gabe saw that it was Weston, the FBI agent, walking towards them. The policeman let him go.

When Weston got to them, Gabe gestured towards the stretcher. "Is that . . . her?" he asked the man who had brushed him off a few days before.

Weston nodded. Gabe couldn't read his face. He sprinted off towards the cluster of medical technicians getting ready to load the stretcher into the ambulance. He pushed one of them aside and there, eyes closed, pale as white china, was Christie.

"Who are you?" the technician standing next to him asked, placing his hand lightly, but authoritatively, on his shoulder.

Gabe wasn't about to try to explain. "Her fiancée," he lied.

The man dropped his hand away. "I'm sorry," he said, "we don't have time. We have to get her to the hospital."

Gabe looked at him in surprise. "She's *alive?*"

The man shrugged. "We're going to try to keep it that way."

Gabe's mind exploded with hope and a hundred different jostled thoughts. "I can help!" Gabe cried.

What would they need to know?

"Look, I know what's wrong with her! Aliens booby-trapped her with poison agents, and they've activated them remotely." That sounded crazy. "I know you probably don't believe me, but you've got to listen! You've got to take care of the alien agents inside her!"

The emergency technician's sympathetic demeanor changed to disgusted irritation. Here was a guy bundled up for skiing, talking about aliens. "Right pal, you can explain it to the doctors at the hospital."

The man planted both his hands on Gabe's shoulders now and started pulling him away, but Gabe saw Christie's eyes open slightly. He lunged out of the man's grip and leaned over her. "Christie!" he cried, "You're going to be okay!"

It was more a prayer than a prediction—a demand, really.

She smiled weakly. "Fiancée?" she whispered. "I barely know you."

Gabe's vision blurred as tears welled up unbidden.

"But I accept," she added.

They now moved Gabe firmly aside and loaded the stretcher into the ambulance. He guessed that a fiancée would normally ride along, but they weren't taking any chances with some nut babbling on about aliens.

He stood and watched as the ambulance pulled away, siren screaming.

"I think we got most of it," a man's voice said next to him.

Gabe turned to find Weston standing there watching the ambulance leave. "You know about . . . *them?*" was all Gabe could come up with.

Weston shrugged without looking at Gabe. "I know what she told me. Exactly what part's real, and what, if any, is imagined, I don't have a clue. But I intend to find out. In the meantime, I'm keeping an open mind."

"What did you mean when you said you think you got most of it?"

"The aliens, or whatever they were, inside her."

"They weren't the aliens themselves, just alien agents—devices that could be directed to release poison."

Gabe didn't tell him that he wasn't even sure *he* knew who the real aliens were, the insect devices that he'd electrocuted, or the Source that had been hanging in his attic.

Weston looked at Gabe a moment, and then replied, "Like I said, I'm keeping an open mind."

"How did you do it? How did you get rid of them?"

Weston grinned. He stepped over to his car, reached in, and came back with an empty plastic bottle. "I was supposed to get a colonoscopy tomorrow," he said, handing it to him.

Gabe looked at the bottle. "Citrus of Magnesium?"

Weston smiled broadly now. "It's a fast acting laxative."

Gabe stared at Weston. It had been that easy?

"According to Christie," Weston went on, "it had been a day and a half since she'd ingested them. Most of them were probably already through her system. We just gave the last of them a slippery last push. I wish I'd thought to save the evidence."

Gabe raised his eyebrows.

Weston laughed. "On the other hand, maybe I'm glad I forgot."

"She looked half dead. Do you think you really got them all?"

Weston indicated towards the disappearing ambulance. "They think she has a bad case of appendicitis. My guess is that one of the little buggers got stuck in her appendix. It looks like she's going to be a little lighter by the end of the day."

Gabe wished it was going to be that easy. They had no idea yet how bad she was, how many agents were in her when the activation signal was sent. "I've got to get to the hospital," he said, starting away.

Weston grabbed his arm. "Just a couple of minutes, Gabe. I won't take long."

Gabe looked at him, weighing whether to continue towards his car.

Weston must have guessed what he was thinking, for he nodded towards the policeman who had tried to handcuff him.

Gabe sighed.

He talked to Weston while one of the rescue squad cleaned and bandaged the Charlemagne wounds in his arm and hand. Gabe gave him a summary of the last few days. During it all, the medical technician pretended he didn't hear a word. He probably heard more bizarre stories on a daily basis.

When his arm was done, they took a walk up the street to gain some privacy. Weston, in turn, explained that he had become interested when the British Prime Minister's visit was announced exactly as predicted by Gabe. His investigation had started with Gabe as a possible terrorist suspect, but as he began gathering data, he'd decided that Gabe was either on to something important, or just plain nuts. He had arrived at Crabnuckle's an hour before, just after Gabe had left to go back to his own house. He'd actually come as a result of a neighbor's complaint about the noise from the band. He had asked the police to inform him of any activity at the two addresses. They had fortunately interpreted "any" literally. He wanted to call in backup and nab the remaining two terrorists, but had held off until after 2:00 at Christie's urging. Nabeeh and Abdul-Baari received cuts and bruises from the cup-bomb, but were fine otherwise and in custody.

"There's a dead body lying in that garage," Weston added. "You're in line for some hard questions."

Gabe nodded. He'd almost forgotten that. "The autopsy will show that he died of an extreme allergic reaction to a bee sting on his arm."

Weston looked at him searchingly.

Gabe shook his head. "I didn't do it. It was one of the assassin bees."

They walked on in silence awhile. Weston finally said, "You exploded a homemade bomb in a location where people could have gotten seriously hurt or killed. You've probably broken half a dozen laws with that one act."

Consequences were coming home. "I've already explained that—"

"My report will say that you tried to warn me about the terrorist plot, but that there was confusion about the meaning of 'alien.' You meant alien as from another country," here Weston gave him a meaningful look, "while I foolishly dismissed you as some nut talking about space aliens. You discovered the terrorists as a result of your pet sitting activities with their neighbor, Mrs. Crabnuckle. Since you couldn't get help from the FBI, you decided that your duty as an honorable citizen was to try to stop them yourself. You thought you could destroy their nuclear weapon with your homemade bomb. You're essentially a hero."

Gabe walked along looking at the ground. The man was handing him his freedom. Did he thank him, or play along?

"But," Weston continued, "you did break laws and they'll have to charge you. With my testimony, though, and some luck, you could get off with a slap on the wrist."

Gabe nodded and gave Weston a grateful smile.

Weston stopped, and Gabe stopped too. "But, if you start talking about space aliens," Weston warned, "I can guarantee that they'll either send you to jail or an institution. Going on about speaking with aliens from other planets is one thing. Adding homemade bombs to the mix is a whole other ballgame."

Gabe nodded understanding.

They started back towards the bustling activity of San Diego's emergency agencies in action. News crews were starting to arrive. "I've got to get away to the hospital," Gabe said.

"You do," Weston agreed.

Gabe knew he should let it ride, but he couldn't help himself. "Why do you believe us?" he asked. "Why did you wait until 2:00?"

Weston didn't answer right away. When he did, he spoke quietly, almost as though he was talking to himself. "Sometimes you have to go with your intuition. You measure people, and make a judgment. You decide whether you're going to believe them."

Gabe smiled, thinking of previous conversations with his former friend. "That's how we beat them," he said.

Weston lifted an eyebrow.

"The aliens. They couldn't lie, and so didn't understand trust."

Weston shrugged. He probably didn't know what the hell Gabe was talking about. "If you're going to make it to the hospital," the FBI agent warned, "you'd better high-tail it. I see some pretty women with skirts and microphones headed our way."

Gabe sprinted off towards his car. *Trust*, he thought. *The poker chips in the game of human life.*

Chapter 19

six days later

Gabe looked around the hospital lobby a third time, and then walked over to the admissions counter. "Excuse me," he said to the bored woman. "I'm here to pick up a patient who was supposed to be released this morning. I've called her room, but she's not there. Can you tell me where she might be?"

"What's the patient's name?" she asked.

"Christie Owens."

It felt good to say her full name, as though it implied a special intimacy.

The woman tapped on her keyboard, and looked at the monitor. "She hasn't been released yet." She shrugged.

Gabe had always wondered why people exit trains and check out of hotels, but are released from hospitals. It sounded as though they'd completed their incarceration.

He must have looked pitiable. The woman picked up the phone and said, "Let's see if somebody at the nurses' station knows." When she hung up she told him that Christie was talking to the surgeon in the recovery section's lounge. She gave him directions.

Gabe found Christie in a tiny room with three padded chairs. She was dressed in street clothes and sitting in a wheelchair talking with a doctor Gabe recognized. This elderly man had breezed in to her room each day along with an entourage of interns, completely ignoring Gabe. Like a professor lecturing on a subject he'd covered uncountable times, he had explained her condition, treatment, and prognosis to his protégés in incomprehensible terms, and then, almost as an afterthought, he'd ask Christie how she was doing. Gabe didn't even think the doctor listened to her answer as he scribbled something on his clipboard, and then reassured her she was doing fine before gliding away to the next subject.

When Christie saw Gabe, her face lit up and she waved him over. The doctor looked annoyed at the interruption.

"They want me to stay for more tests."

As she said this, her brow wrinkled with disappointment.

Gabe looked at the doctor. "Are there complications?"

He hesitated ever so slightly, as though weighing whether Gabe even deserved an answer. "Not exactly. We just want to understand better what's happened to Christie."

Doctors in hospitals always say "we" when they have unwelcome news to deliver. "I thought it was appendicitis," Gabe said.

The doctor nodded. "Appendicitis is a general term for inflammation of the appendix. It's the closest term we have to describe Christie's ailment. Frankly, I've never seen or heard of anything like what I found. Normally, appendicitis begins with an irritation that causes the appendix to fill with puss. If untreated, the appendix can swell and eventually become perforated—burst. In Christie's case, the appendix didn't so much burst as dissolve. Something was destroying her organs indiscriminately."

Gabe shrugged. "You have her appendix. What have you found?"

The doctor sighed. "There lies the problem. We've found nothing that would explain it . . . although, there wasn't much left to work with."

"What good would it do to keep Christie here? What more could you learn from her?"

The doctor seemed clearly irritated to have to answer questions from somebody not even related to Christie. "We're discussing approaches," he replied testily.

"Maybe we should continue this discussion when you know. In the meantime, we can go home."

"Look! That's this young woman's decision, not yours."

Gabe looked at Christie. She smiled. "Let's go home," she said.

The doctor frowned. He wasn't used to being stymied. "You could be in serious danger. We have to understand what happened."

"If you don't understand what happened," Gabe reasoned, "how can you assume she's in further danger?"

"I saved this young woman's life!"

Meaning, Gabe thought, *that I'm the doctor, and you're just a person.*

Gabe's court hearing about the homemade bomb was coming up, and he knew it was important not to talk about the aliens, but Gabe couldn't help himself. "What if Christie was implanted with an alien substance that was designed to do its damage, and then deteriorate so that it couldn't be detected later?"

Gabe didn't expect the doctor to take that seriously, and he didn't. "Look, I can declare a quarantine situation and force Ms. Owen to stay here."

Gabe had started it. He might as well go for broke. "So you *have* isolated a contagious agent?"

The doctor was red in the face. Gabe knew that he'd called the man's bluff. "Come on, Christie," he said, "let's go home."

ж ж ж

Gabe stood by while the orderly helped Christie into the car. He would have rather done it himself, but he thought it would seem pushy. He snatched the parking citation from under the windshield wiper, tossed it on the back seat, pulled away from the curb, and headed home.

The two of them, going home. That sounded good. He'd suggested that she stay with him until she recovered, and she had agreed as though he had asked her if she'd like a mint.

"I hope I didn't step on your toes back there with the surgeon," he said. "I didn't give you much chance to talk."

She grinned. She seemed happy to be out in the sunshine again. "I appreciated the help. He was intimidating. When a doctor has saved your life, it's hard to turn him down. I think he saw me as his ticket to professional fame. 'The doctor who discovered Owen's Disease.' He had no way of knowing that it was a one-shot deal."

Gabe's mood sobered at the thought.

"Hey!" Christie said, "Why the gloomy face?"

Gabe laughed. He wasn't used to somebody being tuned in to him. "I just wish I *knew* it was a one-time thing."

Now Christie looked concerned. "Why? What's happened?"

"Oh, nothing new. I was just thinking about some of the things Ronny had told me. His colleagues—he always called them that—320 light years away received one message from Earth saying basically, 'The water's great, come on in. We'll tell you when and where.' Then nothing followed. They'll obviously assume something went wrong and send another advance party."

"Maybe they'll think humans are too tough for them, and leave us alone."

Gabe shook his head. "Ronny told me that over the last million years they've encountered dozens of intelligent species. None have survived the encounter for more than a few hundred years. At this point, I don't think they're scared of any living beings."

"When do you think they'll . . . you know, get here?" she asked kind of panicky.

She had a very personal reason to be frightened of them.

"Oh, I don't think we need to worry just yet," Gabe said, trying to sound reassuring. "Ronny said it took his crew years to get to Earth from their entry point out of hyperspace, and he thought that they'd been very lucky to get even *that* close."

This seemed to mollify her a little, but she still seemed a little nervous. *And well she should be*, Gabe thought. She stared out the window, and Gabe left her to her thoughts.

"Why did the bee sting the dog—Charlemagne?" she asked, out of the blue. "I mean," she added, "wouldn't it have known he was one of them?"

It was odd that he hadn't thought about this since the great Battle for San Diego. He remembered the same question flitting through his mind at the time, but so much happened afterwards, he'd then forgotten about it. What little reflections he'd made about the whole alien battle always ended in despair and self-recrimination for not preventing Ronny's destruction.

"Ronny explained that the bees were not very intelligent. None of his colleagues wanted to volunteer their service—as he'd done for his role with the raccoon—and they didn't have time to develop special pilot versions. The bee's brains were apparently general-purpose factory models, and not the sharpest knives in the drawer. My guess is that Ronny managed somehow to transfer a bee that was wiggling its way into his own fur to Charlemagne's without the bee realizing it."

Christie placed her hand lightly on his knee. "He saved your life."

"More than once." *And I wasn't able to do the same.*

Gabe drove along thinking, as he did practically every hour of every day, of his friend. "Do you recall how Ronny seemed depressed and lonely after the aliens cut off his communications?"

Christie smiled, remembering. "He turned downright needy."

"I don't think it was his colleagues he was missing."

"You think it was that information storage thing?"

"The Source, yes. I'm glad he was already gone when I smashed it. It probably would have been like witnessing the destruction of your whole family—your whole race."

They rolled on through the California sunshine in silence for a while. Christie took his hand in hers. "Ronny turned from his kind to save us," she said, "and he got what he wanted."

Gabe glanced at her and smiled. They drove on towards home.

ж ж ж

Gabe helped Christie into the house. She could walk, but it hurt, and she needed him to steady her. He sat her on the living room sofa and made a second trip to take her bags into the spare bedroom, which he'd cleaned out. He'd only been able to cover the window he'd broken with a temporary screen, but she had reassured him that this was fine. She welcomed all the fresh air she could get after the hospital.

When he came back to the living room, Christie was leaning over, peering into a clear plastic storage box that was sitting against the wall. "Are those the . . . ?"

"Aliens? Yes."

He slid the box over closer to her and lifted the lid. Christie jumped back in alarm, and Gabe laughed. "Don't worry. They're harmless."

These were the two remaining guards that had been left to watch over the Source. Gabe had come back to the house to find them crouched among the rubble of their ruined city. They had made a half-hearted effort to avoid him, but in the end, it was pretty easy to catch them. Since then, they hardly moved. Gabe felt almost sorry for them, and had tried to relieve what he imagined to be extreme boredom by placing them in front of the TV, or next to the radio. He'd even put books in the box with them, but they seemed to take no notice, only moving when he disturbed them.

"Why are you keeping them?" she asked distastefully.

She clearly didn't like being near them, and Gabe closed the top and picked up the box. "I thought I might need them in case the hearing doesn't go well. If all else fails, I might have to actually tell the truth."

He carried the box of aliens off to his bedroom. "Also," he called from the hallway, "I was thinking about the bigger picture. It seems certain that we'll eventually have to confront their kind again, and it can't hurt to study them beforehand."

He set the box down in his closet and looked at the raccoon lying on his bed watching him. The little guy seemed content to live with Gabe, and he was grateful for that. "Hey!" he called out to her, picking up the raccoon. "I have someone here you might recognize."

When she saw it, hope and joy filled her face for a fleeting moment until she too understood that this was nothing more than a normal raccoon now. But she smiled and took the animal from Gabe with affection.

"Rocky seems to remember you," Gabe observed, watching the raccoon settle immediately into her lap.

"*Rocky?*"

Gabe shrugged. "I couldn't go on calling him Ronny. It seemed . . . disrespectful somehow."

She scratched his chin like he used to enjoy when he was an alien, while Gabe gathered the things he'd need for the day's pet-rounds.

"Gabe," she said, "before you go, could you get the laptop from my bag? I'll finish that email to my mom that I've been writing for a week."

One of her friends had lent her the computer while she was laid up, recovering. Gabe retrieved it, and then strung an extension cord so that she wouldn't have to run on batteries. She gently set the raccoon next to her, opened the computer, and pushed the power button. Gabe was heading for the door when he heard her say, "What's this?"

Gabe walked over, and she pointed to a window that had opened on the screen. It was some sort of network connection software, probably built in to the operating system. In the domain server name field windows Gabe saw: SPACE_ALIENS_INC. The cursor was blinking next to the question: *do you want to connect now?*

Christie looked at Gabe, eyes wide. "Do you have wireless service?" she asked.

Gabe just shook his head slowly. *Space Aliens, Incorporated?*

Christie moved the cursor over the "yes" button on the screen and looked at him questioningly. He shrugged, and she clicked the select function.

The network configuration window disappeared and was replaced with the Internet browser, which immediately displayed text that read:

Hello Gabe and Christie. This is your friend, Ronny.

Gabe and Christie looked each other, dumbstruck. The text changed to a new message:

You don't believe it's me? Did you hear the one about the alien who lost control of his host raccoon, so his friends started calling him Rocky for spite?

"Where *is* he?" Gabe asked, looking around the room.
The text changed again:

Right next to you—where I've always been.

Gabe and Christie looked down at the raccoon, which lay there, half asleep. "The raccoon?" Gabe asked.

Of course. I've been trying to contact you ever since my colleague disabled my control outputs. You assumed, quite naturally, that I was completely destroyed. That would have been the case if you hadn't thrown the rest of the broom into the defense field area, Gabe. Luckily, that drew all the reserve power and my ex-colleague was not able to finish the job.

Gabe squatted down in front of the raccoon. "You can hear me through his ears?"

I can hear, see, and feel—I just can't control him. Of course, I only see what he's looking at. Right now he's staring at Christie's knee. He's daydreaming about fish in a nearby pond.

It was beginning to sink in. "This is *great*! You're alive, you silicon button-brain!"

Actually, my circuitry is made from molecules more complex that silicon. But I'm happy to say I'm as alive as I've ever been . . . which in itself has, I guess, been open to interpretation.

Gabe, could you please go get your iPod, radio attachment, and the dual earphones? Tune the radio to 100.0 megahertz.

Gabe glanced at Christie only a second before running off. He returned some minutes later to find her asking, ". . . and what did Gabe do when Charlemagne attacked you?"

"He's lying," Gabe accused, "he's trained to do that. He can't help it."

Christie was reading the screen intently. "No," she said, looking up, "it looks like you're a bona fide hero. I may have to marry you some day after all."

Gabe could feel himself blushing. That was the first time that had been mentioned, even in jest, since she'd stood at death's door. He sat down on the other side of Christie and handed her the second set of earphones, while he put the first set on himself, then tuned the radio.

"Hello, my friends," Gabe heard. It was the same calm voice that had spoken directly into his ear through the worm.

Christie laughed out loud. "You sound like my Uncle Paul."

"Would you prefer this?"

Gabe looked at Christie, confused. He realized that Ronny was imitating Christie's voice.

"No," Gabe protested, "that's way too whiny."

Christie punched him on the shoulder. It hurt.

"Before we continue," Ronny said, reverting to his original Uncle Paul voice, "let me caution you not to let me—this raccoon—too far from your sight. He seems content enough to be with you, but I'm not sure he'd return if he found himself outdoors."

Gabe realized what a disaster that could be—Ronny lost in the wild, helplessly riding along with a wild raccoon. Ronny's radio signal couldn't be very strong. Their friend would have no way of contacting them. Gabe shuddered as he thought how careless he'd been with the raccoon over the last week, how many times it could have easily escaped had it been inclined.

"Do you need anything?" Christie asked.

"I now have what I've craved these long days."

Gabe smiled. "Christie scratching your chin?"

"That is a bonus. I've had a lot of time to think. You've probably surmised that the alien enemy—my former colleagues—will return."

"We talked about it," Gabe confirmed.

"We have to prepare."

Gabe raised one eyebrow. "Three of us? Against an alien race millions of years old?"

"No. Of course not. We'll need to prepare the people of Earth."

"I'll go make some signs." Gabe said. "We can each stand on a different street corner. They'll read: 'Prepare! The aliens are coming!'"

"There was a time when I might have thought you were serious, and sadly stupid. It will indeed be a tricky business convincing people of the truth—"

"Because we're such persistent liars."

Gabe suddenly realized that he was going to have to lie about the aliens at his upcoming hearing *because* humans are so very capable of lying. If he told the truth, the judge would interpret it as lies. No wonder lying confused the aliens.

"Yes. It comes down to credibility. It's on your shoulders, Gabe, at least the first big step. First, you have to go back to college and get your doctorate degree—"

"Whoa!"

"What's wrong?"

"I can't even afford to finish my four-year degree."

"I've thought of this as well. You're going to become moderately wealthy as an inventor."

Gabe grinned. "Am I, perchance, going to be getting some help from somebody already familiar with the inventive ideas?"

"I don't think the US patent office will allow a raccoon as a co-inventor. Don't worry, my ego will survive."

"I'm listening."

"Your patent portfolio will serve two purposes: first, as mentioned, it will bankroll your education, and second, it will help establish your reputation and credibility as a science genius."

"Oprah, here I come."

"You'll have to convince her to let you bring along a raccoon, otherwise you might make a fool of us all. But seriously, there's an additional danger that is even more daunting. The alien horde will be keeping their eye trained in our direction. It's not likely that they could react in time to a random hyperspace perturbation, but there's a possibility that they could."

Gabe shook his head. "This science genius isn't following you."

"Nuclear explosions on Earth could now potentially open the door for an alien hyperspace marker."

Ronny was silent as Gabe and Christie absorbed this.

"The ultimate MAD," Christie finally offered.

"I don't understand," Ronny confessed.

" It stands for Mutually Assured Destruction. It was the watchwords—the morbid peacekeeper—of the cold war years. All three superpowers had the ability to destroy the others, so anyone attempting to wage nuclear war would be assured of being destroyed themselves."

"I see. Yes, any use of a nuclear weapon could now spell the end of the entire human race."

Gabe took a deep breath. "I'd better hit the books. They don't hand out doctorates like candy, you know."

ж ж ж

Gabe turned his car onto Mission Canyon Road. He wasn't at all comfortable about this, but the sooner he tied up loose ends, the sooner he could get down to the business of saving the Earth from aliens.

He parked in front of Mrs. Crabnuckle's house and surveyed the scene. Police tape still barred entry into the former terrorists' house. Rumors had indeed begun to circulate the web that a terrorist bomb, possibly even nuclear, had been found here. Word had obviously come down from on high—probably as high as it comes—to control the media exposure. November elections were on the horizon, and it would be better to let the public rumor-mill spread the idea that the government had been on the ball, had nipped the plot in the bud. No fanfare, please, just doing our jobs, folks.

No need to advertise that the atom bomb was a couple of days from being detonated over Las Vegas, and that a young man, along with his raccoon and jump-blues band, had stymied them.

Gabe understood that it was this desire to veil the truth that had resulted in the speedy resolution at his hearing. But Weston had also explained afterwards, somewhat sheepishly, that the case could be re-opened if Gabe made trouble.

Well, they'd have to see about that.

He got out of the car, walked up to Crabnuckle's door, and rang the bell. After a minute, the old woman opened the door, and then swung it wide. "Well, if it isn't our young secret agent."

She was still convinced that Gabe and Christie, and maybe even Randy, were with the CIA. She wasn't sure about Derrick. It was hard for anybody to believe that Derrick could be trusted with a gun.

"Sorry to bother you," he said, walking in past her, "but I wanted to stop by and make sure we didn't leave anything behind."

At the sound of his voice, Punky came tearing in from the back rooms. He tossed himself around like he was having one granddaddy of a grand mal seizure. Gabe tried to ignore him, and

Mrs. Crabnuckle yelled for 'Pinksty' to shut his trap, which he did, knowing from experience the consequences otherwise.

"No," she said, "that friendly fellow, Derrick, came by to get the last of it. Quite a hoot he is. We had a few whiskies together. I haven't been intoxicated in years."

"Oh, good."

Gabe knew he had to get to it sooner or later. "Well, I also want to pay you for any damages."

"Pooh!" she said, waving him off. "None to speak of."

Gabe pulled a ten-dollar bill from his wallet. "At least let me pay for the shotgun shells we used."

"Ha!" she laughed. "You think I would ever use them?"

"I insist," Gabe said, pressing the bill into her hand. Somehow, this payment was important, a token.

She looked at it a moment, then shrugged and took it. "I'm not going to argue with you," she said. "Would you like a drink? Maybe a whisky? I've gotten kind of fond of the stuff."

"How about an iced-tea?" Gabe said. He could feel that his palms were sweating.

"Bah!" the old woman snorted. "A tea-toddler. Very well."

She shuffled off towards the kitchen.

Gabe watched until she disappeared, then squatted down and waved Punky over. "Shhh!" he said, putting his finger to his lips as the dog ran over, wagging his tail. Gabe grabbed the wriggling ball of fur and ran for the door.

When Gabe got to his car, he threw Punky headlong in the back and jumped in the driver's seat. Mrs. Crabnuckle rushed out of the house. "You won't get away with this, young man! CIA or not!"

Gabe pulled away. He would have squealed the tires if the engine had been up to it. As it was, he slowly accelerated away from the figure standing in the road waving her fist at him.

Punky jumped into the front and began reapplying the layer of saliva that had been missing for far too long. Gabe used one hand to wrestle with him.

The space alien defense squad was now intact and open for business.

About the Author

Blaine C. Readler is an electronics engineer, inventor, and writer (although, that's rather redundant considering the context). He lives in San Diego, from where he ventures forth in spring and autumn when the rest of the country is habitable. He has half a dozen published books under his belt, none (yet) nominated for a Pulitzer.

He encourages you to visit him:
http://www.readler.com/

www.ingramcontent.com/pod-product-compliance
Lightning Source LLC
Chambersburg PA
CBHW020757250626
47155CB00003B/1119